3800 16 0080211 4

HIGH LIFE HIGHLAND

Doug Johnstone (@doug_johnstone) is the author of six previous novels, most recently *The Dead Beat* (2014). A freelance journalist, son~~g~~w~~riter~~ ~~and musician, he is also a~~ Royal Literary Fund Fello~~w~~ ~~at Edinburgh University.~~ He lives in Edinburgh.

www.dougjohnstone.com

Further praise for *The Jump*:

'All the time that the tension builds, so too does the detail in Johnstone's picture of a once-happy family ground down by sorrow. He is a master of the magic and mundanity of marriage, of the way that as we age and change, so too does the love that we feel. But there's the odd, brilliant flash of black humour that twinkles through even the darkest of moments, thanks to Ellie. I would have been happy to read chapters and chapters more of this book, not least because I longed to spend more time with the complicated, thoughtful Ellie, but then again, perhaps *The Jump*'s brevity is what makes it so satisfying.' Rebecca Armstrong, *Independent on Sunday*

'Johnstone tells his story so efficiently that if it were a TV drama it would be a straight one hour fit . . . Although this book is a thriller what it says about parenting is just as important – that behind the teenage mask of boredom and disgust they're often quite scared.' David Robinson, *The Scotsman*

HIGHLAND LIBRARIES

WITHDRAWN

'The writing is clever, the narrative style is addictive and the character building is superb – as well as that the setting is vivid and the whole thing has a completely authentic feel to it.' *Liz Loves Books*

'If you have yet to read anything by this author then I suggest you do so, without delay. His words always have a particularly hard-hitting edge to them, that lingers when the book is done and safely on your bookshelf.' *Eurocrime*

'This is a very absorbing and thought provoking read. A difficult subject is handled sensitively, in an emotional and very believable thriller.' *Northerncrime*

---

also by Doug Johnstone

Tombstoning
The Ossians
Smokeheads
Hit & Run
Gone Again
The Dead Beat

HIGHLAND
LIBRARIES

WITHDRAWN

The Jump

DOUG JOHNSTONE

HIGH LIFE HIGHLAND LIBRARIES	
38001600802114	
BERTRAMS	14/02/2017
GEN	£7.99
AF	

FABER & FABER

First published in 2015
by Faber & Faber Ltd
Bloomsbury House
74-77 Great Russell Street
London WC1B 3DA
This paperback edition first published in 2016

Typeset by Faber & Faber Ltd
Printed and bound by CPI Group (UK) Ltd, Croydon CR0 4YY

All rights reserved
© Doug Johnstone, 2015

Extract from 'Swim Until You Can't See Land' reproduced with the kind permission of
Frightened Rabbit

The right of Doug Johnstone to be identified as author of this work has been asserted in
accordance with Section 77 of the Copyright, Designs and Patents Act 1988

*This book is sold subject to the condition that it shall not, by way of trade or otherwise, be lent, resold,
hired out or otherwise circulated without the publisher's prior consentin any form of binding or cover
other than that in which it is published and without a similar condition including this condition
being imposed on the subsequent purchaser*

A CIP record for this book
is available from the British Library

ISBN 978-0-571-32158-2

FSC
www.fsc.org
MIX
Paper from
responsible sources
FSC® C101712

2 4 6 8 10 9 7 5 3

In memory of
Gayle Edington
and
Mark Smith

A salute at the threshold of the North Sea of my
mind,
And a nod to the boredom that drove me here
to face the tide,
And I swim

'Swim Until You Can't See Land',
Frightened Rabbit

There were widows and orphans, but why wasn't there a word for a parent who lost a child? Because it was too awful to contemplate, too terrible to give a name.

The thought buzzed in Ellie's brain, just as it had every day for the last few months, as she stood on the shore at the Binks, a rocky wart sticking out into the Firth of Forth. To her left was the road bridge, a concrete javelin suspended across the river from two giant supports. Beyond that she could see the yellow cranes working on the new bridge foundations, emerging from the water like sleepy krakens. In the other direction, past the low harbour wall and the Craigs, was the more famous rail bridge, the rusty red squeezebox of criss-crossed struts, with the smudge of the BP tanker berth lurking behind.

The road bridge loomed over her, as always. She and Ben should've moved away from South Queensferry after it happened, made a clean break. But she was secretly glad they hadn't, she liked the constant reminder, the open sore that she couldn't help touching. Besides, she could never leave Logan behind.

Thirty yards back was the house she shared with Ben. Just Ben. It wasn't a home any more, not without Logan. Greystone terrace, two bedrooms, though they didn't need the second bedroom now. She hadn't been able to clear away Logan's stuff yet.

Every day at the shore the light was different. Today it felt like the start of autumn, sharpness in the bluster of wind from upriver sweeping into the wider firth, high feathery clouds making the light somehow milky.

She looked at the distance from the centre of the road bridge down to the choppy surface of the water. Forty-five metres. She knew that from a leaflet she picked up at the bridge visitor centre. Not so far, you might think, but it was easily enough to kill you if you jumped. It was the method of suicide with the highest success rate. 97 per cent died. She wondered if Logan knew that before he jumped. If he'd Googled it, found the surest way. She'd checked his laptop browser history some-time after, when she briefly emerged from the blackness, but there was nothing unusual on there. Maybe he looked it up on his phone. It was still in his pocket when they recovered the body, but broken, obviously.

She took a deep breath and closed her eyes. Counted to six. Opened them again and looked at the bridge. Imagined his body falling through the air. She'd watched hundreds of videos of people committing suicide this way since Logan jumped, amazing how many attempts had been caught on film. Mostly it looked peaceful, somehow casual. Just a simple step off a ledge, a tiny splash of white spray on entry. But she knew the truth was different. You could reach seventy miles per hour. Hitting the water was like hitting a pavement, legs pulverised, spine col-lapsed, internal organs crushed, arms wrenched from sockets.

She wished for that oblivion. Less often than she used to, but still every hour, every day.

Ben had identified Logan's body. She wondered over and over if that was a mistake. She couldn't really remember the events of that day, just the call at her desk, the frantic drive across Edinburgh, then people she didn't know telling her things she couldn't understand. Her fifteen-year-old son was dead. He'd jumped from the bridge.

A maintenance worker saw it, radioed in to control. The coastguard called the safety boat from the bridge-works at Port Edgar to go fish the body out. Not even worth scrambling an official sea search. He was only ten minutes in the water. Not that time mattered, of course, he was dead on entry, body smashed by the laws of physics.

Back at Port Edgar someone in the coastguard office recognised Logan as Ben's boy. Ellie felt sorry for the man, suddenly given the burden of that information. He called Ben, who sprinted the short distance along Shore Road to the marina and confirmed what they all knew.

Ellie felt excluded. By the time she'd got through traffic, Logan had been taken away. At first she thought it was a horrible joke, the sickest prank imaginable. But the look on the men's faces, on Ben's face, made the truth clear.

No note.

No previous attempts.

No cries for help.

No overdoses or slashed wrists.

No self-harming or mood swings or depression, no trouble at school, no bullying they could uncover.

He'd been quiet, but then he'd always been quiet and thoughtful, a good boy, never ran with the gang of loud, obnoxious kids at school. Preferred his own imagination, books and games to macho bluster or petty squabbling. He was respectful, polite.

And now he was dead.

It was unbearable.

She closed her eyes again and listened. The same two things she always heard when she stood here. The thin shush of waves on the shore and the rumbling thrum of traffic on the bridge, commuters, delivery drivers, people heading north or south to visit loved ones, friends and family. Mums and dads. Sons and daughters.

She opened her eyes and took her phone out of her pocket. Her finger hovered over the Videos icon. She was trying hard not to look at that any more. She had the footage from the CCTV camera on the bridge. It had taken two months of pestering John, the security guard, to get it. Pleading, crying, threatening to sue, offering money. Once she went up to the control booth drunk and tried to unzip his trousers, getting on her knees and grabbing at his crotch. He gripped her shoulders and pulled her to her feet. Looked at her with kindness and told her to get help. She cried all the way home.

In the end she wore him down and he gave her the footage. Strictly against policy but maybe he realised she needed it to cling to. So now she carried it around with her, her boy's last moments. A grainy image of him walking to the middle of the bridge, the highest point in the gentle curve of the road, looking out for a few moments, elbows on the railing, flicking his hair out of his eyes like he always did, then climbing over in an agile movement, not looking around or down. A step forward, one step, and he was gone.

She didn't press Videos. Instead she opened Facebook, checked his page. No one had posted anything since last night. Had his friends forgotten him already? In the blur of their busy lives, was he just a memory now?

She typed quickly.

Miss you so much it hurts every moment.

Wish I could have you back.

Mum xxx

She flicked through the pictures of him, snapshots from old parties or muckabouts in the park. One of him with his arm around Jackson, another of him looking shyly at Kayleigh amongst a group outside the chip shop. He had a thing for her, but nothing ever happened that Ellie knew of. Just one of an infinity of missed chances. She felt vertigo at the thought of her son's non-existent future, all the possibilities branching off into fog. It was a familiar feeling and she was comforted by it. The sickness in her stomach, the dizziness, these had become more reliable to her than breathing in the last few months.

She went back to Logan's profile page.

Refresh.

Refresh.

Refresh.

Nothing. Of course. No likes for her comment. Why would anyone like it?

She put her phone back in her pocket and picked up two stones from the beach. She put one in her pocket and felt the heft of the other in her palm, the solidity of the earth it had once been a part of. She hurled it as hard as she could into the water, yanking her shoulder and elbow in the process.

She was weak these days. She'd lost weight in the last six months, and she didn't have a lot to lose in the first place. But eating seemed irrelevant. She was wasting away, on hunger strike against the oblivion of the universe, refusing to take part in the basic chemical process of converting food into energy.

She rubbed at her throwing arm, felt the raw skin. Pushed her sleeve up to examine the tattoo. It was a decent likeness of the bridge, not perfect, but good enough. Still scabby and sore. She liked that period best, when the tattoos hurt. It was her seventh in six months, up her arms, across her back, down her sides. All connected to Logan and the firth. The road bridge, his name, his dates, the rail bridge, a boat and an island. A porpoise arching up her leg. She used to call Logan her little porpoise when he was a toddler, after they saw one together from the Binks, its snubnose pushing through the wash.

Ellie knew the tattoos were compulsive but she didn't care. Ben never said anything. He had his own strategy to get him through, they didn't judge each other for coping however they could.

She scratched at her scabby arm, gazed at the water and thought about what lay under the surface. Junk, sunken boats, dead bodies, the ones they never recover. All of it hidden in hundreds of millions of tons of water. Imagine if the seas of the world dried up, what treasures we would find.

She looked at the bridge again. Tried to think about breathing. In and out, in and out. She turned to walk up there.

'I'm coming,' she said.

2

It felt good to be moving. That's something she'd learned over the last six months, physical exercise was a way of keeping the worst of it at bay.

She strode up Rose Lane away from the Binks and the waterfront, on to Hopetoun Road then left, away from Shore Road and up the hill. After a few minutes the road went under the approach to the bridge, colossal concrete legs supporting the thunder of traffic overhead. She turned left again up the steep access road, feeling the gradient, pushing her legs into it, enjoying the strain on her calves and thighs.

For the first two months after Logan died she did nothing. She took the pills they gave her, cried in her sleep and awake, puked most things she tried to eat, and thought about killing herself. She sat in the house or on the beach, staring at the bridge, wishing she was dead.

Then one day she went in the water.

A paddle at first, just to feel the waves on her toes, to touch the body of water that had killed her son. Then she stripped off and dived in, right there on the Binks. The cold of the firth was shocking, but she embraced it. It was the first time she'd felt alive since it happened. She'd been a strong swimmer before, capable and determined, with solid technique, but she'd grown soft in her time away from the water, and she struggled. That was good, though.

She swam east along the coast, round the harbour, the old town of South Queensferry on her right. Her breathing was heavy, pressure on her lungs, her arms and legs stinging with cold and tiredness, her mind empty of everything except trying to keep going. But her heart was raging with power, she could feel it trying to escape her chest.

She headed back into shore at Hawes Pier, where the tourist boats left for Inchcolm Island. She was gasping for air, bent over in just her bra and pants, a drookit skeleton of a thing, her pallid flesh slick and oily from the dirty water of the firth. The tourists on the pier gawped at her, a monster from the deep, as they sat licking their ice creams.

She walked back along the town's main street, dripping and shivering, everyone pretending to ignore her. Maybe some knew what had happened to Logan. None of them wanted to get involved with a crazy woman, half-naked and shaking. She began to feel like she was slipping into death again, so she started running, bare feet slapping the pavement, dodging round mothers with buggies, old couples taking in the sea air. She wanted to stop and scream at them all that it wasn't worth it, that all the love in the world would die when their loved ones died. But she didn't, she just kept running and running.

And then she was back where she started, at the Binks, her little pile of clothes like a deflated human being, crumpled on the pebbles.

She was at the top of the access road now. She U-turned on to the approach to the bridge. A maintenance van was parked by the visitor centre, and she recognised the man inside. Gerry. She'd spoken to him often, he was nearly pension age, had kids and grandkids, and he knew about Logan. He'd stopped to chat to her on the bridge several times over the months. The day after her swim along the firth she came up to the bridge, and had done so every day since. It was company policy for bridge employees to engage in conversation with anyone lingering on the bridge. The staff had all done suicide prevention training as standard procedure.

So when she'd stopped at the place Logan had jumped from, in the middle of the bridge, it was only a few minutes until the little yellow van came out to see her. Not that five minutes was quick enough to save Logan, who was up and over the railing in thirty seconds. She didn't blame the bridge staff, she didn't blame Logan. She only ever blamed herself.

Since that day it had become a familiar routine. Go down to the waterfront, stare out to sea, look at the bridge, imagine it all, churn it around. Sometimes go for a swim, depending how dead she felt. Then head up to the bridge and chew it over again from up there. It probably hurt more than it helped but Ellie didn't care, the methodical repetition of it gave her something to hold on to.

She turned away from Gerry's sad smile before he could open the van window and speak to her. She didn't feel like engaging with him today. She walked along the bridge approach. As always she was amazed by the roar of the traffic, the brazen exposure to the elements up here, the scale of this massive intrusion into nature.

She looked at the warning signs, like she did every day.

PERSONS UNDER 14 MUST BE ACCOMPANIED BY AN ADULT

Logan was fifteen, so that wasn't a problem. Had he wanted

to do it for years, but waited to make sure he obeyed the law? Stupid, stupid.

IT IS AN OFFENCE TO THROW OBJECTS FROM THE BRIDGE

Did that include yourself? She knew now that suicide itself wasn't a crime in Scotland, but if you fucked it up and lived you could get done for breach of the peace. Imagine the indignity of that, not only had you failed to die but you'd turned yourself into a criminal in the process.

Ellie stroked the smooth stone in her pocket, the second one she lifted from the Binks. She'd done this every day too, taken something from the shore, brought it up and dropped it over. She didn't know why, just needed to do it. What were they going to do, arrest her?

WARNING

LOW RAILINGS WITH WIDE GAPS

YOUNG CHILDREN MUST BE CLOSELY SUPERVISED

AT ALL TIMES

How young was young? Had she supervised Logan closely enough? Every day as a parent you had to strike a balance between protection and independence. The first walk to school alone, the first sleepover, staying out after dark. That loss of control over your child was a terrifying slow death. At some point you have to let them grow up, that's what they say about teenagers. But what if they choose not to grow up at all?

She turned away from the Samaritans sign and looked out.

The tops of birch trees planted down below were at the same height as the road she was on, crows nesting in the branches, cawing loudly, protecting their young.

She stepped on to the bridge and felt the comforting vibrations under her feet. Something she hadn't really thought about before Logan jumped. She'd been across the bridge plenty of times but never really paid attention. Now, since the jump, her senses were sharpened, every observation acute, every thought poignant or profound. Like those people who had near-death experiences and found a new joy in the mundane nature of life. Except in her case it was the opposite, it had taken the suicide of her son to make her more attuned to the presence of death everywhere.

She placed a hand on the railing and felt the throb of the traffic. When a lorry went past, the road beneath her shook and swayed. It was terrifying and exhilarating. It was a suspension bridge, and only once you were on it did you realise what that meant, that it was suspended from its giant supports, millions of tons of it kept in position by thin steel cables. It swayed in the wind, shook with the traffic. One day it would come crashing down into the water and all this engineering brilliance would be lost.

She strode towards the centre of the bridge. The camber was large, another surprise to her tuned senses the first time up here after Logan. She walked past the SOS Crisis phone for drivers, the first set of CCTV cameras, then the traffic warning signs. She looked out across the expanse of water. North Queensferry huddled into the hillside on the opposite bank, the rail bridge sturdy and implacable over Inch Garvie, then back the way she'd come, her and Ben's home nestled at the water's edge between the older flats by the harbour and the new developments closer to the marina.

She stopped and looked up at the cabling, felt dizzy. Closed her eyes and leaned back against the railing, let the tremors overtake her body. She sensed two lorries raging past, her body shaking in unison with them. It felt good to be connected.

She opened her eyes and kept walking towards the middle of the bridge.

As the camber levelled off, she saw a figure up ahead. A teenage boy or a young man, tall and thin, standing where she was heading for, the centre of the bridge. For a moment, a tiny gasp of time, she thought it was Logan.

She took a few more steps then realised the person wasn't on this side of the railing. He was already over it, standing on the thin metal ledge beyond, holding on to the railing behind his back, looking down at the water.

3

She tried to shout between breaths as she sprinted towards him.

'Wait.'

Gulping in air.

'Stop.'

He was fifty yards away, still looking down, rocking backwards and forwards, his elbows bending and straightening as his fingers gripped the grey metal behind his back.

Thirty yards.

'Hold on,' Ellie shouted.

The traffic noise was all around her, seeping into her, pervading everything. She didn't know if he hadn't heard or was just ignoring her.

Fifteen yards.

'Stop.'

His body jerked and he turned his head towards her. His face was crumpled and tears were streaming down his cheeks, snot from his nose. He was taller than Logan, maybe a couple of years older, but he had the same hair flick covering his eyes. The breeze blew his hair about, swirling around them both. He wore a blue-and-grey-striped hoodie, jeans, Adidas, standard teenage stuff. Logan had similar clothes in his room right now, washed, put away forever.

'Logan?'

She didn't know why she said it. She didn't even realise it came from her mouth until it was out. She knew it wasn't him, crazy to even think it.

He looked confused. His breath was catching in his chest from the crying, his body shaking with the bridge as a truck hammered past. Ellie turned and stared at the road. No one would pull over. The drivers probably hadn't noticed anything, and even if they did it was madness to stop in the middle of a dual carriageway when you were travelling at sixty miles an hour. And anyway, there was no way to get from the road to the footpath of the bridge without climbing across the gap between, where the cables stretched to the top of the support tower. You had a pretty good chance of killing yourself doing that.

She glanced at the CCTV cameras, then looked both ways along the path. No sign of the yellow van. It took five minutes, if they were even watching the monitors.

It was down to her.

'Don't do this,' she said.

He shook his head, then stared at the water past the rail bridge, the firth widening to the sea.

'No,' Ellie said. 'Turn round. Look at me.'

He didn't turn. He began rocking forward and back, as if geeing himself up for a dive into a swimming pool.

'Please turn round and talk to me.'

Ellie knew all about this now. She'd spent night after night looking up suicide-prevention techniques online, official strategies on SAMH and Choose Life websites, anecdotal stuff on message boards from people who had tried and failed, as well as people who had been talked out of it. All of it, that mass of loneliness and distress, boiled down to one thing. Get them talking. Engage. Be there, and help them to reconsider.

'Please,' she said.

She took three steps closer. He was only a few feet away now, shoulders shaking, legs jittery. He was thin, like Logan, gangly, as if his bones didn't quite fit together yet. His clothes were too baggy, hanging off him. She stared at his hands on the railing. She prayed for those hands to hold on, as if they were separate from his willpower, his decision making. He had long, thin fingers and slender wrists.

Another step closer. She could almost touch him.

'My son did this,' she said. She tried to speak calmly but she wanted to be heard over the rage of the traffic. 'Six months ago. Don't do it. You think this is the only way, that you're never going to feel better, but you're wrong. We can get help. Think about your mum. Your family.'

His left hand came off the railing. She reached out towards him. He swung round to face her and grabbed hold of the railing again, this time with his back to the water, away from the drop.

She put her hands on his hands. Her spindly little bones dwarfed by his. He was a foot taller than her, around six feet, maybe seventeen years old, close to being a man. Closer than Logan was ever going to get. He had a beautiful face, smudged by tears and confusion. Big brown eyes, some thin stubble across his chin and lip.

Ellie rubbed her hands up and down his on the railing.

'Come over to this side,' she said.

His chest was heaving as he tried to get his breath back, tried to compose himself. Ellie knew from all those suicide videos that nothing was predictable, nothing made any sense in the face of this moment. She moved her hands up to his wrists and held on tight. If he went over, she would go too.

'Please, just come back to me.'

He avoided looking at her, turned to stare both ways along the bridge, then down at his feet. Ellie followed his gaze and felt vertigo, the huge drop a few inches behind him. Seeing what Logan must've seen just before he jumped. It took real bottle, that's what she'd come to understand. Her son had a lot of guts. This wasn't a coward's way out, this wasn't pills or wrists or whatever. This was brave and strong and she was perversely proud to have produced such an independent human being from her own tiny body.

She reached up and stroked this boy's cheek, then held his jaw so that he had to look in her eyes. He could've pulled away, he was strong enough, but he didn't.

'Come back to me,' she said.

The railing between them was four feet high. He could swing his leg over and it was done, but there was no way Ellie could pull him back if he didn't want to. It was his choice.

'Maybe I should come over there to you,' she said.

He looked surprised, shook his head.

'Don't do that,' he said.

His voice was deeper than Logan's, but still somehow not fully formed.

'Please,' she said. 'Come over. So we can talk.'

He took a large breath then released it. Looked up and down the bridge again. Then shifted his weight and lifted his leg so that his foot was on top of the railing. She had to move backwards to make room for him, but she held on to his wrists.

With a flex of muscle he was up then over, the same movement Logan did in the CCTV footage only in reverse, from the bad side to the good. From death to life.

Ellie put her arms around him and felt him squirm. It was inappropriate but she didn't care, she wanted to hold on to him and never let him go. The size of him towering over her was comforting. She hadn't felt that strange sensation in months, the weird dislocation of touching a teenage boy already taller than you, marvelling at the physical presence of the thing you'd created, something that was no longer part of you at all, completely alien.

She was still holding him, and she felt his arms go round her. She began crying. He took hold of her shoulders and prised himself away.

She wiped at her tears and looked up to see him doing the same. She laughed.

'I'm sorry,' she said.

He shook his head.

Behind him, Ellie could see the orange flashing light on the maintenance van as it approached.

'What's your name?' she said.

He took a long time to answer. He was trembling. 'Sam.'

She noticed a dark stain on his jeans where he'd wet himself.

'Will I take you home?' she said.

He shook his head, panic on his face.

She rubbed his arm. 'It's all right, you can come back to my house, we'll get you sorted, OK?'

He thought about it then nodded.

The van arrived and Gerry got out. 'Everything all right, Ellie?'

She put on a smile. 'Fine, Gerry, thanks.'

'Got a call from the office, is all.'

'It's OK, really.'

Gerry looked undecided. He couldn't leave them standing here on the bridge in case of a change of heart, she understood that.

'We're just heading home,' she said.

She guided Sam away, back towards the south end of the bridge.

Gerry scratched at his beard and called after her. 'If you're sure you don't need any help?'

She looked at Sam, his hair flicked across his face, and turned back.

'It's fine,' she said. 'I've got him.'

4

She had her arm around his waist as they walked, trying to help him put one foot in front of the other as if he was an injured passenger being led away from a car crash.

'We'll get you sorted,' she said, rubbing his side.

He didn't react, kept his head down, feet plodding on like he was in a trance.

She'd forgotten about the awkwardness of teenage boys.

The rumble and judder of traffic continued to swamp the pair of them, hundreds of people driving to their destinations regardless of Ellie and Sam's little drama. It must've been the same when Logan jumped. Did anyone driving across the bridge that day even realise something had happened? Hundreds of cars must've passed Logan as he walked towards the middle of the bridge. Dozens more in the few moments he stood there. And yet more as he climbed over and stepped off.

But the drivers' eyes would've been on the road ahead. People only realised something happened if the bridge got closed to traffic, and they never did that. One incident Ellie remembered from a long time ago was when someone, instead of jumping off the bridge, climbed the suspension cables and threatened to jump off. They had to close the bridge that day. In the end the guy never jumped, and he was charged with breach of the peace when he clambered down. Road users were furious. The same kind of people who tut on a train when someone jumps in front of it, because they're going to be five minutes late for a meeting.

Twenty people kill themselves by jumping off the Forth Road Bridge every year. They were about to celebrate the bridge's fiftieth anniversary soon. That added up to a thousand people. But it only rarely made the news, partly because it wasn't deemed newsworthy, partly because journalists had guidelines about reporting suicide. If you made a big deal about it in the papers you got lots of copycat deaths. Imagine sitting at home reading about someone killing themselves and thinking, oh yeah, that's what I want to do.

Ellie looked at Sam. Maybe that's what he'd done. Maybe he knew Logan, or had heard about Logan jumping, and thought he would do the same. Or maybe there was another kid who'd jumped off more recently, a friend of Sam's. She knew that in South Queensferry, in the shadow of the bridge, there was a higher suicide rate than elsewhere. Experts put it down to simple opportunity. People saw the bridge every day out their windows, on their way to work or school, and thought, why not?

They were at the end of the bridge now. Sam began crying again, staring at his hands as if he might find the answer to life there. Ellie wanted to tell him it wasn't that easy, there were no answers.

'I'll take care of you,' she said.

They stepped off the bridge and the vibration under their feet stopped, though the rumble of traffic noise was still everywhere.

Ellie ushered Sam round the corner on to the access road. As they headed downhill the noise reduced, leaving an oppressive murmur, the crows from earlier cawing and flapping in the tops of the trees.

'I live down at the Binks,' Ellie said.

It was awkward to keep walking with her arm round his waist as they headed downhill, so she removed it and took his hand in hers. He let her. It felt odd, the slope pushing them forwards, holding hands as if they were a couple, this half-boy, half-man towering over her, her hand engulfed in his like she was the child. But she felt a thrill, too, an electricity running from his touch through her hand and up her arm.

For a moment she considered what it would look like if they met anyone she knew. She was twice as old as him, and he was far too old to be holding hands with his mum. Not that she was his mother of course.

At the bottom of the hill she pointed right. 'This way. It's not far.'

He walked in the direction she indicated. She wondered what was going through his mind. What had driven him up there today? What was so awful in his life that he couldn't see any alternative? She was used to the wondering. The lack of answers burned as much today as it did the first day, and it would burn just as ferociously on her deathbed. At least with Sam she had a chance of finding an answer.

'You OK?'

He shook his head.

'Let's get you home,' she said.

5

'Try these on.'

She held up a pair of Logan's jeans. Dark green, skinny fit. She remembered when he brought them home, one of the first things she'd let him buy for himself, on a trip into Edinburgh shopping with mates. Just one of a million little independences, all the ways in which children grow into their own lives, away from their parents.

Sam was a couple of inches taller than Logan, but they were both thin and bony, the jeans would still fit.

Sam sat on Logan's bed, his hands over his lap to hide the wet stain on the front of his trousers. Ellie hadn't mentioned it but the offer of trousers meant he knew that she knew. She was thrilled they shared a secret, only the two of them knew what just happened on the bridge, it connected them forever, no matter what came next.

Sam's eyes darted round the room as he took the jeans and held them like ancient relics.

Ellie looked round the room too. It wasn't a shrine, she wasn't insane, thinking Logan would come back one day and slot back into his old life, she just couldn't bring herself to clear his things out. His plain blue bedspread, nondescript after a childhood of cartoon characters on there. His music posters, Frightened Rabbit, Chvrches, Haim, Lorde. She was glad about that, strong female figures among them, talented, independent women, no R&B idiots in bikinis. His PS3 and Xbox and iPod and laptop sat in a corner, his neatly ordered bookshelf full of zombie stories and graphic novels.

And this new boy sitting amongst it all.

She realised he was waiting for her to leave so he could get changed.

'Oh sorry,' she said, turning her back. 'I won't look.'

She felt him hesitate then heard him begin to untie his trainers. She looked at the television on the dresser. She could see his shape reflected in the black glass as he peeled his damp jeans off. She realised something and opened the drawer in front of her, pulled out a pair of Logan's underwear. He preferred trunks, tighter than boxers but not as skimpy as briefs. Without turning, she held them out behind her back.

'Here, you'll need these.'

She felt him take the trunks, and caught a little of his deodorant smell. Not exactly the same as Logan's, but in the same ballpark, and too much of it, like all teenage boys. Probably Lynx, that's what they all wore because of the ads with the half-naked girls all over the guys who used it.

She looked back at the television. Saw Sam slip off his shorts, his back to her, pale buttocks in the glass of the screen. He wiped at his crotch and legs with his scrunched up shorts, then pulled on Logan's underwear, stumbling to get his foot in the first hole, yanking them up, pulling the jeans over them. Ellie squinted as she watched him in the glass, imagining Logan.

She turned round. 'Sorted?'

He nodded, looked at his clothes on the floor. Ellie picked them up without a fuss and rolled them up in a ball in her hands. 'I'll get these in the wash.'

Sam shook his head. 'You don't have to.'

'It's no problem.' She moved to the door. She wanted to ask him so much, but didn't want to scare him away. 'Come on, I'll put the kettle on.'

She went downstairs, heard his footfall behind her as she turned into the kitchen. She threw the jeans and shorts into the washing machine, poured some liquid in and switched it on. The machine shuddered as she took the kettle to the sink and filled it. When she turned back he was standing in the doorway. She pulled a chair out from the kitchen table, nodded at it.

'Sit down, love.'

He took the seat and picked at his fingernails.

She switched on the kettle, came over and sat next to him.

'Want to tell me what that was about, on the bridge?'

'No.'

He began crying again. Ellie was starting to see a pattern, periods of near catatonia, followed by tears. He was getting himself het up now, his breath catching, like a panic attack. His shoulders shook with it. She got up and put her hands on his neck muscles, felt the tension and knots beneath her fingers.

'Hey, it's all right,' she said, almost a whisper. 'Whatever's the matter is outside that front door, OK? Nothing can hurt you in here, you're safe now.'

It was a litany, under her breath, the tone reassuring more than the words. She meant it, though, she would take care of this boy, never let any harm come to him.

He began to calm down. She made green tea for them both, and got a couple of pills out a drawer. A sleeping pill and a mood stabiliser. She couldn't remember the brand names. She brought the tea and the pills over to the table.

'Take these,' she said. 'They'll make you feel better.'

He frowned.

'They work, trust me,' she said.

He picked them up and took them, sipping at his tea to wash them down. She sipped from her own mug as she sat.

'What's your surname, Sam?'

He hesitated, looked out the kitchen window. They were at the back of the house, the view of the bridges, the massive lines of them framing the whole world, pointing their eyes towards North Queensferry on the opposite bank.

'Look at me,' Ellie said. 'I promise I won't let anything happen to you.'

'McKenna,' he said.

'Do you go to the High School?'

'Just finished.'

'Sixth year?'

He nodded.

'So you're seventeen, eighteen?'

'Seventeen.'

Two years ahead of Logan, then.

'Did you know my son, Logan?'

Sam shook his head.

'But you know what he did?'

He nodded. It was the talk of the school for weeks, maybe months. They had a memorial for him, some words at assembly from the head teacher. Ellie was invited but hadn't gone, couldn't stand having all that youthfulness and vitality in her face.

'It's not the answer, Sam.'

She took his hand but he pulled it away.

'You don't know,' he said.

Ellie sighed. 'You think I don't? What I've been through with Logan?'

He fiddled with the zip on his hoodie, head down. He jumped like he'd got a fright, then pulled the zip up to the top, hands shaking, eyes wide.

Ellie thought she'd seen something.

She reached out to his hand on the zip. 'What's that?'

He brushed her hand away, but she put it back a second time and he didn't resist. His eyes looked around for something to distract himself.

She peeled his fingers away and pulled the zip down, pushed the material aside. His blue T-shirt underneath had marks spattered across it. Dark stains.

'Is that blood?'

His breathing was erratic again, his body shaking.

She tried to unzip the hoodie the whole way. 'What is it, Sam? Are you hurt?'

He knocked her hand away, hard this time, and pulled the zip up.

'I'm fine,' he said, through stuttering breaths.

'Then . . .'

She heard a noise. A car pulling into the driveway.

Ben was home. Ellie looked at Sam. She didn't want to share him, not yet. It was their little secret, Sam and Ellie. And there was the bloodstain to think about.

She heard the car engine switch off.

'Come on.' She took Sam's hand and yanked him out of his seat.

She pulled him up the stairs and into Logan's room as she heard the front door open.

'Hi, honey.' Ben in the hallway.

She pushed Sam on to Logan's bed. 'Stay in here and keep quiet.'

She heard footsteps coming upstairs. She backed out of the room, closed the door and turned.

Ben was halfway up.

'Hi,' she said, keeping her voice level.

'Hey.' Ben looked at her, then beyond at Logan's bedroom door. 'What were you doing in there?'

'Nothing.' She walked downstairs past him. 'Just putting something away.'

He followed her into the kitchen.

'Are you all right?' he said.

'Fine.'

'Who's that for?'

She turned. 'What?'

He was pointing at the two mugs of green tea on the table.

'You,' she said. 'The kettle boiled just as I heard you pull up.'

He frowned at her for a moment. She examined him. He hadn't shaved in a week, the stubble greyer than it used to be, a white patch on the side of his chin that was never there before. He needed a haircut, messy at the sides, too long at the back. He looked tired, dark pouches under his eyes, hollow cheeks, and he seemed to be squinting into the light all the time. His checked shirt and jeans needed washed. She caught a little of his scent, the smell of nervous sweat. He always seemed to be nervous now, nervous about what shit life would deliver next. She knew that feeling well enough.

'I can't really stop,' he said. He picked up Sam's mug and

took a sip. 'I don't know why you try to get me to drink this stuff, you know I can't stand it.'

'It's supposed to relax you. Clean the system.'

'I know what it's supposed to do.'

She looked at him for a moment. 'What are you up to?'

He patted at the satchel over his shoulder. 'More flyering.' He pulled a leaflet out, handed it to her.

This was how Ben filled the void since Logan. While Ellie had resorted to physical routine to blot out the blackness, Ben had jumped straight down the conspiracy-theory rabbit hole. It wasn't Logan's fault according to Ben, it couldn't be, he was under some kind of external influence, something made him do it, no son of mine could ever think about taking his own life. Denial, obviously. He wasn't stupid, though, deep down he must realise it was ridiculous, just as her swimming and running and walking to the bridge was a coping mechanism, nothing else.

So he buried himself deep into suicide conspiracies. He became an expert on cluster points, where you got a spate of suicides in one place, very often teenagers who all knew each other. There was a small town in Wales where dozens had done it within months of each other, and Ben knew all the stats for that place, comparing them to the numbers for South Queensferry. He spent countless hours on websites and online chatrooms, dabbling in stuff that even David Icke might baulk at. Satanic cults, mind-altering drugs, school vaccinations, food additives, computer games, side effects of prescription medication, washing powder, the signal from mobile-telephone masts causing depression, anxiety and suicidal thoughts.

She looked at the leaflet in her hand. This was his latest crusade, the Queensferry Crossing, as it had been named. The new road bridge across the Forth was being built just to the west of the current one, hitting land right next to the marina where Ben had worked until recently. He'd stumbled across the idea on some crackpot website that either something in their internal communication network was sending signals into the ether that changed the wiring of kids' brains, or there was something in the building materials giving off a gas that poisoned everyone's minds. It was ridiculous, of course, and she'd told him so umpteen times, but he never heard. She understood, it was hard to hear the truth, that Logan just killed himself and there was no answer, no resolution. No comfort. Easier to believe that the government or building contractors or phone companies were to blame.

Ben's leaflet had quotes from building trade 'insiders' confirming that dangerous, cheap non-EU chemicals were being used, and that there had been other clusters of suicides at major building projects using the same method in the Far East.

Ellie closed her eyes and tried to remember their wedding day. Tight-skinned and happy, the two of them waltzing in a small marquee, their lives ahead of them, Logan not even an idea then, let alone a dead one. All she could see was Sam standing on the bridge, his hands tight on the railing, his body swaying back and forth. Her eyes went to the ceiling. Logan's room was directly above them, if Sam walked around they would likely hear him.

Ben took another sip of tea and made a face at the taste. 'I really need to get going, deliver these.'

Ellie wondered what the neighbours thought of Ben's steady stream of lunatic leaflets through their letterboxes. To begin with maybe there was some sympathy, he'd lost his son after all. But now, six months later, wasn't it time to move on? But it was never time to move on, that's what she'd come to realise.

'Stay a minute.' She went over to him and touched his arm. 'Sit down. I feel like we haven't talked in ages.'

'If you're going to go on about the leaflets, I don't want to hear it.'

'I won't.'

He sat down, the same chair Sam had been in a few minutes before. Ellie listened for noise from upstairs, but there was nothing. The washing machine chugged away in the corner of the kitchen, throwing Sam's trousers and pants around.

She knew she should tell Ben. Keeping it to herself could only push them apart. But she had to figure out what it all meant, had to understand the gift she'd been given first, before she could share it.

'Remember when we saw that porpoise, when Logan was little,' she said.

He shook his head. 'I remember.'

'He was three, I think?'

Ben nodded. 'Three and a half.'

'He kept saying "dolphink", "dolphink".'

'Then you said, "No, it's a porpoise".'

Ellie laughed. 'And then he wouldn't stop saying "purpose", "purpose".'

They were both smiling now. Their little purpose. Ellie tried to think when she'd last seen Ben smile.

'Our little porpoise,' she said.

Ben sighed, the smile gone. 'Yeah.'

Ellie looked up at the ceiling, then out at the Forth. 'What if we got a second chance?'

'What do you mean?'

'Imagine we got to live our lives over,' Ellie said. 'What would you do different?'

'Don't, Ellie.'

'Go on.'

'I can't do this. I don't want to hear you talk like this.'

'But if we got a second chance?'

Ben stood up, knuckles on the table. 'There are no second chances. You know that. Stop talking this way, please.'

She got up too, hands out, pleading. 'What are we going to do, Ben? There's no end to this, is there?'

He shrugged and headed for the door.

'No,' he said. 'It never ends.'

She heard the front door open and close.

She breathed in and out a few times, trying to get the hang of it, then looked at the ceiling.

She went upstairs and opened the door to Logan's room, careful not to make any sound.

Sam was sleeping on top of Logan's bed, hands under his cheek, face slack. Ellie went to a drawer and took out a blanket, draped it over him. She pushed his fringe away from his face, tucked a stray strand of hair behind his ear. She let the backs of her fingers rest on his cheek for a while, feeling the movement of his breathing, watching his chest rise and fall, peaceful for now.

There are no second chances.

6

Inchcolm Terrace was a suburban cul-de-sac like any other. Fifties-built detached houses, pebbledash, steep roofs, garages. Family homes with trampolines and scooters in the small gardens.

Ellie walked along, checking the numbers. She stopped at number 23, Sam's place, same as all the rest. It had taken ten minutes to walk here from her house at the shore, up The Loan then nipping in to the right, easy enough to find. She'd never been up this street before, but then you wouldn't unless you knew someone who lived here, it wasn't a road to anywhere.

She'd checked the phone book, only one McKenna in South Queensferry. She thought about phoning but didn't, this felt like a conversation that needed to be face to face. She wasn't even sure what she was going to tell them about Sam, if anything. Where do you start? But she wanted to see their faces, see the family he'd come from, the people who had created and shaped him. Were they worried about him? Had he shown any of the signs of mental-health problems? Where did they think he was right now?

She dragged a hand down her face, felt the slackness of her skin, then walked through the gate and up the path. She rang the doorbell and waited. Nothing. Rang again. Silence. She looked at the neighbouring houses, wondered about curtains twitching but didn't see any movement. She rang a third time.

She tried the front door. It opened and she leaned in.

'Hello?'

She stepped inside. Coats were piled on the end of the banister, shoes on a low shelf unit by the door. Looked like four people, including a girl. Perfect little family unit – mum, dad, son and daughter.

She closed the door behind her.

'Hello?'

A bowl on the hall table with car keys, small change, golf balls, Post-its, a phone charger. The stuff of life. She couldn't picture Sam as the golfer, it must be his dad. Sanded wooden floor, an IKEA runner rug on top, she recognised it from last year's catalogue.

She looked up the stairs. Thought about going up there, wondered which room was Sam's, if it looked anything like Logan's. What about the sister, was she a chintzy pink princess or old enough to be a moody emo by now?

She heard a noise, maybe a voice, from the direction of the kitchen.

'Hello, the door was open. Is someone there?'

She crept down the hall, listening. That noise again, a grunt. She got to the kitchen doorway.

'Holy shit.'

Lying slumped against the fridge was a man with a kitchen knife in his gut. Stocky, receding hairline, in his forties. His eyes were closed and his forehead creased with deep furrows. Blood was soaked into his white shirt and black trousers, and had pooled around him on the tiled floor. He let out a pained breath.

Ellie took two steps forward. 'Can you hear me?'

He didn't move or speak. His chest rose and fell, small movements.

She took another step.

The fingers on his right hand twitched. His hand lifted off the bloody floor for a moment, as if he was trying to reach for the knife, then it dropped back down with a little splash of blood.

She looked around the kitchen. No sign of any other disturbance, nothing smashed or broken. Sliding glass doors led into the back garden. They were closed, no obvious sign of a break-in.

She looked at the man. He didn't look like a burglar. She thought about the bloodstains on Sam's T-shirt. Looked at the knife in the man's belly. It had a serrated edge, wooden handle, she had one similar at home.

'Mr McKenna?'

He gave out a breathy moan.

She stood absolutely still, trying to think.

The man's fingers twitched again and one eye opened. He looked at her, but his gaze was unfocussed. She didn't know how conscious he was, how aware. He grunted again then his eye closed and he gave a heavy sigh, as if the effort was all too much.

Ellie heard another noise. The scrape of a key in a lock, then the front door opening, a bag being dropped on the floor.

'I'm home.' A woman's voice, shouting up the stairs. 'You lazy gits up yet?'

The man on the floor wheezed.

Ellie stepped over him, careful not to stand in the blood, and ran to the patio doors. She slid the snib up then pushed the door open just enough to squeeze through, gliding it shut behind her.

She ran to the side of the house, out of view, then climbed over a low fence of wooden slats into the neighbours' garden. At the bottom of the garden were a couple of cooking-apple trees. She sprinted down to them and launched herself at the stone wall behind, scrambling up and over. She dropped down without looking, desperate to get away. She hoped no one was in the neighbours' kitchen or she was spotted for sure.

She glanced around as she got her breath back. She recognised where she was, Ferrymuir Gait. Over the embankment across the road was the A90, heading to the bridge. Further round the road she was standing on were the visitor centre and the offices for the new bridge. Back the other way was the cemetery where Logan would've been buried if they hadn't decided to have him cremated and scattered in the Forth. Everything so close by, everyone in the Ferry living in each other's pockets, the road and the railway and the bridges slicing through it all.

She waited and listened. After a few minutes she heard a siren, and imagined the ambulance arriving.

Now she had her bearings she knew there was a quicker way home, past the visitor centre and down the access road, the same road she'd walked with Sam earlier today. She headed in that direction.

7

She let herself in the back door and went through the rooms, checking Ben wasn't there. She hadn't come directly back to the house, instead ducking left off Hopetoun Road on to Shore Road, then cutting down to the beach, avoiding the police station two minutes away from the front of her house.

The house was silent. She listened for sirens from the cop shop. Nothing. You hardly heard them here, the Ferry wasn't exactly a hotbed of crime. No sound from upstairs either. She went up and stopped outside the door to Logan's room. Rested her fingers against the chunky wooden letters that spelled out his name. She ran her hand from the L to the O and slowly onwards, stopping with her fingers pressed against the N. The sign had been on Logan's door for ten years, and he'd moaned about it being childish when he hit his teens, but he never took it down and neither did she.

There was a rough splinter of wood at the end of the N, it had been like that for as long as Ellie could remember. She deliberately snagged her thumb on it, feeling the skelf push against her skin. She remembered for the hundredth time that day that her son was dead, that she would never see him again, then she breathed and pushed the door open.

Sam was still asleep, blanket pulled over him. Ellie sat on the edge of the bed and ran her hands through his hair, brushing against his ear.

He moaned in his sleep.

She moved up the bed, still stroking his hairline along his forehead, behind his ear, letting her hand linger on the nape of his neck for a moment, before starting again. She breathed in through her nose, caught the smell of Lynx and urine and something underneath, his unique scent.

He was coming round. She didn't want to disturb him, but she had a stronger urge to hear him speak, to hear his voice and reassure him. He looked like he was having a good dream, and she wondered how that was possible. She tried to remember when she'd last had a good dream.

His eyes fluttered open and he looked at her, confused.

'Shhh,' she said. 'You're safe.'

She saw it on his face as he began to recognise where he was and who he was with, as he remembered what had happened. The confusion turning to distress, panic.

She was still stroking his head, but he pushed her hand away and tried to sit up.

'It's OK,' she said. Her hand lay limp on the bedclothes where it had landed. She looked at it as if it wasn't part of her.

Sam seemed more together than he'd been earlier, more aware of his situation. He went into the pocket of his hoodie and pulled out his phone. Checked for messages with a trembling hand, then pushed call and held it to his ear.

Ellie could hear it from where she sat. She prayed for it to go to voicemail. Five rings, then it did. Sam hung up without leaving a message.

'Who are you trying to get hold of?' she said.

He shook his head, trying to drive the sleep away.

'Is it your little sister?' Ellie said, thinking about the coats and shoes in the hallway earlier.

He stared at her. 'How do you know I have a little sister?'

She tried to put her hand on his, but he slipped away from her touch.

'I just want to make sure you're OK,' she said.

'How do you know about Libby?'

'Libby, that's a lovely name. How old is she?'

'I asked you a question.' He shuffled back against the headboard. 'Who are you?'

'You know who I am,' Ellie said. 'Do you remember being on the bridge earlier?'

'Of course.'

'I found you. Brought you back here to get you sorted out.'

He glanced at his phone then rubbed his face. 'How do you know about my sister?'

She looked at him, held his gaze. 'I've been to your house.'

'What?' He seemed younger than his age suddenly, had the scared look of a toddler in trouble.

'I was worried. You fell asleep. I wanted to get in contact with your parents, let them know you were safe.'

He rubbed at his fist with his other hand. 'And?'

She shook her head. 'I didn't. At least . . .'

'What?'

She took his hand. 'Why don't you tell me what happened at home?'

He pulled away from her and sat up, swinging his legs off the bed in a tangle of blanket. 'I need to speak to my sister.'

She put a hand on his thigh, felt his muscle through the

38

material of her son's jeans. 'Wait, I can help. Tell me what happened and I'll help you find Libby.'

He looked at her hand on his leg. 'I can't.'

She stood up, positioning herself between him and the door, arms folded across her chest. Not that it would do any good if he wanted to leave.

'Let me tell you what I found,' she said. 'I went to your house, 23 Inchcolm Terrace. There was no answer but the door was unlocked, so I went in. I found a man in the kitchen with a knife in him. I think that man is your dad. He was still alive. I heard your mum come in the front door and I ran out back. A few minutes later I heard an ambulance arrive, then I came home.'

He looked down at his lap and played with the zip on his hoodie. Ellie thought about the bloody T-shirt underneath.

'Now your turn,' Ellie said.

'Do you think he's still alive now?' Sam said, his head staying down.

'I don't know. I think so. He opened his eyes when I was there.'

'He saw you?'

Ellie nodded. 'But I don't know how aware he was of anything around him.'

Sam sat in silence.

'Is he your dad?' Ellie said.

A nod.

'Who attacked him?'

Sam rubbed his hands.

'Was it you?' Ellie said.

Sam closed his eyes, pinched at the bridge of his nose.

'I saw blood on your T-shirt.'

He nodded again.

'Was it an accident?'

Sam raised his head and looked at her. 'No.'

Ellie thought for a moment. Sam looked at his phone.

'Is this to do with Libby?' Ellie said.

He picked up his phone and tried to call her again. Still no answer. He nodded as he threw the phone on to the bed.

'Were you protecting her?' Ellie said.

Sam hesitated. 'I was trying to.'

Just then the front door opened downstairs. Ben was home. Sam tensed up at the sound and Ellie put her hands out to placate him.

'It's just my husband,' she said. 'He doesn't know you're here, doesn't know anything about this.'

A voice from downstairs. 'Ellie?'

Ellie walked across the room, placed her hand on the door handle. 'Stay in here, it's safe. I'll go and speak to him. I won't tell him about you.' She looked at the floor. 'Don't walk about or we'll hear you downstairs.'

She opened the door, looking at Sam. 'OK?'

'OK.'

8

Ben spoke as she entered the kitchen.

'Something's happened.'

He'd already flipped open the laptop on the table and was typing in their password.

Logan1.

Ellie's hands had typed that password into countless computers and online accounts over the years, she could hit the sequence of keys every time at speed without thinking or looking. A muscle memory, completely subconscious. If she slowed down to think about it, it felt clumsy and awkward, and she would get it wrong. Like glimpsing something in the corner of your eye that disappeared if you tried to look at it directly.

Ben fired up Twitter. He was much more internet savvy than she was, all that time in obscure conspiracy chatrooms and the like. Ellie thought about Logan's Facebook page, felt a familiar itch to check in and see if anyone had posted anything. Then she thought about Sam upstairs. When she got a moment she would look him up on Facebook, his sister too, find out all about his life, family, friends, whatever it was that had brought him to her. She looked at the ceiling. How many inches away were his feet? The ceiling was covered in grease and cooking stains, cobwebs strung across the corners. Who ever cleaned their kitchen ceiling?

Ben was typing away. Ellie didn't do Twitter, didn't understand the appeal. Just lots of celebrities showing off, and angry, lonely people shouting into the void. Every second news story these days was about people being abusive on Twitter, misogyny, racism, all the bitter bile of humanity in one handy place.

'What's happened?' she said.

'There's police everywhere,' Ben said.

She looked over his shoulder.

He typed in: 'Why are there police all over South Queensferry?'

Then he searched #queensferry #police.

He turned to her. 'I was flyering up The Loan when three cop cars went bombing past, sirens and lights on. By the time I got to Kirkliston Road one of them was parked across Viewforth Place blocking the street. I spoke to the officer but he wouldn't tell me anything, just that there was an incident and they'd cordoned off the area. So I went round the back way, but Loch Place and Lovers Lane were blocked too. That means about ten streets are closed. That's some incident.'

He didn't wait for a reaction from her, but turned back to the laptop, his conspiracy brain kicking in. Before the jump, Ben had not exactly been a passive acceptor of authority, but since Logan died he didn't trust anything that anyone in power told him. Watching the news, he provided a running commentary on the lies they were being told and why it was exactly what they wanted you to think, how big corporations or government or the police were covering up dark secrets, misdirecting public attention, treating us like idiots. Ellie had some sympathy for the point of view but he'd gone too deep. You had to trust someone or something at some point, didn't you, or else how do you go about living in a society? Of course, how you went about living was a question she hadn't yet found her own answer to.

Ben pointed at the screen. 'Look at this.'

He scrolled down through the feed. A handful of people had posted.

WTF I cannae get to my fkn house, cops have closed roads. #viewforthroad #queensferry

Some shit going down in Inchcolm Terrace, crawling with polis. #queensferry

#queensferry Counted 6 cop cars, a van and amblnc in Inchcholm Terr, number 25?

Holy fukk!!! Guys in they white forensic suits in garden of 23 Inchcolm Terrace #queensferry #CSIshit

Two filth at door just asked if I'd seen anything!! Fuck! #queensferry

'What do you think?' Ben said.

'I have no idea,' Ellie said.

Ben clicked Refresh again and again. One or two new posts appeared but no new info. Ellie thought about the people in white suits going over the garden, the house, the kitchen. Her fingerprints on the doorbell, the front door handle and the glass of the patio. She tried to remember if she'd touched anything else. What about the neighbours, had anyone seen her walking down the street earlier, going up the path, opening the front door? Or running out the back and over the fence? Had they seen Sam or Libby running from the house earlier? Was there CCTV around there, or neighbourhood watch? She thought of the footage of Logan on the bridge. She thought about being up there this morning with Sam, there would be footage of that too. We are always being watched.

The Twitter feed began to fill up with news flashes. Local STV and BBC services were reporting an incident, but they were an hour behind the action, as always. Then Ellie read something that made her fists tighten.

My m8's dad is a cop, says another cop's been stabbed in his house on Inchcolm T!! At hospital now, could die. #copkiller #queensferry

Cop killer. This was instantly picked up by other tweeters, the network going at it.

Polis stabbed at home in #queensferry. His kids missing apparently. Revenge by a crim?! Cop into dodgy shit? Domestic? Shitting hell.

The speed of it all terrified her.

Ben was on Refresh.

Refresh, refresh, refresh.

More opinions, more facts, more bullshit and nonsense, teeming into the ether like an airborne virus it was impossible to escape.

She turned away from the laptop and went to the window, looked out at the Forth. The sea was a constant. Changing all the time, yes, but somehow also reliable. It took her son and it would take others too. If sea levels rose, this house would be one of the first to go, submerged beneath all that implacable calm. She pictured water pouring in through the doors and windows of her home, imagined being swept up in it, the taste of salt on her lips as she swallowed it down. Maybe a handful of molecules from Logan's ashes slipping down her throat.

The sea had almost taken Sam this morning but Ellie had stopped it, she challenged the water and won. She was scratching at her most recent tattoo. She pushed her sleeve up and looked at the patch of red skin. Maybe it would never heal, maybe it would stay raw and bloody forever.

'What do you think?' Ben said.

She clenched her teeth and turned away from the bridges.

'About what?' she said.

He pointed at the laptop. 'All this.'

She shrugged. 'I don't think anything.'

She heard something, a movement upstairs maybe. She went over to the kettle and switched it on to cover the noise, glanced up at the ceiling once Ben had turned back to the screen.

The air filled with the hiss and rumble of water boiling. She went over to the washing machine. The load from earlier had finished, Sam's jeans and pants inside. She could see them bunched in the bottom of the half-empty drum. She wondered about forensics and evidence. She found herself reaching over to push the door button on the washing machine, force of habit, not wanting to leave the sodden clothes in there to go mouldy. She pulled her hand away from the button and turned.

She should go to the police station round the corner and give Sam up, that was the right thing to do. Then again. She tried to work out the different paths the future could take, depending on what she did right now. The multiverse theory. But there were too many variables, too many potential futures, she couldn't get her head round it. She just needed everything to settle down, needed time and space to think it all through, then she could be sure about making the correct decision.

Meantime she had to keep it a secret, even from Ben. Before Logan died she could never have imagined keeping secrets from her husband, they were such a tight unit, best friends as much as lovers. Their relationship didn't feel like either of those things now. She didn't want to keep this a secret from him but the truth was that it would be easy. Their lines of communication had been eroded so much it made her want to weep right here in her kitchen, in the house they shared. But mostly, right now, she wanted him out the house so that she could deal with everything at her own pace.

Ben shook his head. 'Mental.' Refresh, refresh. 'Doesn't look as if there's much new info coming out.' He straightened up.

'Why did you come back?' Ellie said.

'What?'

She pointed at the laptop. 'Couldn't you have checked all that on your phone?'

'I needed to get more of these.' He pointed at the pile of flyers on the far corner of the table. 'I ran out quicker than I thought. Still got a fair bit of leafleting to do.'

The kettle had boiled.

'Don't you want to stay for a cuppa?'

He looked at her. 'I can't believe you're not more interested in this thing up at Inchcolm Terrace.'

She shook her head. 'We don't know any of the facts. I prefer to wait until I know what's happened before I get outraged about anything.'

'But someone's been stabbed, ten minutes up the road,' he said. 'A cop, that's crazy.'

She slung a green teabag into a mug, poured in the water, felt the steam swirl around her face.

'Maybe,' she said.

'Don't you want to know what happened, the details?'

She shook her head as she dipped the teabag in and out of the mug. 'Dwelling on the details doesn't make any difference to the truth, does it?'

She felt him looking at her as she kept her head down. It made her uneasy, and she couldn't believe that being watched by her husband, the man who was supposed to be the love of her life, made her feel like that.

'You're talking about Logan now,' Ben said.

She sighed as she carried the teabag to the bin, her other hand under the spoon to stop drips on the tiles.

'I'm always talking about Logan, Ben. Everything is always about Logan, you know that. You know what it's like. It's always there, in every single word that comes out of our mouths.'

He came towards her and she felt the muscles in her neck and back tighten as he stroked her arm. His hand was right where the new tattoo was. She wondered if that was deliberate, if he was trying to hurt her. No, just an accident, his touch was meant to be supportive. He was rubbing at the ink under the surface of her skin, and she felt like she deserved the discomfort. She flinched but didn't move away.

'I know what you mean,' he said. 'It's just . . .'

He squeezed her shoulder, more pain under her clothes, then he placed his lips against her temple, kept them there for a second. For a moment his bulk was reassuring, the smell of him, and she felt a remnant of the gravitational pull that used to draw her to him.

He pushed himself away, checked Twitter one last time then closed the laptop. Picked up the flyers from the table and put them in his bag.

'I'd better get going,' he said.

She stirred her tea. 'OK.'

He hesitated a moment, silence between them, then left.

9

Sam stood at Logan's window staring at the road bridge. Ellie watched him. He hadn't turned when she opened the door, as if he was transfixed by the view. She imagined Logan standing on the same spot, gazing out to sea. Was that all it was, proximity? Had Logan killed himself because he saw that damn bridge every day when he opened his curtains? Maybe he wasn't any more depressed or angry or suicidal than any other teenager, it's just that he had the idea implanted in his head by that metal-and-concrete monstrosity looming over his life. There were increased suicide rates near high buildings and bridges. Many more suicides in countries where guns were easily available. And there were clusters, Ben was correct, but Ellie knew in her heart that was just down to human nature. Not exactly peer pressure, kids weren't egging each other on to do it. It's just that once you saw it was possible, a viable alternative to living, that really opened your eyes. She knew that from her own experience. Since Logan, she'd thought about following him into the water every day. The truth was she didn't have the nerve.

Sam turned. He had tears in his eyes. 'I can't believe we were up there. It seems like a dream or something. A nightmare. This whole thing is a nightmare.'

Ellie went over to him. 'I know.'

She looked at the stubble on his chin. He was definitely older than Logan, whose facial hair had been wispy fluff. Sam's was more like Ben's, but many years away from going grey.

Sam wiped at his nose with his sleeve and she wanted to tell him to use a tissue. All those years of motherhood ingrained in her now, impossible to shake off. Not that she wanted to shake it off, once she was no longer a mother, she was nothing.

She put an arm round him but he pulled away. Already she longed for the closeness they'd had earlier, when she'd helped him back to the house. That was real mothering, like looking after a toddler whose every need is your responsibility. She craved that burden on her shoulders.

He had his phone out his pocket.

'I need to find Libby,' he said.

'I'll help you,' Ellie said. 'But you can't go out looking for her just now. The police are everywhere.'

He stared at her, doubtful. She needed to be an authority, needed to control this situation before it got away from her, like everything else.

'And you can't stay here either,' she said. 'Ben will be back soon.'

He glanced out the window. 'Maybe I should go to the police.'

She reached out and touched his chin, moved his head until he was facing her.

'No,' she said, her voice steady. 'You want to protect your sister, don't you?'

He nodded.

'Think about it,' Ellie said. 'What you did was attempted murder. You're old enough to go to prison, then who would look after Libby?'

He was shaking with sobs. She stroked his face.

'Shhh, it's fine, I keep telling you I'll take care of everything.'

His breathing calmed and he nodded.

She had the urge to say 'good boy', as if he was a three-year-old who'd eaten his broccoli, but she held back. Her hand was still on his cheek, wet now with tears. She took it away and sucked at her finger, the saltiness that had been part of his body until a moment ago now inside her, part of her.

'The first thing you need to do is get out of that T-shirt and hoodie,' she said.

He frowned.

'The blood?'

A look of realisation on his face. Had he really forgotten he was walking around with his father's blood on his clothes?

She began undoing the zip on his hoodie but he put his hand on hers.

'It's only on the T-shirt.'

Ellie shook her head. 'It could've transferred. Better take both off to be sure.'

She turned to Logan's drawers. Opened the top one, full of the stuff he preferred to wear. She thought about what had been biggest on him, oversized, so that it might fit Sam better. There was a baggy red Superdry top, but red was stupid, too easily spotted and remembered, better to have something dark and anonymous. No brand names or logos either. There was no chance of that though, not in a teenage boy's wardrobe. The best she could find was a black Adidas hoodie, the three white stripes small on the chest. She pulled a T-shirt out of the drawer, a plain green thing that Logan had got from French Connection, way overpriced, she remembered, the stitching flimsy along the seams.

When she turned round Sam was naked from the waist up, holding his T-shirt and hoodie scrunched up in his fists. Good muscle definition, flat stomach, hairless chest. Definitely a couple of years older than Logan, closer to being a man.

She handed him the clean clothes and took the bloody ones from him. Watched as he pulled the clothes on then checked his phone again.

He was now dressed entirely in Logan's clothes. Ellie closed her eyes for a moment, then opened them and sighed. She looked down at the stained bundle in her hand. This was bad, all of it, but she was still in control. That's what she told herself, she was still in control of this situation.

10

She led him out the back door and locked it behind her. It was twilight now, street and house lights coming on across the water, the orange sheen from the bridge lights making the churn of the Forth look radioactive. The gloom would help them, though.

She pushed Sam ahead of her, down to the beach. The clatter of pebbles and shingle under their feet was loud in Ellie's ears. She had a small rucksack slung over one shoulder and was clutching a Tesco carrier bag with all Sam's clothes in it. She wasn't sure how yet, but she would have to get rid of them.

They headed west along the beach, the backs of the posher houses overlooking them. Hopefully it was dark enough now that they couldn't be seen, or maybe just mistaken for a couple of dog walkers. The tide was out so they could get quite far along on the pebbles before they reached the larger rocks of the embankment under the road bridge. They passed the converted steading and the residential home then reached some oak trees and trudged up through them till they came out on Shore Road directly under the bridge. The concrete supports were fenced off, barbed wire across the top, security signs everywhere. Inside the fenced-off area were diggers, giant rolls of metal wire, huge pipes. It was like a kid's play set on a massive scale.

They risked a hundred yards on Shore Road then ducked through some more trees and across the car park at the back of the marina. It was dark here, not enough money to keep the security lights operating, they had brought it up at marina committee meetings, Ellie remembered. Long, thin warehouses and boat sheds were all around them, boats parked up on lanes and alleyways as well, from tiny dinghies through bigger sailboats to macho powerboats.

They went round past the toilets and block of changing rooms rather than risk walking past the yacht clubhouse or the coastguard Portakabin. Not that there would be anyone inside at this time, skeleton staff on reduced shifts these days.

Ellie and Sam skirted the last of the boats in the dinghy park then rounded the workshop nearest the quay, the slipway down to the water's edge a mess of mud and seaweed. They clambered on to the pier then scurried along it. At the marina shed they walked past the weather-beaten sign prohibiting the landing of foreign animals, then Ellie stopped at the security gate that led down to the berths.

She looked around but couldn't see anyone. She didn't want to run into one of the old seadogs tinkering on their boats. She turned to Sam and nodded at the gate.

'I'll show you the code in case you need to come and go. It's C0604, then you turn this dial.' She showed him carefully, and the door clunked open.

Sam looked round. 'I've never been here before.'

Ellie closed the gate. 'Now you try. The "4" is a bit stiff.'

He opened it no problem and she ushered him down the steps. There were four rows of pontoons leading off from the main one, all pointing at the breakwater further out. The harbour walls either side meant the water was calm and the pontoons only swayed a little under their weight.

'We're D8,' Ellie said, pointing. 'This way.'

Up the last pontoon, along to the eighth berth and there was the Porpoise, the boat she and Ben had owned for a decade. Named after their little purpose, of course. A scruffy 1980s Hunter Horizon, twenty-three footer, twin keel, with a crappy four-stroke outboard slung on the back. Off-white with blue trim and in serious need of a paint job. She wasn't much but she was all they could afford.

Ellie pulled on the mooring rope to bring the bow next to the pontoon, held it tight for Sam to get on board then followed him.

'This is yours?' he said, taking it in.

'Mine and Ben's.'

'So you can sail?'

'Ben's the real sailor, but yeah, I can sail.'

The mast and rigging clanked as the boat rocked. There wasn't much room on deck with the two of them there, and the motion of the boat made Sam stumble then steady himself.

'It's better below deck,' Ellie said. 'Come into the cabin.'

There was a padlock on the small wooden door to the cabin. She took out a key and unlocked it, then went inside and sat down. He followed, ducking to avoid banging his head. They sat on opposite benches with the tiny mess table between them. She put the plastic bag of his clothes down and took the rucksack off her shoulder.

She pointed to the forward cabin, where a snug berth was squeezed into the space. 'That's your bed for tonight. There are blankets in the drawer underneath.'

She unzipped the rucksack and began pulling things out. She'd spent five minutes at the house packing a bag, trying to think what Sam might need. She laid it all out on the table now. Cheese sandwiches, crisps, three Wispas, bananas and a large bottle of water. She pulled out a metal box. 'This is a portable battery. I presume your iPhone is running out of juice?'

He checked his phone and nodded. 'Ten per cent.'

She pulled a connector out and plugged it into the battery. A small blue light went on. She offered the other end of the connector and he inserted it in his phone.

She pulled toilet roll out the rucksack and pointed a thumb to the side of the entrance. 'There's a chemical toilet over there.'

He nodded.

'Are you hungry?'

A shake of the head.

'You should eat,' Ellie said. 'Here.'

She picked up a Wispa and undid the wrapper for him, handed it over. He bit and chewed like it was made of dust.

'And drink plenty of fluids,' she said. 'It's important.'

She pointed to the small stove in the corner. 'There's a kettle, coffee, teabags and UHT milk in the cupboard above the ring. You want a cup of tea just now?'

'No.'

He put the chocolate down and reached for the water bottle and she watched as he glugged, Adam's apple rising and falling.

'Get some sleep,' she said.

She took two pills out her pocket and placed them on the table.

'They're herbal,' she said. 'Nothing to worry about. They'll just help you to go over, that's all.'

He stared at them but didn't speak.

'Stay here for now,' she said, 'until I find out what the situation is out there.'

She pointed towards the porthole behind him.

'You said we were going to find Libby?' he said.

Ellie nodded. 'I am. That's the first thing I'm going to do.'

She got her phone out her pocket and nodded at his phone on the table.

'I presume you've got a picture of her?'

'Yeah.'

'Send it to my phone, and forward me her number too.'

Ellie told him her number and he began pressing buttons. She got the picture on her phone and looked at it. A selfie taken in a bathroom, lips pouting, obvious make-up, blonde hair tumbling over her shoulders like she'd just shaken her head a second before. She wore large-framed geek glasses and a white T-shirt with a small black heart over the breast. She was still a kid, trying to be a grown-up like all girls that age. She was pretty in a gawky kind of way, a seriousness in her eyes that made her look older.

'She's eleven, yeah?'

'Eleven.'

'And your dad has been hurting her?'

His head still down, looking at his phone, a slight nod.

'How long for?'

He didn't speak.

'Sam, it could be important.'

He looked up. 'Why?'

'It just might.'

'I don't know.' Sam's hands began to shake. 'Today was the first time I actually saw anything but . . .'

His chest rose and fell, sharp breaths.

Ellie put her hand out and took his.

'Take it easy,' she said.

'I've been thinking about it all day,' he said. 'She never said anything to me, not exactly, but I think she might've been trying to let me know. She used to come into my room late at night and just sit around. Like she was nervous. I thought she was just being a pest. I used to chuck her out. If I'd been a better brother, maybe she could've told me. I should've asked if anything was wrong.'

'You can't blame yourself. Your dad's the one who's been doing awful things, not you.'

Sam held her gaze. 'Do you blame yourself for your son jumping off the bridge?'

Ellie took a deep breath. 'It's different.'

'How?'

'It just is.' She hated the tone of her voice, like a strict schoolteacher. 'Look, can you tell me exactly what happened today?'

He shook his head.

'It might help.'

'I can't.'

His body was shaking again. He was on the edge of coming apart all the time. Ellie knew how that felt.

'OK,' she said. 'But Libby left the house?'

'After . . .' He stopped, scratched at his hand. 'I was just standing there looking at him. Then I went to find her but she must've run out the house. I was kind of in a trance or something. I don't even know if she has her phone with her.'

'Where might she have gone?'

'I don't know.'

'Could she be back home by now?'

'I don't think so.'

'Why not?'

'She saw me, and Dad. Saw the knife and everything.'

'So?'

'Would you go back if it was you?'

Ellie thought. 'Maybe, if I had nowhere else to go.'

'There is nowhere else.'

'What about a secret place she likes to hang out?'

He shook his head. 'Nothing like that.'

'Are you sure?'

He looked up. 'Shit. There was somewhere she mentioned, I never thought before.'

'What?'

'She's been smoking with her friend Cassie. I told her it's stupid. Cassie's dad has a lock-up garage, they go there. I think it's on the lane under the rail bridge, past the Hawes Inn?'

Ellie nodded. 'I'll try there first.'

'And if she's not there?'

'I'll try your home.'

'That's too dangerous.'

Ellie got up. 'I need to find out what the situation is with your dad anyway.'

'How are you going to do that?'

She put her phone in her pocket. 'I don't know yet. I'll find Libby and I'll find out what's happening, then we can start getting things sorted.'

'This is never going to be sorted,' Sam said.

Ellie looked at him. 'It will. Things won't be the same again, but there's still a way out of this for you, I promise.'

'You can't promise that,' Sam said.

Back on the pier she stared at the old crane perched at the end of the quay, all rust and flaky paint. She turned to take in the marina. Decay everywhere. Port Edgar was going to the dogs and it was only going to get worse with the closure of the sailing school. Ben had worked there for seven years and they were shutting it down. The council said they would try to get him something else but that was just talk, they couldn't afford to keep on staff, and besides, there wasn't anywhere else on the east coast that taught sailing through local authorities.

She looked at the Porpoise. She was a rickety old thing, and they might have to sell her soon anyway. With Ben out of a job and her still signed off long-term sick from Marine Scotland they couldn't justify it. The government's enthusiasm for renewables meant that her research into the effect on marine life was bulletproof for now, but she couldn't imagine ever going back to work. Sitting in that office, having meetings, taking minutes, working on action plans, giving presentations – it was meaningless now. Logan's death had robbed her of any confidence that she knew what she was doing, so how could she sit there and tell others how to do their jobs? She had an appraisal meeting with HR coming up, assessing her fitness to return to work. She wasn't fit, they would likely cut her loose, then she and Ben would be in much deeper water. Or maybe she would have to pretend to be capable, keep them afloat. Neither option held any appeal.

Beyond the boats and the breakwater, giant yellow cranes sat on barges in the water. The new bridge supports were just breaking the surface of the Forth. Work had been carried out underwater for months, structures being built unseen by anyone. She couldn't imagine what the engineering involved, the scale of it eluded her. She tried to picture the finished bridge arching away into the night, but couldn't. She wondered if the new bridge would help the marina, if Port Edgar would get a new lease of life from its proximity, but she couldn't see how.

She wondered if Sam would take the pills, if they would work.

She walked to the end of the pier clutching the plastic bag of Sam's clothes in both hands. She'd thrown a handful of stones from the Binks into the bag and she felt the heft of it now. She checked the knot in the top was firm, then looked back along the pier. No one in sight. She narrowed her eyes looking for CCTV, but the only camera was down at the entrance to the berths, pointing at the gate. She heaved the plastic bag with both hands and watched as it landed in the water then sank, dragged to the bottom by the ballast inside. She watched the ripples where the bag had been then turned away.

She looked at her phone, flicked to the picture of Libby. Zoomed in closer and she could make out spots beneath the foundation on the girl's skin. She tried to imagine having a daughter, a female companion, but nothing came into her head. She wondered about those women on television who said their mums were their best friends. Had she been best friends with Logan? It never felt like it. She was always too much of a mother for that, too protective. And anyway, he didn't live beyond the stroppy teen years so she would never know if they

could've been grown-up friends. She liked to think so, imagined them going to gigs together, or out for a meal. Or maybe
the three of them out for dinner, her and Ben proud parents,
him keen to head off to meet his mates and go clubbing, her
and Ben sharing a knowing, worn smile, this is what we made,
between us, this one good thing.

Thinking like this was destroying her. Or maybe it had
already destroyed her.

She walked down the pier, past the coastguard hut and the
tumbledown storage buildings, cracked windowpanes, weeds
tangled in drainpipes, crumbling brickwork.

She stopped at a memorial stone, wreaths of poppies round
it. It was the one thing in this place that was well kept. She'd
walked past it many times and never paid much attention.
She read it now. It was a remembrance stone for the Navy's
minesweeping service that had trained here during the Second
World War, erected by the Algerines Association, whoever they
were. At least somebody cared, it was obviously looked after.
Across the top of the granite stone was a line:

'Let there be a way through the water.'

She stared at it for a long time, then turned and walked to
Shore Road, heading towards town. She went the front way
this time, past the police station then past her own house. The
downstairs lights were on, so Ben was back. She'd been right to
get Sam out of there when she did.

She kept walking, past the Binks then the harbour, along
the old High Street, charity shops and pubs, cobbles underfoot.
She was striding by the time she got to the long stretch of
seafront where the shows pitched up a couple of times a year,
cars parked up there now, a middle-aged couple sitting in one

eating bags of chips and staring at the view. That could've been her and Ben if things had worked out differently.

She thought of everything they'd been through together, more than twenty years. They met as students at Edinburgh Uni, both doing marine biology and ecology. They hadn't hit it off initially, took three years of circling each other, dating others, before they got it together.

They had so much in common. Both from small coastal towns, her North Berwick, him Anstruther, both in love with the sea. Keen sailors and swimmers, as much at home on the water or in it as they were on land. He was almost a year older, born at the tail end of '69, a running joke between them that he was a child of the sixties, an old hippy, while she belonged to the brave new world of punk.

Ellie had stayed on at uni after her degree, the offer of a PhD too good to ignore, while Ben scrabbled around doing the usual shit – pub jobs, office temp work, slowly getting a foot in the door with the marina and the sailing school, helping out in his spare time until they offered him shifts covering for other tutors. After her PhD, a lack of jobs for Ellie, no Scottish government then, no renewables programme, the only jobs in her field in London, a place so remote she could hardly imagine it.

Then marriage, a move to South Queensferry, the small seaside town that was theirs together. Ellie got a job working at Deep Sea World across in North Queensferry. She was stupidly over-qualified but she got to work with animals all day, getting into the tank to feed the sharks in front of gawping children, letting them handle starfish and crabs, making sure the rest of the fish were fed and cared for.

A string of miscarriages, six in three years. That seemed

startling but it wasn't so uncommon, she was on the statistical curve, not exceptional, just had to deal with it. After the first one she and Ben performed a little ceremony, a remembrance thing, and gave the baby a name, Stuart. They got the idea from some website and while it seemed new-age nonsense at first, it helped. But successive miscarriages numbed them, each dead foetus mocked the sincerity and sombreness of that first time with Stuart, and they didn't give the others names. In Ellie's mind they just piled up like the death toll of a tsunami only worse, a nameless horde of dead babies, mocking her inability to carry a child in her womb like the billions of women before her.

Then Logan came along.

No one could blame her for being over-protective. Seventh time lucky. Neither she nor Ben ever mentioned the others, not once they had their hands full with nappy changing and colic and six feeds a night and Logan's hernia that had to be operated on, just a normal procedure they said, it happened to a lot of boys. They were lost in the fog of fatigue for a while but gradually found themselves again, discovered themselves as a family.

When Logan was around three, once Ellie felt ready, they tried again for another. Two quick miscarriages then a trip to a specialist who told them to cut their losses and count their blessings. Something had happened to Ellie's insides giving birth to Logan. It was incredibly unlikely she could hold on to an embryo long enough, and she might kill herself trying.

So Ben got the snip and they settled down as a trio, the three stooges, the three musketeers, all that. They joked that the best things always came in threes anyway, happy just to have each other.

Ellie walked past the boarded up Two Bridges restaurant. There was a rumble up ahead then a train thudded out over the rail bridge heading north across the water. As the clack-clack faded Ellie strode past a bistro then the motorbike shop and the Hawes Inn, a picture of Robert Louis Stevenson, their most famous customer, on the chalkboard outside.

She crossed the road at Hawes Pier. The Maid of the Forth bobbed in the water, waiting to scoot tourists to Inchcolm Island tomorrow. Ellie had set off from this pier six years ago on a sponsored swim, back when she was really fit, when she was at her best. A team of eight of them in dry suits, the middle of summer, the most benign conditions possible, and still it nearly broke her. It wasn't the distance, not much more than one and a half miles, but the height of the waves, a tidal range of over six metres to compete with. They had to alert coast-guard and the harbourmaster beforehand, check for shipping traffic. But it had been worth it, the eight of them raising twenty thousand for the Sick Kids, and she was immortal for a brief moment afterwards. Staggering up the slipway at North Queensferry, hands on knees, she felt a mix of immense tired-ness and overpowering adrenalin, bone-weary but unable to sleep until the small hours of the morning. It felt like she'd achieved something useful, and the glow of it had stayed with her for weeks.

She was directly under the rail bridge now, passing the huge stone legs supporting millions of tons of red steel. She wanted to feel the shudder of a train overhead, but none came.

It was only once she reached the lock-ups that she realised she didn't have a clue what to do if she found Libby. There were six garages in a row, all in darkness, no street lights here. She went to the first one, listened. Silence. She tried to open the corrugated door but it was locked. She knocked on the door, which rattled in its fitting.

'Hello?'

She went along the row doing the same, listening, trying the lock, knocking, but if Libby was in one of the later ones she would've heard Ellie coming, and would surely stay quiet.

After shaking the last door handle Ellie stood looking out to sea. The lights of the rail bridge stretched into the gloom over the Forth, like the promise of a brighter tomorrow. The sound of the waves, the salty smell, so familiar to her.

She unlocked her phone and opened Facebook. Checked out Logan's page. A heart and three kisses from a girl called Melissa. A picture of the two of them together, in what looked like her bedroom. Ellie didn't recognise her. How could your son be friends with a girl you've never heard of? How could he spend time in a teenage girl's bedroom and you not know about it?

She typed in Sam McKenna, three mutual friends, apparently. She clicked through but it was no one direct, always once removed. That was the problem with Facebook, once you had a few hundred friends you were connected to the whole world, we're all intertwined now, whether we like it or not.

She looked at Sam's profile, not much there. Logan's was the same, none of the kids cared about filling in their lives because they hadn't lived much yet.

One hundred and thirty-five photos. She swiped through them, barely stopping to register. Gangs of mates hanging around the seafront, at school, in each other's houses. Holiday photos. She slowed down at those, checking out his sister in a few of them, his mum and dad. Jack and Alison. They weren't tagged in the pictures, so maybe they hadn't succumbed to social media. Ellie tried to remember a time before she'd been on Facebook, but struggled. Just another crutch now.

She looked closer at the holiday pictures, flicking back and forth, then stopped at one that must've been taken by Sam. Libby and her mum and dad standing on a Scottish beach somewhere. Ellie zoomed in. What could you tell from the look on a face in a photograph? She stared at Libby, large-framed glasses on her face, a cluster of spots in the space between her eyebrows, those eyebrows brown but her hair tied in a blonde bun, so she was old enough to be dying her hair.

She clicked on Libby's tag and went through to her page. Two hundred and four pictures. Swipe, swipe, swipe. The most recent ones all moody, fish-faced selfies, in a bathroom or bedroom, wearing make-up in a haphazard way, always trying to look older, more sexual, hand on hip, chin out, the universal teenage pose for social media. Ellie wondered where they learned it. At that age Ellie had been a bumbling, childish mess, painfully shy, no social skills. She could never have imagined posting pictures of herself in a tight dress for everyone to see, opening herself up to so much hurtful spite, psychological damage. What was the obsession with being connected?

She flicked back to Logan's page and posted quickly.

So missed, always, xxx

She clicked 'like' on Melissa's comment then turned away from the sea and back into town.

12

The street looked normal. No flashing lights, no police cars, no news reporters hanging around. Ellie didn't know what she was expecting, but maybe in the back of her mind she thought there would be a fuss, a sign that something out of the ordinary had happened here. But of course that's not how it worked. Someone gets stabbed, taken to hospital, the police ask around then leave. That absence seemed the most obscene thing. When Logan died she wanted people to stay around forever, fussing about it, collecting information, seeking answers. As soon as they were all gone and she was alone in the house with Ben she thought she would die. She wanted to die. As long as other people were there, distracting her, she could keep breathing.

As she walked down Inchcolm Terrace she thought about being here earlier today, touching the front door, seeing Sam's dad on the floor, running out the back door.

She approached Sam's house making sure to keep her pace steady, one foot in front of the other. She walked past it, only glancing at the house casually, as if it was any old place. The lights were on all over the house, curtains closed. She pictured Sam's mum sitting with her head in her hands. A large brandy at her side, maybe. How much did she know? Where did she think Sam was?

Ellie walked past two more houses until she was at one with

no lights on. Without breaking stride she turned up the path, round the side of the house into the back garden. Over the wall, into a crouching run across the neighbours' grass, then over the low fence into the McKennas' place.

Lights were on at the back of the house, the kitchen where Ellie had been earlier. She pictured her fingerprints on the patio door. A movement inside the kitchen made her shift back into the shadow of an elm tree. Alison, a tousle of dark hair, hoodie and joggers, her face crumpled with worry. She held a large wine glass loosely by the stem, dregs of red in the bottom. She stood at the sink and stared out the window, then grabbed a wine bottle and filled her glass up, took a big swig.

Alison turned and Ellie saw Libby come into the kitchen. She was wearing an oversized Aran jumper and checked jammy trousers. Alison spoke but Libby ignored her, opening the fridge and taking out a can of Diet Coke. Alison moved towards her, spoke again. Libby closed the fridge and left the room without making eye contact. The silent treatment, not even a hard stare. Alison rubbed at her forehead and took another slug from her glass.

Ellie had seen enough.

She left over the back wall, landing in the same street she'd been in earlier, the approach road to the bridge just over the embankment. She began walking home past the bridge visitor centre, through the tour-bus car park. She stopped to watch the traffic on the bridge. It took on a different character at night, more lonely and somehow ominous, as if each vehicle carried an individual's fragile hopes with it, people striving to get somewhere. The street light near her buzzed and she felt a thrumming energy through her body.

She checked the local news apps on her phone. No updates on Jack McKenna that she could find. She wondered about Twitter, if there might be more stuff on there. She should set up an account, get Ben to show her how it worked.

She headed down the access road, felt her heart sink as the traffic noise receded. All those people zipping overhead, trundling along in their metal bubbles, connected through the concrete and steel of the bridge.

She gave up checking her phone as she reached the bottom of the hill. Stood at the junction and looked both ways. To her left was Shore Road, the marina at the end. To her right were her home and the police station.

She had a thought and checked her watch. 9.45 p.m. Not so late it would seem weird. She walked to the police station, its blue-and-white chequered sign a beacon outside. The station was a jumble of low stone boxes, anonymous except for the sign and the bright blue handrail by the wheelchair ramp outside. A small half-barrel of flowers sat beneath the noticeboard at the front door and two cop cars were parked outside the garage alongside.

She tried the door. Locked. Lights were on inside, though. She pressed the buzzer. A woman, younger than her, peered out from behind a desk and reached underneath with her hand. Ellie heard a buzz-click and pushed open the door. Her breath seemed to be narrowing her throat.

'Can I help you?'

The policewoman had a copy of *Glamour* magazine in front of her and the look on her face said she didn't like being taken away from it.

Ellie put on a smile. 'Hi.'

The officer had a name badge pinned above her left breast. Lennon. She was in her mid-twenties, and Ellie thought of that line about police officers getting younger. Lennon was trying her best with the uniform, the shapeless blouse cinched at her waist to a tight skirt, her hair backcombed in a big bun like girls were always doing these days, subtle make-up, enough for a work situation but not so much to arouse comment. Her nails were impeccably matched to her make-up and her skin looked beautiful and soft. Ellie wanted to reach out and touch her cheek.

'I love your nails,' she said.

Lennon held them out and smiled. 'Thanks. What can I do for you?'

'I was just passing and I thought about that terrible thing that happened today, up the road. The police officer who got hurt.'

Lennon shook her head. 'It was awful.'

'Is the officer OK?'

'Do you know him?'

Ellie tilted her head. 'No, I was just concerned. I only live round the corner from here and thought I'd pop in and ask.'

Lennon sized her up. 'What's your name?'

'Eleanor,' Ellie said. 'Eleanor Sharp.'

Her voice sounded ridiculous in her own ears, wobbly and neurotic. Her pulse roared in her head.

Lennon looked Ellie up and down. Ellie wondered what she saw, a middle-aged busybody sticking her nose in where it didn't belong. She probably got ten of them every shift.

Lennon shook her head. 'I can't say anything, it's an ongoing investigation.'

'Can you at least tell me if he's going to be OK?'

Lennon. 'I'm really not at liberty to say.'

'Is he still in hospital?'

Lennon's gaze narrowed. 'Why do you want to know that?'

'Just wondered,' Ellie said. What was she hoping to achieve here?

'I can't say any more, Ms . . .'

Ellie struggled to remember the name she gave. 'Sharp.'

She turned to go, trying not to move too fast. 'Well, I hope the officer is back home soon with his family. And I hope you find whoever was responsible.'

Lennon sat up straight. 'Don't worry, we will. We don't muck around when it comes to one of our own.'

'I'll bet.' Ellie was heading for the door.

Lennon stared after her. 'Where did you say you lived, Ms Sharp?'

Ellie had the door open. 'Just up the road. Anyway, thanks, sorry to be a bother.'

She turned and left without waiting to see if Lennon had anything else to say. She strode along Shore Road and got her phone out, Googled the number for ERI and called it.

'Hello, could I speak to someone on the ward looking after Jack McKenna please.'

'Who shall I say is calling?' An older female voice.

'It's his wife, Alison.'

'Do you know which ward it is?'

'Sorry, I've forgotten. I was just there earlier, as well.'

'It's OK, dear, I'll search the database.' Ellie heard tapping on a keyboard. 'It's ICU, I'll put you through.'

Hold music, classical and tinny.

'Hello, ICU?' A more serious woman's voice.

'Hi, sorry to bother you. This is Alison McKenna, I was in earlier seeing my husband Jack. I wondered if there had been any change?'

'Just a minute.'

More hold music, a thin swell of strings and brass.

'Hello?' The woman was back. 'Mrs McKenna, the doctor has been round and your husband has seen some improvement. Dr Evans said we'll keep him in ICU tonight, then probably move him to G.I. tomorrow if he continues to get better.'

Ellie realised she'd been holding her breath. 'Oh thank you, that's great news. Thanks so much.'

'No problem, happy to help.'

Ellie hung up. She knew Sam's dad was alive, and that he was still in hospital.

She began jogging along the dark lane, past the legs of the bridge and the old sheds then into the marina, along the pier, punching in the numbers with sweaty hands, her breath heavy from running.

She felt the surface sway under her feet as she scooted over the pontoons to the Porpoise and climbed on board. She looked around, couldn't see anyone else about, just the lights from the bridges and the cranes at the new foundations.

She headed below deck and saw the tiny table where she'd left the sleeping pills for Sam. They weren't there. He was curled up in the single berth at the bow of the ship, squeezed into the space, the small fan heater whirring away on the floor, the duvet and blankets in a tussle over him. He was snoring but not like Ben did, not a big, throaty rasp, more like a gentle collapsing of air, a small animal at rest.

She wanted to wake him up. His sister was OK, back at home, his dad wasn't dead, it wasn't murder. She lay down on the bed facing him and stroked his head. He was so pretty. The small, stubby nose, his long eyelashes, the tightness of the skin across his cheeks. He looked peaceful. She leaned in and kissed him on the lips, just a touch of her skin on his, then pulled away and sighed.

She stared at him for a long time then got up and headed home.

13

She put the key in the door and steeled herself.

'Hi, it's me,' she called.

No answer. But he was in, she knew it. She wandered through the rooms downstairs but he wasn't there. She went upstairs and stopped at the door to Logan's room. Felt the urge to go in but resisted. Felt the itch to check his Facebook, but didn't. She stroked the lettering on his door again, another ritual, touch wood for luck.

She walked to her and Ben's bedroom and stood at the open doorway. Ben was under the covers, laptop open on his knees, creases across his forehead as he frowned in the light from the screen.

'Hey, honey,' he said without looking up.

'Hey.' She walked over to the dresser and opened the jar of Neutrogena, rubbed some into her hands then the skin under her eyes. 'How was the flyering earlier?'

'OK, I suppose.' He looked up from the screen. 'Where have you been? It's late.'

She looked at her reflection in the mirror. 'Just out for a walk. You know.'

He nodded. She often went for long walks, especially in the evening. It was part of the whole thing, the swimming and the other rituals, the physical act helped to empty her mind. She preferred it at night as well, fewer prying eyes, fewer accusations. She liked to think of herself as shrouded by the darkness, letting the essence of it soak into her bones as she drifted through it, osmosis transferring blackness from her to the night and back again, two porous entities combining.

Ben glanced down at the screen then back at her. 'I think I'll go out in the boat tomorrow.'

Ellie rubbed her hands together, letting the last of the cream soak in. Her skin was so dry these days, as if the world's moisture couldn't get any purchase in her body.

'Oh yeah?' she said, putting the lid back on the jar. 'You haven't been out for a while, why now?'

Ben pointed at the laptop. 'I want to go and check out the new bridge foundations again.'

'Why?' Ellie said.

'Been talking to this guy online, says he has evidence they're using chemicals in the concrete process that release toxins into the atmosphere. Stuff that causes depression, hallucinations, all sorts.'

Ellie sighed. 'Who is this guy, and how would he know?'

'Calls himself Truthteller21, says he got sacked by the company for asking too many questions.'

Ellie turned round to face him. 'Really? Come on, Ben.'

'I know, a pinch of salt and all that, but he sounds like he knows his stuff.'

'For God's sake, you say that about all of them. Every bampot on the internet, every conspiracy nut and lunatic loner convinced the world is out to get them.'

Ben stared at her. 'Like me, you mean.'

Ellie rubbed at the skin below her eyes. 'That's not what I mean.'

'I believe all this shit, so that makes me as much of a nutjob as them.'

'I just don't think it's very realistic to believe a respectable company, commissioned by the government under all the strict health and safety checks, is pumping chemicals into the sky that are making people suicidal, that's all.'

Ben shook his head. 'Of course not, that's what they want you to think.'

'Oh come on, listen to yourself.'

'The bigger the lie, the easier it is to make people swallow it,' Ben said. 'I'm telling you, it's right under our noses and nobody is doing anything about it.'

Ellie took a deep breath. 'Anyway, I don't know if going out in the boat tomorrow is such a good idea, the forecast said it's going to be blowy. Up to thirty knots out on the firth.'

'I hadn't heard that.'

'In the morning, anyway, maybe it'll ease off in the afternoon.'

He could check online, of course, and he would, so she didn't know why she bothered saying it. She just had to make sure she got Sam out of the boat before Ben was up and about tomorrow.

She stood up and went over to the bed, sat down next to him, nodded at the half dozen open browsers on the laptop screen.

'Did you find out any more about the thing up the road, the cop that got attacked?'

He brought Twitter up and began searching. 'A little bit. Nothing new in the mainstream, obviously, but quite a lot of chat on social media. The guy's name is McKenna, do you know him?'

Ellie shook her head. It was a fair enough question, it often felt like people in a small town all knew each other.

'He has two kids at the high school, an older boy and a younger girl.'

Ben meant older and younger than Logan. It was an instinctive thing to say, something Ellie found herself doing all the time, but it was redundant now. Logan was never going to age so the comparison was irrelevant. But it was a thing they had together, her and Ben, a frame of reference only the two of them understood.

Ben was clicking and scrolling. 'The interesting thing is that the son is missing. He's seventeen, so he's within his rights to do what he likes, I guess, but it looks pretty suspicious, vanishing from a crime scene where your own dad has been stabbed.'

'The cop was stabbed?' Ellie said.

'Didn't I say that already?'

'Is he going to be OK?'

'The chat is that he'll be fine. You can't keep anything a secret from the collective consciousness, can you? Insiders at the police station and the hospital have already put everything out there.'

'So everyone thinks it was the son who did it?'

Ben shook his head. 'There are quite a lot of rumours that this McKenna guy was into something dubious.'

'Like what?'

'Normal police crap. Backhanders from criminals, payoffs from drug dealers, a protection racket. I don't know. Could be anything. Word is he has a big gambling problem. Some are saying he's had affairs, so it could be tied up with that.'

Ellie let out a breath. 'The internet is such a scurrilous bastard.'

Ben smiled. 'You get a lot of bullshit, but that's the price you pay for the truth to come out as well.'

Ellie looked at him. 'You believe that, don't you?'

He turned to her. 'Of course.'

She put out a hand and touched the rough stubble of his cheek. So different from Logan's soft skin, from Sam's. She tried to remember what Ben's skin had felt like the first time she touched it. She sometimes thought the two of them were aliens inhabiting these worn out bodies they had become. In just a blink of time they'd gone from tight-skinned, giggling sex maniacs to saggy, toughened bags of bones.

Ben looked confused at her touch, as if the very idea of his wife stroking his cheek was weird. She pulled his head towards her and kissed him on the mouth, thinking how different it was from the touch of Sam's lips earlier. This was the man she loved, she still loved him, they just had to find a way back to that.

She kept kissing him, felt his surprise as her tongue explored his mouth. This is what kids did, not a couple in their forties eroded by life. She pulled him close, stroked her hands along his arms and chest. This was her man, still. She felt his hand on her breast and leaned into it. She reached inside the duvet and pushed against his body, rubbed at the crotch of his shorts and felt him harden. She pushed the laptop to the side and wriggled out her jeans and pants, then pulled the covers off and sat on top of him. She was already wet and he slid in. Years of practice, knowing exactly which movements got them there quickest. She moved up and down as he whispered under his breath, looking up at her. She liked that, the look in his eyes, still hungry for her after all these years. She closed her eyes and focussed on the feeling in her groin, but Sam's face appeared in her mind, his skinny cheekbones, his lithe body as he got changed earlier in Logan's room. She opened her eyes again, felt Ben push into her and come inside her, then felt a swell through her own body, spreading through her as she ground her pelvis against his, her legs trembling as she slumped forward and hugged Ben, running her hands through his hair, reminding herself all the time that this was her husband, this was the man she'd promised to love and honour forever.

'It's been a while,' he whispered in her ear, breathless.

'Shhh.'

'That's the first time since . . .'

She kissed him. She didn't want him to end that sentence.

14

Back at the Binks. She cradled a black coffee in her hands, shoulders hunched against the breeze. The sun was crawling into the sky behind the rail bridge, columns of light stretching upriver. Traffic was still light on the road bridge but the noise was there all the same, the never-ending rush of it.

She'd dreamed of Logan again. She knew dreams meant nothing, and she hated hearing other people talk about their own, people's subconscious activities were never as profound as they thought they were. In fact, the subconscious was a pretty blunt instrument. So she dreamed of Logan, big deal, what did that tell you? That she was heartbroken about her dead son. How did that help her in everyday life?

She looked down at her bare feet. She'd come out here to put her feet in the water, wanted to feel her body intermingle with it, feel the force of the waves, the tidal power, the immense connectivity of it all.

She climbed down to the beach, careful not to spill her coffee. Tensed her toes against the tiny stones and shells under her feet. She walked into the water lapping at the shore, held her breath for a moment against the cold. Wiggled her ankles and kicked a stone at the water's edge. A few more steps, nothing crazy, just up to her pyjama shorts. But as she moved deeper into the water she felt the urge to throw her coffee mug away and dive under the surface. She poured the coffee into the sea, watched the brown liquid swirl and disappear as it was diluted. Then she dropped the mug and watched it weave its way to the bottom then nestle in the sand.

She looked out over the Forth to North Queensferry. People over there just waking up, getting ready for work, hurrying the kids along so they weren't late for school. The stuff of life.

She stretched her arms in front of her, put her hands together and dived into the wash, kicking with her legs, pushing the water away with every stroke of her hands, feeling the tension and stretch of the muscles in her arms and legs. The cold hammered at her chest, tried to push the air from her lungs with the shock, but she resisted. A few strokes underwater, shoulder blades flexing, breath held, then she surfaced, already some distance from the shore.

A line from a song came into her head, like it did every time she swam in the firth. That band Logan liked, Frightened Rabbit, Scottish guys singing in their own accents. That had been unthinkable when she was a teenager, there were no Scottish voices in rock music. The line was 'swim until you can't see land'. A lovely idea. Impossible here, though, surrounded on both sides, you'd have to go a dozen miles out into open sea. Suicidal.

She breathed deeply and ducked under the surface. A few long strokes, enjoying the purity of the movement, at one with the ocean and the currents, the seals and the crabs, gliding through this world as if she belonged.

She came up for air. Treaded water as she looked back to shore.

She was not suicidal, not today. Today she had things to do, people to help.

She took a mouthful of seawater and swallowed, the saltiness burning her throat, and imagined grains of Logan's ashes slipping silently through her stomach lining into her bloodstream.

She looked at her house, small from here, like something made of Lego. She turned to the road bridge. The same feeling. She imagined a giant child building all this in their playroom, the town, the bridge, the boats in the marina, all of it. A three-year-old god in charge of their lives. But she knew that wasn't true. No fate, no destiny. We were all in charge of our own lives, for better or worse.

She swam back to shore.

*

Ellie checked her watch as she stepped on to the bridge. Still only quarter past eight. Ben wouldn't surface for a couple of hours yet, he always stayed up into the small hours with his little gang of internet-conspiracy buddies.

She'd gone back to the house to strip, towel off and change, throwing her sodden jammies in the machine. She thought about Sam's clothes, the jeans she'd washed but then dumped in the sea along with the bloodstained top and hoodie. The forensic trails that we left behind all the time, a frightening concept, no chance of living on earth without trace thanks to modern science. Was it so hard to just disappear? The trick was to have no one looking for you, at least not in the right place, then it was easy.

The rumble of trucks and vans as they thudded past was like a hug to her. The shudder of the walkway under her feet was as comforting as old slippers. She strode along the bridge, immersed in the noise, revelling in the anonymity, the wind flicking at her hair. She walked past the first security camera and wondered about the footage from yesterday. Did they have anything of Sam and her? Had anyone in the control room put together the boy on the bridge and the missing boy from the police officer's house? The trick was to have no one looking for you, that's how you disappear.

She was close to the middle of the bridge now. She'd walked along the east side, the same as yesterday, the same as every day, the side Logan jumped from. That meant she couldn't see the marina from here, over to the west. She presumed Sam was still asleep, two of those pills were usually good for twelve hours, she knew from experience.

She got to the spot and stopped, just like every day before. Except this wasn't the same, Ellie felt different. She thought about Sam, here on the bridge yesterday, almost catatonic at her house, nervous and distraught later, then finally sleeping below deck on the Porpoise. She thought about seeing his sister and mum through the kitchen window. She thought about stepping round the pool of blood on the floor as it spread out from Jack McKenna's stomach. Had Sam's mum cleaned up yet?

Ellie leaned over the railing and looked down. Light from the sun scudded off the ripples in the water, blinding her for a moment. She raised a hand to shield her eyes and thought she saw something down there, a dark shape shifting through the water. Could be a seal, a basking shark, a piece of junk, anything. A porpoise, maybe, in its element, living only for the moment.

She leaned back, gazed out past the rail bridge and thought of Logan. Pictured him standing in the hall of their house, thirteen years old, playing with his hair and peering at the mirror, the smell of Lynx wafting into Ellie's nose as she watched from the kitchen doorway. He was going out on his first date, at least the first that she knew about, with a girl called Maddie. Going to the cinema then Pizza Hut up the road. Logan was trying to pretend it wasn't a big deal, shrugging his shoulders and avoiding Ellie's gaze, but she knew different, could tell straight away that he liked her. She worried, of course, he was her baby, going into the world to get his heart broken a hundred times by a hundred different girls. Or maybe he was out there breaking hearts himself, either way it was horrible to think about. She didn't mind the physical stuff so much, the idea of him doing things with girls. They'd had the talk a long time before, he knew all about being safe, even at thirteen. It was the emotional stuff. He wasn't a typical boy, full of bravado and bluster. He was soft and kind and cared about what people felt. That was better, of course, she was proud that she and Ben had raised such a caring person, but it also left him open to hurt. By girls, by other boys, by the world. And she couldn't do anything to protect him, that was the worst of it. She just had to be there and cuddle him when it went wrong. Except she never got that chance.

She thought again of Sam in the boat, closed her eyes and held tight to the railing, the tremor in it carrying up her arms. She had to save Sam. She still didn't know how, but she would save him.

'Thank you,' she said. 'Thank you for this second chance.'

15

The lone clank of a hammer on metal greeted her from one of the boat sheds. She walked past the cafe and clubhouse, then the coastguard Portakabin, no activity there. She went past the Bosun's Locker supply shop. Rumour was the rich owner was going to buy the marina from the council, reopen the sailing school. Ellie would believe it when she saw it.

She hurried past the boats in the dinghy park, their worn undersides exposed to the elements, then she turned on to the pier. Punched the code into the door lock and scurried down the stairs to the berths.

One or two old men were tinkering on their boats. This was the sailing fan's equivalent of a shed, retired men came here and hid from their wives, women who were equally keen to get their husbands out from under their feet. The vast majority of boat owners were old men, partly because they were the only ones who could afford them, partly because they were the only ones who had the time to dedicate to such an all-consuming hobby. Not that they would call it a hobby, to these salty dogs it was a way of life, just as it had been for Ben before the sailing school had closed down.

Ellie had a sudden flit of tension in her chest – what if Ben had got up early and come here already? But then Ellie spotted the Porpoise in its berth, scruffier and smaller than the boats on either side, needing a paint job and a caulking coat. Ellie and

Ben's ability to focus on such things had evaporated in the last six months, no energy to think about anything other than their grief, so the Porpoise was in need of some serious TLC. Ellie resolved to take care of it once this was all over.

She was at the boat now, no sign of life. She tugged on a rope, pulled the vessel alongside the pontoon then climbed on board. She had a quick look round. Just the same old men fiddling with brass fittings, sails, ropes. She ducked below deck.

She knew straight away he was gone.

She rushed to the berth in the forward cabin, just a jumble of sheets. She flipped the covers over, picked them up and shook, as if he'd tumble out somehow. She lifted the pillow to her face and breathed in. His smell. She looked round the tiny cabin, checked the toilet. It had been used, water droplets around the sink. She opened the bin in the main cabin, just the remains of food packaging in there.

She glanced round the cabin one last time, picturing herself spotting something like a television detective, but it was just her little boat, giving away nothing.

She hurried up the steps and out on deck. Looked around, more urgently this time, watching for any human movement amongst the bobbing boats and swaying masts. The clack of rigging filled the air with a constant chatter. You got used to it down here, but suddenly it seemed like gossipers to Ellie's ears, mocking her attempt to control this situation.

She saw old McNamara working on his keel boat a few berths down, and leapt off deck towards him.

'Hey, Ronnie,' she said.

He looked up and smiled. All these old guys felt paternal about Ellie, especially since what had happened with Logan.

She liked that but also hated it a little, an uneasy mix of comfort and condescension. Ronnie had wild eyebrows and leathery skin, a lifetime of wind and waves toughening his face into a mask.

'Ellie.'

'Have you seen anyone down here this morning?'

'You mean Ben?'

Ellie thought for a second. 'Yeah, he said he was going to take the Porpoise out today.'

Ronnie shook his head. 'Haven't seen him.'

'Have you been down here long?'

'A while. I don't sleep like I used to, like to come down and potter about.'

'Have you seen anyone else come along this pontoon since you got here?'

'Like who?'

'Just anyone.'

Ronnie frowned. 'Is there a problem with your boat? Has someone tampered with it?'

Ellie shook her head. 'No, nothing like that, I was just wondering.'

Ronnie gave it some thought. 'No dear, there's been no one near the Porpoise that I've seen. I was below deck for a few minutes, but I've mostly been up top.'

'When did you get here?'

'Are you sure everything's OK?'

'Fine,' Ellie said. 'Just, when did you get here?'

'About an hour ago.'

'OK.'

Ellie began to walk away.

'Ellie?' It was Ronnie behind her.

She turned. 'Yeah?'

'If there's anything I can do to help, just let me know.'

Ellie nodded. 'I will.'

'Take it easy,' Ronnie said.

'Thanks,' she said over her shoulder.

She walked along the pontoon and pulled her phone out, dialled Sam's number as she went. Straight to voicemail. She hung up.

She jogged up the steps and along the pier then stopped and surveyed the scene. There were a million places to hide in the marina, boat sheds, yachts, the abandoned warehouses, but why leave the Porpoise if you just intended to hide somewhere else?

She skirted round the coastguard hut and popped her head into the sailing clubhouse. Empty. She went through to the changing rooms and looked into the men's locker room. No one there.

She ducked out and strode to Karinka's Kitchen, the greasy spoon. It wasn't always open, but the sign was out and she smelt burnt fat and coffee. She opened the door. A couple of old timers were getting bacon rolls for breakfast, a guilty little secret from their wives after their bran flakes at home. Ellie could ask Karinka behind the counter but she was already wary of arousing suspicion, so she turned and left.

She'd known she wouldn't find him in either of those places, they were long shots. She thought she knew where he'd gone, and began running as she headed away from the marina towards town.

16

She rang the doorbell, the same button she pressed yesterday, and stared at the door. She was out of breath from jogging up the hill to Inchcolm Terrace. She felt a thin smear of sweat on her forehead and wiped it with her sleeve. Her armpits and groin were wet from the exertion. She hadn't thought this through. She'd broken into a run leaving the marina and got into a rhythm, the repetitive pound of her feet on the tarmac soothing her mind, the physical superseding the mental.

But now she was standing at the McKennas' house, waiting for the door to open. Her heart pounded and her lungs made her chest rise and fall. She rubbed her hands on her thighs, trying to wipe them dry. Thoughts crept in, and she was about to turn and leave when there was a noise behind the door, then it opened.

It was Libby. She looked younger than in the pictures Ellie had seen. Ellie could see the spread of acne between her eyebrows, her jaw set in a pubescent overbite. The way her left ear stuck out a little more than her right reminded Ellie of an untrained puppy. She would most likely grow into this face, that body. She would be beautiful one day, probably soon, but not quite yet.

Her blonde hair was tied up in a rough knot to the side of her head, roots showing. She wore the same outfit as last night, jammy trousers and a jumper. Ellie wondered if she'd slept well.

She didn't look frightened or distraught, but she had that mask, the sheen kids that age have, a barrier to the world made of disinterest, boredom and disgust. Ellie knew from Logan at the same age that it was a front, and there was a scared human underneath.

'Hi, Libby,' Ellie said.

Libby had one hand on the door frame, the other on her hip, a nonchalant stance but also on guard.

'Who are you?' she said. 'How do you know my name?'

'I'm a friend of your brother.'

That got her attention. 'What are you on about? You can't be Sam's friend, you're like forty or something.'

'I've been helping him,' Ellie said. 'Have you seen him since yesterday?'

'None of your business.' Libby was already closing the door.

Ellie put her hand out. She thought for a moment then placed her fingers on the door handle and smeared her palm around it.

'Let go of the door,' Libby said.

Ellie took her hand away.

'Look,' she said. 'I just need to know if you've seen Sam, that's all.'

'What's it to you?'

'I know,' Ellie said. She opened her eyes wider, gave Libby a look she'd used a hundred times on Logan, a look that meant she wasn't pissing about, she was to be taken seriously.

Libby shrugged, pretended not to care or understand, but it had got through, Ellie could tell.

'I don't know what you're talking about,' Libby said.

'Yes, you do.' Ellie looked up and down the street. 'Has he

been in touch since yesterday? He was trying to call you all day.'

'How do you know?'

'He's been worried sick about you.'

'I can take care of myself.'

Ellie tilted her head and made a show of sizing the girl up. 'I'm sure you can, but he's your big brother and he was trying to help you. You know what I'm talking about.'

Libby shook her head. 'I really don't.'

Ellie moved closer, put a foot on the doorstep, and lowered her voice. 'Listen to me, I found Sam on the bridge yesterday, did he tell you that?'

The look in Libby's eyes said that he hadn't.

'He was going to jump because of what he'd done. Do you understand?'

Libby's eyelids flickered.

Ellie continued. 'I talked him out of it and took him somewhere to pull himself together. Away from anyone who might be looking for him. So you see, I am his friend, I'm looking out for him. And I'm looking out for you too.'

Libby was softening, Ellie saw it in her face.

'I need to know where he is,' Ellie said, 'so that I can protect him properly. You understand, don't you?'

A slight nod from Libby. She was working out how much of what Ellie said could be true, how much tallied with what Sam told her, if he'd even been in touch. It suddenly occurred to Ellie that Sam might've just handed himself in to the police.

'So has he been in touch?' Ellie said.

Libby looked down at her bare feet. 'He was here earlier, but he's gone.'

'Where?'

Libby was about to speak when a voice came from behind her.

'Who is it, Lib?'

Libby's eyes widened. Footsteps padded down the wooden stairs as Libby let go of the doorframe and stepped aside.

It was Alison. She was the same height as Libby but stocky, broad shoulders, heavy breasts, a thick waist. Her features weren't unattractive but her face was getting jowly and she wore a lot of her life in the lines around her eyes and across her forehead. She had bleary eyes and Ellie could smell stale wine on her breath.

'What do you want?' she said.

Ellie took a deep breath. 'I'm sorry, my name is Eleanor, I live down the road. I hope you don't think I'm intruding, I just heard about what happened here on the news and I wanted to say how sorry I was for your trouble. If I can help in any way?'

It was pathetic but maybe Alison was hungover enough to buy it.

Alison turned to Libby. 'Go and get dressed.'

Libby didn't move and Alison turned back.

'What did you say your name was?' she said.

'Eleanor.'

'Thanks for your concern but this has nothing to do with you. Unless it was you who stabbed my husband in the stomach?' She spat the words out, sarcasm and hatred in them.

'I'm so sorry,' Ellie said. 'I shouldn't have come.'

'That's right,' Alison said, 'you shouldn't have.'

She was closing the door.

'It's just . . . I know what it's like,' Ellie said. 'To have trouble

93

in the family, I mean. My son was the boy who jumped off the bridge six months ago.'

Alison stopped. 'You're his mum?'

Ellie tried to speak but was surprised to find the words stuck in her throat. She nodded.

Alison sized her up. Ellie must've weighed two stone less than Alison. She wondered what Alison thought of her, the mother who couldn't keep her son from killing himself.

'Well, I'm sorry for you,' Alison said. 'Thanks for your concern but this is totally different. My husband was stabbed by a burglar and my son is missing. We don't want people intruding on family business.'

'Of course.' Ellie nodded. 'I completely understand. I don't know why I came, I'm sorry.'

Alison had a look of pity in her eyes. 'Just go.'

She stepped back to close the door and Ellie got a better view of Libby behind, looking confused.

'OK,' Ellie said, 'sorry to have bothered you.'

She looked over Alison's shoulder as the door closed. Libby was mouthing a word to her. 'Hospital.'

Ellie smiled. 'And goodbye Libby, it was nice meeting you.'

She was doing eighty-five round the bypass, Radio Forth blaring, trying to keep the thoughts at bay. Lorde came on, that song that was everywhere at the moment. Logan had been into her early on, before the song had broken through and become a hit. He'd downloaded her first EP on to his iPod, she'd heard it through the wall and was surprised at his taste, how good it was. To his credit, he hadn't abandoned her once she became famous, something Ellie might've done in her teenage days. Back then selling out was to be avoided at all costs, now it was an aspiration. The musical landscape was so different for kids like Logan, but good stuff still crept through, like this girl. Some teenage New Zealander selling millions, imagine that happening before the internet. She had a whole lifetime of making music ahead of her, a career Logan would never see.

Ellie turned off at Sheriffhall and up Old Dalkeith Road as the new Rihanna tune came on. She was so glad Logan was never into her, at least not that he admitted to. Ellie was all for female empowerment and women should be allowed to do whatever the hell they want, but dancing naked for the titillation of others wasn't her idea of empowerment. Maybe Logan secretly wanked off thinking of Rihanna writhing around, but Ellie hoped not. She didn't mind the idea of him wanking. She knew other mums would have wrinkled their noses up at the thought, but it was a natural thing for a teenage boy to be doing, it meant he was developing a normal sex drive. She was more worried about what went on in his head. She hadn't cared one way or the other whether Logan was gay, straight, bi, whatever, the key thing was respect. Show other people respect, and hope that it comes back your way. But it was so hard to teach boys about respect. Women were depicted everywhere as objects or sluts, often by other women, so how do you get through to your son that girls and women were equal in every way? How did you make a boy emotionally literate? It was all a million miles from her strident feminism of the eighties as a young woman.

But having Ben as a dad had helped, a good male role model made all the difference. Ellie saw the reverse in the playground, then later with some of Logan's friends. Their dads spouted the usual sexist drivel, jokes and slights, unintentional or otherwise, and the boys mimicked them. She was proud to see Logan squirm at some of the comments of his mates. She would've been prouder still if he'd spoken out against them but that was asking a lot of a fifteen-year-old boy, drowning in peer pressure, the emotional chaos of hormones and all the rest. She was confident he would grow into a good man.

'Would've', she corrected herself, not 'would'.

So much for the radio drowning out her thoughts.

She turned into the ERI's car park and struggled to find a space. This was where Jack had been brought, and she presumed Sam had come to see him. What was he thinking, coming here after what he'd done?

She strode to reception and gave Jack's name. The man behind the desk was almost pension age, thick hands, heavy eyebrows and a tremor in his neck that made his head judder. His nametag said George.

'Are you a relative?' he said.

Ellie nodded. 'Sister.'

That seemed to be all he needed.

George punched his stubby fingers at the keys, squinted at the screen.

'Your brother's in Ward 107, G.I. general surgery.'

'G.I.?'

'Gastro-intestinal.'

'He's not in intensive care?'

'No.'

That meant it wasn't too serious, he was going to be fine. He would survive and get out of hospital. Then what?

'Which way?' Ellie said.

George looked at his watch. 'You're a bit early for morning visiting.'

'Which way?'

George pointed at the floor. There were a dozen different coloured lines painted on it, heading in different directions.

'Follow the yellow line to the lift, then up one and look for the signs.'

'Thanks.'

George called after her. 'They might not let you see him, depends what mood the ward sister is in.'

Follow the yellow brick road, thought Ellie, as she ducked along corridors and round corners. Eventually she found the lift and went up. Came out and followed the signs. By the time she got to Ward 107 she'd lost her bearings completely, had no idea where she was.

She went through the double doors and was spotted by three nurses chatting around the reception desk.

'I'm here to see Jack McKenna,' she said.

'You're early,' said the nearest nurse, Gibbs on her breast badge. Judging by her uniform, she was in charge.

'Just a few minutes,' Ellie said. 'I'm his sister, I've driven a long way, I came as soon as I heard about the stabbing.'

Gibbs narrowed her eyes and pursed her lips. 'I think he's sleeping.'

'Can I just see him for two minutes?'

Gibbs turned to one of the other nurses. 'Carol, take this lady to see her brother.'

Carol smiled and got up, waved at Ellie to follow. Past four doors then in to the right, a small room with four beds. The two beds at the window were empty. To Ellie's right was a woman in her eighties, half wasted away, skin hanging loose from her neck. To her left was Jack.

Ellie turned to Carol. 'Thanks.'

'Two minutes,' Carol said, turning to leave.

Ellie walked over to Jack's bed. His eyes were closed, he was on a drip and he had the covers pushed down to his waist. His stomach was heavily bandaged, thick layers of wrapping, his body rigid.

Ellie watched his chest rise and fall.

She wondered if Sam had been here. Surely he couldn't say he was Jack's son, the nurses must watch the news, they would know he was missing and would report it. Would he have lied to them? What if they recognised him anyway? Maybe he sneaked in. She looked at the door, no police presence. She'd thought maybe there would be an officer on guard, but presumably they didn't think it was necessary.

She had no idea what she was doing here or what she hoped to achieve. She imagined lifting a pillow from one of the empty beds and pushing it into Jack's face, picturing a hundred clichéd murders on television and in the movies. Was it really as easy as that?

She crept closer. Jack's eyes remained closed.

She leaned in and whispered. 'Can you hear me?'

Nothing.

She thought about the last time she'd seen him, on the kitchen floor in a pool of blood. She wondered if he'd seen her then, could identify her.

'I said, can you hear me?'

She saw movement under his eyelids and his breathing became less deep. She knew from years as a mum what it looked like when someone was pretending to be asleep.

'I know you're awake,' she said in his ear. 'I know everything. I know who stabbed you and why.'

Her pulse pounded in her ears as she took a breath.

'Listen carefully,' she said. 'If you implicate Sam in any of this I will expose the kind of man you are. I have evidence. Do you understand? Then I will kill you. I'm a guardian angel to your children, protecting them, and I'll be watching you every minute of every day.'

His Adam's apple rose and fell.

'Do you understand?'

His eyes moved under the lids, he swallowed, his breath came in and out of his nostrils.

'I will come for you,' Ellie said, patting his hand. 'Don't think I won't. I have nothing to lose.'

She straightened up and took her hand away, then turned and smiled at the old lady in the other bed, who didn't seem to see her at all.

On the way out she stopped at the reception desk.

'Thank you,' she said. 'That's laid my mind to rest, I'll be back soon to visit.'

Gibbs nodded.

'Just one thing,' Ellie said. 'Has anyone else been to see him this morning?'

Gibbs shook her head. 'No, why?'

'Just wondering.'

Ellie walked away, taking her phone out her pocket and dialling Sam's number again.

18

Ellie was back on the bypass when her phone pinged with a text. She was in the outside lane passing an IKEA lorry as she lifted the phone from the passenger seat and looked at it. Sam. She unlocked the phone and read it.

Back at the boat. Don't know what to do.

Her stomach fluttered as she glanced up. A Toyota in front of her braked sharply and Ellie did likewise, pushing her foot hard on the pedal. The seat belt cut into her chest as she was pushed forward by her own momentum. She was only a couple of feet from the car in front, her right leg straight, stamping on the brake, when the Toyota's brake lights went off and it pulled away. The IKEA lorry hammered alongside her, then it edged ahead, its lane clear.

She pulled into the slow lane behind the lorry and set a steady pace fifty feet behind. She still had her phone in her left hand. She texted with her thumb, looking up to the road then back at the screen.

Don't worry. Wait, I'll be there soon.

She pressed send. The IKEA lorry turned off at Straiton and she pushed forward into the gap. She still had the phone in her hand when it rang. She looked at the screen – Ben. She breathed a couple of times then pressed answer.

'Hi,' she said.

'Hey, where are you? You were gone when I woke up.'

'Just out and about,' Ellie said.

She'd caught up with a Tesco van in front. Kept her distance, but then two cars slid in between them from the slip road. She eased off the accelerator.

'Sounds mysterious,' Ben said.

'Just shopping,' Ellie said.

'Are you driving?'

'Yeah.'

'I'll keep it quick then. I'm going out in the boat, wondered if you wanted to come, I could use an able seawoman.'

Ellie noticed her speed had gone up and took her foot off the pedal. Her right hand was tight on the steering wheel, her left gripping the phone. Her ear was warm with the phone pressed against it.

'I don't think that's a good idea,' she said, her voice level.

'I checked the weather reports,' Ben said. 'Don't know what you were on about last night, conditions are perfect.'

'Must've got the wrong end of the stick.'

'So you want to come out? Clear our heads?'

Ellie had to brake as another truck came in from the next slip road. 'OK, when I get back.'

'How long are you going to be?' Ben said. 'Don't want to hit the turning tide.'

'An hour, maybe.'

'That long? What are you shopping for?'

'Bits and bobs.'

'Fine,' Ben said. 'I'll go down to the Porpoise, get her ready for action.'

A string of brake lights up ahead, Ellie too close to the car in front, had to brake hard.

'Don't do that,' she said.

'Why not?'

Doubt in his voice.

'Just wait for me at the house, yeah? I want to go over to the marina with you.'

'But I could be getting her shipshape.'

'Just please wait for me at home. Promise.'

Silence for a second. The cars in front were speeding up again. This traffic was shit, same as always on the bypass.

'What's going on, Ellie?' Ben said.

Ellie's ear burned. Her hands were sweaty and the tremor in her stomach was spreading to her chest. She imagined pushing the accelerator to the floor and crunching into the car in front.

'Just please promise,' she said.

Maybe he heard something in her voice, a desperation.

'I promise,' he said.

'Thanks, I'll be home soon.'

'Take it easy,' Ben said.

She hung up and threw the phone on the seat. She indicated and slipped into the fast lane.

*

Port Edgar was busier than earlier, old men tinkering, some

more-serious crews busying themselves on the decks of the bigger racers. She scurried along the pontoon, nodding at the folk she knew, and clambered on to the Porpoise, then down below.

Sam was sitting at the table in the middle of the room, checking his phone and sniffling, wiping his nose with his sleeve.

Ellie was halfway across the room, arms wide, about to hug him when he looked up and shrank away from her. Of course, too intimate, stupid thing to do. This boy wasn't hers, she had to get a grip. She changed her body shape at the last second, dropping an arm and rubbing his shoulder, a gesture of reassurance.

She sat down next to him, their legs touching on the narrow bench. Sam was still wearing Logan's clothes. Couldn't he have picked up some of his own stuff when he was at the house seeing Libby? Maybe he didn't get the chance.

'How are you?' Ellie said.

He put his phone down and shook his head. 'I don't know what to do.'

He began sniffing again, tears in his eyes. Ellie put a hand on his thigh.

'I'll take care of everything,' she said.

'How?' Sam had a confrontational look on his face. 'You said that yesterday, and I believed you, but this isn't yesterday any more. How can you fix things?'

This was too soon for Ellie, she didn't have an answer.

'I wish you hadn't found me yesterday,' Sam said. 'I wish I'd jumped.'

Ellie moved her hand to his cheek and turned his face toward her.

'Don't ever fucking say that again.'

That shocked him. As if women in their forties weren't supposed to swear, weren't allowed to care deeply about things, care so much they would do anything to make everything right.

'I went to see your dad in hospital,' she said.

He stared at her. 'Why?'

'I was looking for you.'

'I went there but I didn't go in. I couldn't. How is he?'

'He's going to live.'

'Did you speak to him?'

Ellie nodded. 'I told him to leave you and Libby alone.'

Sam shook his head. 'It won't make any difference.'

'I think it will.'

'You don't know him,' Sam said. 'He won't be scared of you.'

'He should be.'

'Why are you doing this?'

Ellie looked round the cabin then got up, walked to the doorway. 'We can't stay here, it's not safe.'

Sam followed her. 'What do you mean?'

'My husband is coming, he wants to go out in the boat. We have to move you.'

'Where to?'

'I know somewhere.'

Ellie pulled open a drawer and yanked out a baseball cap. Black, no logo, not memorable. She handed it to him. 'Put this on.' She went to the forward cabin and folded up the bed sheets and covers, pulled a kitbag from underneath the bed and stuffed the lot inside. Pulled the cord tight and slung it over her shoulder.

'Come on.' She walked past him and put her foot on the first step of the ladder.

Sam put the cap on and followed her above deck.

Ellie stood surveying the scene. Most of the berths were occupied, half a dozen boats with people working on deck between them and the quayside. She looked out to sea, had a faint shudder as she took in the road bridge. The sound of the traffic was soothing from this distance, a soft murmur.

She turned to Sam and pulled his cap down, hiding his face as much as possible.

'Walk next to me and don't talk to anyone.'

She jumped off deck on to the pontoon and held a side rail till Sam had done the same, then they walked at a clip along the rocking pontoon. Ellie nodded at anyone who acknowledged her, tried to keep her eyes facing front. No point trying to make a story up, no need to stop and explain, that would just get them in deeper water.

She breathed easier when they were up the stairs and on to the pier. She put a hand on Sam's elbow and hurried him as they walked away from the main boat sheds, past a handful of old keelboats on raised platforms, and up towards an abandoned warehouse. Its brick walls were crumbling. The corrugated iron roof was red with rust, thin patches where the metal had almost been eaten away.

Ellie glanced over her shoulder then walked to the back of the building, where the glass of the windows had been put in. She picked up a stick and pushed out the remaining shards in one window frame, then threw the kitbag through and clambered inside, Sam following.

Ellie knew this place. She'd come exploring here with Logan one time. Nothing much to see, lots of pigeon shit and rotten stonework, but it was dry inside. Ellie dumped the kitbag in a corner then turned to Sam, who'd taken his cap off and was looking around.

'It's only for a few hours,' Ellie said.

Sam nodded, scuffed his shoe in the dust.

'I'll be back soon,' Ellie said, then she left through the same window.

19

She prayed no one said anything. She was walking back along the pontoon towards the Porpoise, this time with Ben at her side, only half an hour after she'd been going the other way with Sam.

Ellie had placed herself at the side where more people were on deck, so she could ward them off, prevent Ben from stopping and chatting. She nodded and waved and turned away each time, Ben giving her a funny look.

'Are you OK?' he said.

'Fine.'

He looked at the sky then out to the Forth. 'Perfect day for it.'

They climbed on board. Ben began sorting through the rigging, checking ropes and sails.

Ellie went straight below and had a quick check to see if there was any sign that Sam had been here. She couldn't see anything.

She poked her head back up from the cabin. Ben was loosening off the boom ties, inspecting the main sail, going through the checklist, assessing the electrics and GPS. Beyond him, Ellie could see the warehouse where she'd left Sam. She'd driven straight home, met Ben in the kitchen in front of the laptop. He'd asked about her shopping, she said she was trying on clothes, couldn't find the right sizes. It wasn't like her, she wasn't a fussy shopper, or much of a shopper at all, but he accepted it.

Ben wanted to head out to the new bridge foundations. This stupid idea that they were using some chemical in the building process that somehow caused depression, hallucinations and suicide. She had a quick look at his evidence, making air quotes in her mind around that word. It was garbage. He'd gone on about the technical stuff of building, using engineering and construction lingo like caissons, piles and cofferdams, and she hadn't really followed, especially when he got on to the dubious chemistry of the theory.

But she was here now and going out sailing with him, partly to show him how ridiculous he was being. She pointed out that if they went to the new foundations and came back without suffering hallucinations or feeling suicidal, that would surely be proof he was talking rubbish. Well, not feeling any more suicidal than usual. But he would find a way round that, reasoned argument didn't hold sway, it always came down to 'that's what they want you to think'.

Ellie wondered about hallucinations. What if she was hallucinating this whole thing? What if there was no boy on the bridge, no body in the kitchen at Inchcolm Terrace, no little sister and drunk mother? Maybe the grief had finally got to her.

She went to the bin and opened it. The evidence of Sam's presence, a Wispa wrapper and a banana skin.

He was real. This was real.

Ben poked his head in as she closed the bin lid.

'Ready to cast off?' he said.

'Sure.'

Up on deck, he pointed to the stern. 'Want to take the tiller, steer us out?'

He yanked the starter cord on the outboard and it rattled and thrummed. Ellie unlocked the tiller and throttled a little in reverse, just to get a feel for the power under her hand. Ben scurried portside and began unhooking the mooring lines, wrapping them round the cleats, keeping everything in place. He jumped on to the pontoon and untied the final rope, threw it on to the boat and scuttled back on deck, pushing away from the edge as he did so.

The bow moved to starboard and Ellie corrected for it. The boat alongside theirs was an expensive SEPA motorboat, it wouldn't do to leave a dent in their hull.

The boat edged away from the berth into the shallow water behind. When it was clear of the pontoon Ellie switched to dead slow forward and headed towards the breakwater.

They picked up speed and headed past the low wall at the entrance to the harbour. Ben ducked into a storage box and pulled out two life jackets. He strapped one on and threw the other to Ellie. She caught it and put it on. It was standard practice to wear a life jacket, compulsory for sailing school and some races, but she didn't know how much use it would be. She could swim better without it. When she was fit she could swim back to shore in calm weather long before a coastguard boat would make it out to rescue them if the Porpoise capsized.

Not that there would be any capsizing today, conditions were calm.

Ben undid the final hooks on the boom.

'Coming round,' he shouted.

Ellie was nowhere near the arm, standing at the stern, but it was good practice to shout it out. If it came round and someone was standing in the middle of the deck they'd be over the side of the boat with concussion before anyone knew what'd happened. She'd seen it once before, not on the Porpoise, but a racing boat she and Ben had crewed years ago. Some novice with a sickly pallour stood up at the wrong time as half a ton of plastic and metal came swinging, the full sail whipping the arm as the boat changed tack. He took the brunt of it on his shoulders rather than his skull, which was just as well. They fished him out the water after barely a minute, but had to return to dry land because of a broken collarbone. The rest of the crew were furious at missing a day's racing, and the kid never appeared on the boat again.

The water today was royal blue. The colour of the sky always made a big difference, the sea mirroring what was above. On a dreich day the water was a mucky grey-brown, but today it was clearer.

The main sail was unfurled now and they tacked into the breeze. Ellie cut the engine. They would sail for a bit out to the bridge foundations, then pull the sail in once they were there, easier to control the boat that way.

Ben looked at the cofferdam around the nearest of the new bridge legs. There were three foundations stretching across the firth, one near each shore and a third one splitting the gap between them in the middle of the Forth. They'd had to remove a historic lighthouse from Beamer Rock in the middle of the waterway so they could build the foundation there. For almost two hundred years it had marked the way to Rosyth and upriver, and they'd carefully taken it down then blown the rock up to make way for twenty-first-century engineering.

As they got closer to the foundation Ellie felt the presence of it. In today's world everything seemed smaller, more contained, lives played out in front of computer screens, the scale of everything diminishing. But this was gargantuan, human endeavour writ large, millions of tons of material shaped into an object that would be seen for miles, seen from airplanes, that would serve an actual, physical purpose. It made Ellie feel connected to the world, this harnessing of nature, even though nature could never really be harnessed, you just had to look at the billions of gallons of water under their hull to know that.

They sailed on for a while, Ellie staring at the cofferdam and the two crane-barges alongside. They passed the yellow navigation buoys that had appeared recently, a thin attempt to keep unwelcome visitors at bay. As they got closer the size of the thing became overwhelming, even though it was hardly even out the water yet. Ellie tried to imagine what it would be like when the bridge was finished.

She'd had a few close encounters with large ships in the past, but never right alongside. The girth of the oil tankers downriver was staggering. They filled up at the terminal on the other side of the rail bridge, and she and Ben had come within a hundred feet once or twice, close enough to know they would crush you in a second and not even notice.

She felt a throbbing through her body. She turned. Ben had pressed ignition and was locking the boom arm, furling the sail up.

She unlocked the tiller and aimed for the bridge leg, the propeller churning the wash at the stern. She looked back to shore but the old warehouse was tiny now, just a red dot in the distance, almost hidden against a backdrop of trees. It was amazing how little time it took on the water before you got that perspective, the insignificance of everything on shore. That was one of the things she loved about sailing, leaving the land and all the problems waiting there.

Ben had his phone out and was taking pictures with the zoom fully extended. The pictures would be fuzzy, what was he hoping to gain from this? Someone else to blame for Logan's death? There was no one else to blame, and this was the worst of his excuses. Even the phone mast was better than this, and the school vaccinations or drug taking were far more likely.

Ben brought a gizmo out his pocket and held it up. A small red light flashed on the front as he looked at the digital display.

'What's that?' Ellie shouted over the thrash of waves.

Ben waited a moment, taking a reading of some kind, then turned.

'Measures air purity, amongst other things.'

'Where did you get it?'

'There are websites.'

There are websites for everything, Ellie thought. That wasn't the answer. None of this was the answer. She looked at the bridge leg. The cofferdam was fifty feet above sea level, the colour of rust. It was made of thick corrugated metal with a walkway round the top, a platform hanging over the side nearest them with four orange generators on it. Half a dozen men in hard hats and hi-vis jackets milled about on the walkway, and as the Porpoise got closer they all turned to watch.

Ellie waved to distract them from Ben taking pictures and holding the gizmo in the air. She was used to this, making excuses for her crazy husband. She knew what the guys on the cofferdam thought, wondering who this lunatic was, bringing his wife out to look at some anonymous piece of engineering. A nice, romantic day out.

A speedboat emerged from behind one of the barge-cranes and headed their way. The Porpoise was fifty yards from the cofferdam when Ellie cut the power, and the other boat continued straight for them. In the speedboat were two chunky guys in black waterproofs – bridge security. Ellie had seen them in Karinka's before, private company logos on their jackets, crew-cut hair, chowing down on full Scottish breakfasts. Rumour had it they were ex-army and mercenaries, but they didn't look like trained killers.

The guy at the bow of the speedboat had a loudhailer and was telling them not to get any closer.

'No problem,' Ellie shouted back, as Ben continued taking pictures. Was there a law against that? If so, what could the security guys do about it? If they really gave a shit they could follow them back to harbour and try to confiscate the phone, but by then Ben could've emailed the pictures to himself or posted them online.

'Go round,' Ben said, turning to her.

'What?'

'I want to see the other side.'

'I'm sure it's just the same as this side,' Ellie said.

She started the engine and guided them round the south side, feeling the stares of the security guys as she steered. The guys in hard hats turned away and began chatting amongst themselves as the Porpoise did a slow circumnavigation. There was a big enough gap between the cofferdam and the barge for the Porpoise to slip through. Ellie looked at the crane above their heads and felt dizzy. It was lifting a grey concrete pipe across to the bridgeworks.

Ellie imagined the bridge collapsing on opening day. She'd

seen footage of badly designed bridges, there was something about setting up resonances with the wind that could destroy a bridge in seconds if it got going. Did that still happen?

They were away from the crane now and round the other side, which was lower in the water. She could see inside because of the slope, pipe supports keeping the whole thing together, keeping the weight of the water out.

She heard shouts from the walkway and looked up to see two figures waving and pointing to the water next to the Porpoise. She looked and spotted a rock poking through the waves. She checked the depth gauge and it was almost at zero, stupid she hadn't noticed earlier, she'd presumed the water was deep all the way round.

'Hold on,' she shouted at Ben, then swung the tiller hard to port to send the boat away from the rocks.

Ben was thrown to the deck with the sway of the boat as it pitched in the water. The hull was part way out the firth as they banked steeply, the other side of the deck almost under the surface. Ben was on the wrong side, hanging on. If they'd been sailing he should've been on the starboard side, feet over the edge for ballast and balance, arms wrapped around the guard rails. But as it was he was clinging on to the jib sheet for the smaller sail, and if they didn't right themselves soon he'd be in the water.

Ellie kept turning the boat, leaning over the edge to see if she could spot rocks under the surface. She waited for the sound of ripping, the scream of stone through hull, but it didn't come. She'd experienced it once before, a sickening lurch in her gut as her frame of reference got torn apart, but this time it didn't happen and the Porpoise glided away past the outcrop.

Ellie straightened the steering and the boat righted itself. She turned and saw Ben holding the jib sheet, shaking his head and looking into the water.

'You OK?' Ellie said.

'Lost my air monitor into the drink,' he said.

It was a small price to pay for not being shipwrecked, but it was Ellie's fault in the first place, she hadn't checked the readings, hadn't been watching things as closely as she should.

20

Ben was fumbling with his key in the front door when Ellie felt an overwhelming rush of sorrow wash over her. She reached for him as he pushed the door open and wrapped her arms around him from behind. The sudden hug threw his momentum, making him stumble and put an arm out against the door jamb to balance. She couldn't even cuddle right.

'Hey,' he said.

She held on tight. He tried to turn and face her but she strengthened her grip. He squirmed round, keys still in his hand, and put his arms round her waist. She was surprised to hear sobs coming up her throat, then felt tears in her eyes.

'It's OK,' Ben said, rubbing her back. 'Shhh.'

He dropped his kit bag on the ground with a thud. Ellie buried her head into his chest, scared to look at him, afraid to let him see her crumpled face. She squeezed his body tight, trying to get comfort from the heft of him. He felt so solid compared to her, she was a ghost drifting through her own life, a lost spirit. Ben felt real, made of flesh and bone and muscle. She pictured him on the boat earlier, almost overboard because of her stupid mistake, because she wasn't paying attention. But how could you pay attention to the world when you were barely in it?

She imagined Ben tipping over the side of the Porpoise into the same sea that took her son. But that was wrong, that's not what happened, the water didn't take Logan, he went willingly into it, gave himself to it.

She was aware of how awkward this was, standing in the doorway, hugging and crying. She sensed people walking past in the street, felt Ben acknowledge them with a look and a nod of the head. She didn't care. Let them all see what the world can do to you. Eventually her crying began to subside. She felt like she wasn't in possession of her own body, she'd lost all control.

Ben gave a final rub of her back then eased himself from her grasp.

'You OK?' he said.

'Not really.'

'Come inside, I'll put the kettle on.'

In the kitchen, everything looked like it always did. Same scuffed table, same worn worktops, same bridges skulking outside the window. She felt like an impostor in her own house, like the real Ellie would ring the doorbell any minute and claim her house and husband and son back.

She scratched at her arm, that damn tattoo. She pulled the shoulder of her cardigan down, examined it. Red raw still, angry. Was that pus, was it getting infected? She dug her nails into the skin, felt relief with the pain, then covered her arm up.

They'd walked back from the marina in silence. They hadn't spoken before that either as they brought the Porpoise back to berth, pressed the kill button on the outboard and switched on the bilge pump under the floorboards of the cabin. They'd taken on a fair amount of water but nothing too dangerous, the level was quickly down. After securing the boat they got changed out of their wet gear in the locker room, then began the walk back. Ellie glanced at the deserted warehouse and imagined what Sam was doing inside.

'I thought you were overboard,' she said.

He filled the kettle. 'Is that what this is about?'

'I'm sorry.'

'Don't be.'

'It was my fault, I was in charge of the boat and I wasn't paying attention. You could've died.'

Ben put the kettle on. 'Nobody died.'

There was silence as those words hung in the air like poison. Ben turned. 'I meant . . .'

'I know what you meant.' Ellie's tone was gentle.

She thought of sitting at this table, talking to Sam yesterday morning. Trying to bring him down from the edge, keep him alive. She preferred being the one doing the comforting, it was a million times easier. She rubbed at the surface of the table where Sam's cup of tea had been, wiped away imaginary biscuit crumbs, just as Ben placed her own tea in the same spot.

'I need to tell you something,' Ellie said.

Ben sat down opposite. 'What?'

He had his mug in his hand. Ellie stared at it. It was from the high school up the road, picked up at a spring fair the first year Logan was there. It had the school crest on it, an abstract thing with a yellow cross and three red flowers. It said *Mente et Manu* underneath – 'with mind and hand'. That had always seemed so vague as to be almost meaningless. She knew what they were getting at but it was hardly inspirational. She stretched her fingers out in front of her and stared at them. Her hands seemed so disconnected from her mind, as if she had no power over them. She imagined her hands slapping her cup of tea on to the floor, or rising up to her own throat and squeezing, or picking up a kitchen knife and burying it in the belly of a child abuser.

She should tell Ben, she knew that. Now was the time, before things unravelled. But they'd already gone too far, she couldn't imagine starting this conversation now. She tried to think of all the different ways into this story, what had happened since yesterday morning, but in the bleached autumn light coming through the window they all felt ridiculous. What seemed like a simple case of doing the right thing had become more tangled. She'd wanted to help someone in trouble, and she still wanted to help, but her possible courses of action were disappearing. As long as she didn't tell Ben she had a sliver of control over this whole situation.

'Nothing,' she said. 'It doesn't matter.'

He blew the steam from his tea and stared at her. 'Are you sure?'

She knew he wouldn't force it; that was one of the million little things she loved about him.

'Yeah,' she said.

'OK.'

She lifted her own mug, blew on the tea and tried to smile.

21

She checked the local news app on her phone as she strode back to the marina. The grumble of traffic overhead as she walked under the bridge made her feel insignificant as always, the thick bridge legs seemingly growing out of the earth.

There was nothing new on the story, the police still appealing for witnesses. She thought about how she'd been at that house twice now. No, three times. She'd been to Inchcolm Terrace three times, hadn't she? God, she was losing it. And the police were still seeking to trace the whereabouts of Sam McKenna, the victim's seventeen-year-old son. 'Seeking to trace the whereabouts' and 'appealing for witnesses' – why did the police succumb to their own clichés of language, their own verbose patterns? It was a unique and awkward vocabulary, as if the public couldn't handle the truth of crime delivered to them in plain language. There was a hint of Orwell about it. Maybe it wasn't sinister, just that the organisation found it easier to fall into that language as a comfort, a code handed down from generation to generation of copper, sticking to their own obscure linguistic rules.

While she still had her phone out she stopped walking and opened Facebook, went straight to Logan's page. Nothing new. She sent a quick message, just *Love, Mum xxx*. She flicked to Sam's page, then Libby's, then back to Logan and swiped through the pictures. Touched her thumb to the screen, zoomed in on one he was tagged in with her and Ben. He'd said it was embarrassing, talked about untagging himself so his friends wouldn't see it, but he never did. They were in France, sitting outside at a table next to a vineyard, three glasses of red wine raised in a cheers. The owner of the vineyard had taken the picture, a fat, happy man who insisted on pouring a glass for Logan even though he was only thirteen. Logan had that weird mix of embarrassment and excitement about alcohol, and they let him drink it. He sipped and winced at first, but kept drinking. She zoomed in as far as possible on the photograph until it was just a grainy blur of colour, the burgundy of the glass, the green of his T-shirt, the paleness of his skin. She rubbed her finger on the screen as if trying to get a stain out.

She closed Facebook and stared at the icons on her phone. Her thumb hovered over Video. She pressed it. Just the one clip on there, from the bridge. She pressed play, stared at the grainy screen, the grey, blank bridge, then the figure of Logan coming into shot, his back to the camera. She wished he'd been facing the CCTV. He stopped at the railing, looked up and down, then faced out to sea. Flicked at his hair. Waited for a moment. Ellie paused the video and raised a hand to her forehead. Closed her eyes then reopened them. Pressed play. Logan hoisted himself up and over the railing, stood on the ledge. She paused it again. Touched the screen. Play. A short wait then her son stepped off the edge and the bridge was empty again. She wiped a tear off the screen and closed the app. She bent double where she stood, and put her hands on her thighs, trying to breathe. She felt something come over here and puked into the grass verge at the side of the lane, her throat convulsing three, four times. She spat sick out her mouth and wiped tears from her eyes. Waited like that, crouched over, for a few moments then straightened her back and put her phone away.

She began walking, stumbling at first like an old woman unsure of her footing. She skirted round the back way to the warehouse, avoiding the likely huddle of activity at the marina this time of day. The wind was fresh and the leaves were beginning to fall from the trees in the woods opposite as the branches swayed in the breeze. They rustled in competition with the bridge traffic and the faint shush of the water. Things were never quiet around here, she couldn't remember a time of peace and tranquillity.

She heard voices and her shoulders tensed. They were coming from inside the warehouse. She crept to the window and listened. Two voices, both young. One a girl, the other Sam. She looked through the empty frame and saw Sam and Libby standing together next to a decrepit workbench in the corner of the room.

'What's she doing here?' Ellie said, clambering through the window.

Sam and Libby turned as Ellie landed in a scuff of rubble.

'I could hear you arguing a mile away,' she said. 'That's not exactly safe. She has to go home.'

Sam approached her, Libby behind.

'I was just telling her that,' he said.

Libby folded her arms. 'I'm staying here.'

Her body language was full of exaggerated, pre-teen melodrama, hip stuck out and pouting.

'You have to go,' Ellie said.

Libby threw a thumb in her brother's direction. 'He's here, why not me?'

Ellie tried to keep her voice calm. 'Because you're an eleven-year-old girl.'

'I'm almost twelve,' Libby said.

Ellie held in a laugh. 'Your brother is technically an adult, but a missing eleven-year-old girl is an entirely different story.'

Sam turned to his sister. 'I told you, Lib.'

'This is bullshit,' Libby said.

'Does your mum know where you are?' Ellie said.

Libby shook her head. 'She thinks I'm at school.'

'But they have an automated system. If you're not in registration, the parents get a text and a call.'

Libby was thrown off. 'I forgot about that.'

Sam raised his eyebrows. 'You forgot?'

Ellie spoke to her. 'We have to get you home right now.'

'No.'

Ellie raised a finger at her, the nagging point. 'Do you want to get your brother into more trouble, is that what you want?'

'Of course not.'

'You've got a funny way of showing it.' Ellie hated how her voice sounded, like her own mother's when she told Ellie off. Falling back on familiar patterns of speech, she was no better than the police.

Libby looked uncertain.

'What's the plan?' Sam said, flicking his hand through his fringe.

Ellie stared at him. 'I still need to work that out. In the meantime we have to get Libby home.'

She turned to Libby. 'Does anyone know you're here?'

Libby made a face like she was talking to a toddler. 'Of course not.'

'Are you sure?'

'Yeah.'

'Have you texted anyone today, posted anything online?'

Libby stuck her bottom lip out. 'I texted my mate Cassie.'

'What did you tell her?'

'Just that I was meeting Sam, that's all, and I'd see her later.'

'When was that?'

'I don't know, an hour ago?'

'Text her now, tell her to delete it and not mention it to any-one.'

'What?'

Ellie moved her face closer to Libby's. She could see clumps of concealer on her face, trying to cover the spots. 'Do you real-ise how fucking serious this is?'

'Of course I do.'

Libby shuffled her feet in the dirt and Ellie could see tears welling up in her eyes.

Sam moved between them. 'Take it easy, she's only a kid.'

Ellie sighed. 'I'm sorry, but you have to understand. I prom-ise I'll take care of both of you, but you have to do what I say. The best place for Libby at the moment is at home, that way the police won't be looking so hard for Sam. Your dad's still in hospital, so there's no danger on that front. We can't arouse any more suspicion.'

Sam was rubbing Libby's arm. 'She's right, Lib. Mum will go mental when she realises you're not there.'

'I suppose.'

'And I'm always on the phone, I've got a battery charger now, so I won't run out of juice like yesterday, Ellie sorted it.'

The tone of his voice had a calming effect on her. Ellie

wondered how Logan would've been with a little brother or sister. Would he have been caring and considerate, or would they have been at each other's throats like so many siblings?

Libby looked at her brother now. 'We can meet up again, yeah? It's weird in the house, just me and Mum.'

Sam gave her a hug. 'Of course we can. We just have to be careful.'

He pulled away as Ellie looked at her watch.

'We need to get you back,' she said to Libby.

The girl looked at Sam for a long moment, as Ellie held out her hand. Then she began walking, dragging her feet, following Ellie.

Libby stopped at the window and turned to Sam. 'See you.'

'See you soon,' Sam said.

22

Ellie waited till they were well away from the marina before she spoke. She turned to Libby who was scuffing her trainers, shoulders hunched in a red hoodie.

'I need to get some things straight with you,' Ellie said.

Libby shrugged. They were heading back under the bridge. How many times had Ellie walked under this thing? Must be hundreds. She imagined the concrete crumbling, huge slabs of the stuff raining down, crushing them, steel cables whipping as they lashed about, cars and vans and lorries piling down and smashing into the dirt around them. She pictured the shockwaves spreading along the length of the bridge, the overhead cables snapping like threads, the entire length of road tumbling into the water, sending a colossal wave to drown the towns and villages along the coast, collapsing the rail bridge and swamping the oil terminal, a chain reaction that would destroy the world.

'If I'm going to help you and Sam I need as much information as possible,' Ellie said. 'Do you understand?'

Libby nodded, just a twitch of her head.

'It might not be easy to talk about,' Ellie said.

Libby looked at her. 'I don't mind.'

'So tell me what happened yesterday.'

'What do you mean?'

'I presume you've spoken to the police.'

'Yeah.'

'What did you tell them?'

Libby shoved her hands further into her pockets. 'Nothing. I said I wasn't home, and I didn't know anything about it.'

'Is that true?'

Libby lowered her head and mumbled.

Ellie ducked closer to her. 'What?'

'No.'

Ellie pointed up the access road to the bridge. 'Let's take the back way, less chance of being seen.'

They crossed the road and headed up the hill, traffic getting louder.

'So,' Ellie said. 'What really happened yesterday morning?'

Libby blew out a big sigh.

Ellie pursed her lips. 'You want to help Sam, don't you?'

'Of course.'

'Well?'

Libby played with her hair, tucked a loose strand behind her ear.

'Sam came home.'

'What time was that?'

'I don't know. Maybe ten.'

'Where had he been?'

'He was supposed to be out with mates, I don't know.'

'When had he gone out?'

Libby slowed her pace. 'Early. I was dreading it. Mum was already at work, Dad had a later shift, so that meant it was just the two of us in the house.'

'What did he do, Libby?'

Libby shook her head. They were at the top of the access

road now, heading left, round the visitor centre and the new bridge information hub. A few work vans parked up, nobody else about.

'I know it's not easy, Libby.'

Libby looked her in the eye. 'You have no idea.'

Ellie held her gaze. 'So tell me.'

'He came into my room. Sat down on the bed next to me. He does this all the time, has done for ages. He started that talk, I'm his special little girl, all that. Says it makes us closer, our wee secret. He thinks he's the first dirty old man to come out with this crap.'

She stalled for a minute. Ellie didn't speak, just waited as they walked together. Eventually Libby spoke.

'Starts feeling me up. Same every time. Tits first, always, then a hand into my pants. That gets him hard. Then I have to suck it. Until . . .'

Libby had stopped walking. Ellie's heart was pounding as she shook her head.

'You get the idea.'

'God, Libby, I'm so sorry.'

Libby shrugged. 'You've got nothing to be sorry about.'

'Why haven't you told anyone?'

Libby raised her eyebrows. 'Like who?'

'Your mum, for a start.'

'I've tried, but it's too hard, I don't know how to bring it up. Besides, Dad says he'll kill me if I tell anyone.'

'What about the authorities?' Ellie said.

'The police?' Libby laughed bitterly. 'He is the police.'

'Someone at school, then, a teacher.'

Libby sighed. 'They're all useless. The women are clueless,

and the men, well, they look at me the same way as Dad.'

They were by the woods now, round the back of the cul-de-sac where Libby and Sam lived. The embankment sheltered them from the traffic noise. It felt suddenly intimate, in that vacuum.

'So what happened yesterday?' Ellie said.

'Sam came back, found Dad in my room with his trousers at his ankles.'

'Jesus.'

'He went apeshit. They argued and shoved each other. Dad tried to walk away as if it was nothing. Sam followed him downstairs and into the kitchen. I came down and Sam was standing holding the knife, pointing it at him. Dad was laughing, said he didn't have the guts. Sam ran at him and proved him wrong.'

'Then what?'

'I ran. Straight out the door and kept running until I couldn't breathe. Just kept going through the woods, along the seafront, anywhere. I didn't have my phone, so I couldn't even call Sam, which was horrible.' She turned to Ellie. 'Was he really going to jump off the bridge and leave me?'

'I think so.'

Libby rubbed at her forehead. 'Stabbing Dad was the best thing he's ever done, I just wish he'd killed him.'

'Me too,' Ellie said.

Libby laughed at that. She stopped and nodded at the fence to their left. 'This is my place over the other side.'

'OK.'

'So what now?' Libby said.

Ellie should take Libby to the police and report it, but it

wasn't as simple as that. She'd have to explain how she knew, then she'd have to tell them about Sam. It didn't help Libby that the stabbing was tied to the abuse. But how else to do it? Libby could go to the police station herself but she already said that was a non-starter and Ellie could see her point. Tell her mum? Maybe Ellie should speak to Alison, but that had the same problem as talking to the police, she would have to explain how she was involved, give Sam up.

'I'm not sure yet,' she said.

Libby snorted. 'You're the worst knight in shining armour ever.'

'I need some time.'

'In the meantime I'm just supposed to sit tight at home?'

'For now.'

'And when Dad gets out of hospital?'

Ellie held Libby by the arms, it was supposed to be reassuring. 'It'll all be sorted long before then, I promise.'

'I wish I could believe you.'

'You can.'

Libby sighed and began to climb the fence at the back of her garden. She spoke to Ellie over her shoulder with a weary resignation.

'Just look after my brother, OK?'

23

It was almost like none of it had happened. Ellie stood in her kitchen like a normal wife and mother, making green tea and wiping the surfaces. Ben was sitting at the table staring at his phone. He always had a screen in his face, ever since Logan, the twenty-first-century addiction afflicting him in his grief, his search for answers.

Ellie dunked her teabag, squeezed it out with a spoon then dropped it in the bin. She needed this time, the quiet, familiar order, to work everything out. Libby was back at home. She'd been on the phone to Sam, apparently she was reported absent by the school, but they didn't have Alison's mobile number, so the automated system left three messages on their home phone. Alison was out at work so Libby erased the messages when she got in. Not exactly a foolproof system.

Sam was back in the Porpoise. Ellie had come straight home after leaving Libby, packed up some more food then jogged along to the warehouse. Dropped off the provisions, handed him the key to the cabin padlock and told him to wait until the sun went down before heading over to the boat, baseball cap down. Part of her wanted to stay with him, keep him close, her maternal instinct kicking in, but she needed time and space alone to think.

Sam had texted an hour ago to say he was on the boat. She liked that he trusted her now. She missed that. But she imagined him on his own, lonely in that cramped berth at the bow of the boat, the rattle of masts and rigging keeping him awake, that and the worry. At least he didn't seem suicidal any more.

She wondered about that. Every case was different, she knew from her research after Logan jumped, you couldn't generalise about suicides and suicide attempts. Some were cries for help, some were spur of the moment things, some were well planned out. Some were the culmination of years struggling with serious mental illness. People who survived all reacted differently too. Weeping with grief that they hadn't managed to end it all, or overwhelmed with relief that their momentary lapse hadn't been successful, realising they had so much to live for. Some found God, some went deeper into a hole, some just walked away seemingly unscathed.

How would Sam be? It was less than two days since she found him on the bridge. But since then he seemed to have pulled himself together, mainly because of Libby. What had he been thinking, trying to kill himself, when he had a little sister who loved him, who needed him around to look after her? But 'what was he thinking' was the stupidest question of all, it presumed a rationality that doesn't exist in the mind of someone contemplating killing themselves.

For a while Ellie buried herself in facts, essays, reports and books that looked at suicide from every side – the social aspect, the cultural angle, the mental-health issues, the reaction of others. But none of it meant anything really, none of it explained away the bare, monstrous fact that her son was no longer around, that he wasn't sleeping in till lunchtime at weekends, hogging the shower at inopportune moments, being sarcastic to her and Ben in a comfortable, familiar way, taking a pretend huff over not being allowed out until he'd done homework or chores around the house.

Ellie thought about Libby, what she'd gone through. If anyone had the right to feel suicidal it was her. Ellie's insides itched at the thought of what Jack had been doing to her. How could anyone do that to any young girl, let alone his own daughter? It was beyond comprehension. Was it just evil, did such a thing really exist? Was it about power? How did a grown man get to the place in his life where making his daughter suck his dick was something to even consider? She wanted to speak to Jack. It was too easy just to brand him a monster, dehumanise him, that's what the liberal in her was thinking. But another, deeper part of Ellie's psyche wanted to destroy him, make him pay for what he'd done.

And what about Alison? Ellie realised she'd been skirting round Alison, leaving her until last in her thoughts. Libby said she'd tried to bring it up with her mum, but Alison had sidestepped it. Could that be true? Did Alison not know anything, or did she suspect in her darkest mind, but refuse to confront it? How could you live with someone half your life and not know they were capable of something like that. Or maybe Alison knew too well what her husband was capable of, maybe that was the problem. Maybe she was scared.

Ellie looked at Ben. How could you live with someone for twenty years and not even know them? She and Ben had seemed like soul mates, whatever that meant, for so long, but Logan, their foundation together, had been destroyed. What did they have in the aftermath of that, did they even know each other now?

'You're in a dwam.'

Ben was looking at her. He was right, 'dwam' was the exact word, she'd been daydreaming, but not the pleasant kind. She smiled apologetically.

Ben put his phone down and got up, walked over to her. He put his hands on her shoulders and she was relieved that she didn't flinch like yesterday. Instead she let him rub at the knots and strains, realising how tense her body was. She used to do yoga, before Logan. She used to do a lot of things before that day, none of it made sense now. Her body was a mess of tight muscles and saggy skin, her flesh covered in ink, her joints achy, as if she was already old. Her son's suicide had turned her into an old woman overnight. Not a widow, something much worse.

She put her tea down and turned to face Ben. Put a hand to his cheek, felt the stubble, pushed two fingers through the grey hair at his temple, looked in his eyes. She always got annoyed in books when people saw things in each other's eyes – recognition, despair, understanding, all that. They were just eyes, the eyes of the man she still loved.

'Are you OK?' she said. 'After today on the boat, I mean.'

He laughed and placed a small kiss on her lips. 'I'm fine. Is that what you were worried about?'

'A little.'

He shook his head. 'I love you.'

She smiled, looked into those eyes again. 'I love you, too.'

24

She looked at the water below. Forty-five metres roughly, depending on the tide. The light today was diffuse, high cloud cover making everything matt and dull. There were no sharp sunbeams bouncing off the water, meaning she could get some sense of the depths below, a feel for the swell of the waves.

The traffic noise thundered at her back, as always. She wondered if the day would ever come when she wouldn't have to come up here. She pulled a pebble out her pocket and dropped it over the side of the railing, watched as it tumbled and turned until she couldn't make it out against the grey below. She waited for a splash but of course it was too small, too insignificant to see from up here. She wondered what kind of splash Logan made as he hit the water, as his body was smashed on impact.

She looked over to the Binks where she'd picked up the pebble earlier. Every day like a pilgrimage. Down there, up here, down there, up here.

She looked at her house. Her bedroom window had the curtains closed, Ben still in bed. The curtains were open in Logan's room, as always. She imagined him standing there in his underwear and T-shirt, stretching and yawning, getting himself together for school before bounding down the stairs in three leaps and shovelling toast into his face while he stood in the kitchen. He never sat down in the morning, there was no calm family breakfast, not for them. Instead they had the typical modern-family rusharound, two parents late for work, trying to find keys, shoving stuff into work bags, finding a moment to talk about bills or tonight's tea or something on the television news in the corner of the room. Their teenage son, their anchor, scurrying between them, mouth full, deflecting enquiries about his day, homework, football training after school.

So ordinary, so boring.

She looked at her watch, almost nine o'clock. She turned from the view and pulled her phone out her pocket. A truck roared past, the bridge rocking under her feet as she leant the small of her back against the railing. She swiped to Sam's number and called, cars blurring past her eye line.

'Hi, Sam,' she said when he picked up.

'Hi.'

'You OK?'

'I guess.' His voice was thick, maybe she'd woken him up.

'Sleep OK?'

There was a pause. 'Not really.'

'Me neither,' Ellie said.

She stretched on to her tiptoes. Past the wash of traffic she could see the cranes at the new bridge. Down to her left was the marina, obscured from view. She imagined Sam under his duvet, cosy in the rocking boat.

'I have a few things to sort,' she said, 'then I'm coming for you. Just stay put.'

'I don't know how much longer I can do this,' Sam said.

'Try not to worry,' Ellie said. 'I said I'd take care of everything and I will.'

'Do you have a plan?' Sam said.

Ellie looked up, her gaze following the sweep of the suspension cables as they curved in a parabola to the tower above.

'I think so,' she said.

'What is it?'

'I'll tell you when I see you,' she said. 'Have you spoken to Libby this morning?'

'Just got a text. Said she was on her way to school.'

'Good.' Ellie had told Sam to get her to act as normal as possible.

'I'm scared, Ellie.'

'It's OK, sweetheart.' As it came out her mouth she realised it was one of the words she used for Logan.

There was a pause, maybe as Sam digested the word.

'This will all be over soon,' Ellie said.

She hung up, took a last look at the firth. The size of the sea made her stomach knot. What was the point of doing anything in the face of such enormity?

*

Ellie pressed the doorbell a second time and waited. Maybe Alison was already at work. The car sat in the drive, but that didn't mean anything, it was probably Jack's. Ellie felt bile rising in her throat. She breathed carefully, pressed a knuckle to her ribs, shifted her weight.

She was reaching for the doorbell again when she saw movement through the bevelled glass. Someone coming downstairs. Whoever it was paused for a while behind the door. Ellie looked for a spy-hole but couldn't see one.

The door opened a crack, still on the chain, and Alison appeared. The word 'haggard' sprang into Ellie's head, unkind but that was the best way to describe her. Her skin was oily and blotchy, hair unkempt, eyes raw, and her downturned mouth made jowls out of her cheeks. She was wearing a baggy hoodie and joggers, frayed cuffs and stains, and she looked confused. Ellie smelt alcohol – last night's or already this morning? Ellie wouldn't blame her if it was the latter.

'What do you want?' Alison said. It wasn't aggressive, just monotone. Sleeping pills maybe.

'We need to talk,' Ellie said.

'No.'

Ellie looked at the chain on the door. Small metal links, like a bracelet. It was the kind of thing you got in B&Q for three quid, it wouldn't keep anyone out. She imagined putting her foot against the door and kicking it in, Alison falling back into the hall, screaming.

'Yes,' she said.

Alison went to close the door and Ellie pushed her foot in the gap. The door rebounded on the chain, almost catching Alison on the chin.

'I'll call the police,' she said.

'Don't.'

'Why not?'

'I've spoken to Sam.'

Alison stopped pushing on the door and Ellie felt the pressure ease on her foot. Alison raised two fingers to her forehead, rubbed at the lines there.

'Where is he? Is he OK?'

'Let me in and we'll talk.'

Alison hesitated, her hand still at her temple. She rubbed at her eyebrow and looked down, then sighed.

'Two minutes, then you're out.'

Ellie took her foot from the doorway and Alison closed the door, slid the chain then opened it. She nodded towards the living room. Ellie walked through and heard the door close behind her.

The decor was like in a TV makeover show, large violet orchids on the wallpaper, mirror over a slate fireplace, black leather sofas and a chintzy mini-chandelier. There were framed pictures on the mantelpiece, school photos of Sam and Libby looking awkward in uniform, a snap of the whole family at a waterpark somewhere sunny. Alison was wearing a one-piece swimsuit, sarong wrapped round her waist, Libby flat-chested in a bikini. Jack had one arm around each of them, Sam on the other side of his mum, held close.

'How do you know my son?'

Ellie turned. 'I met him.'

'Where?'

'In the pub.'

'Which pub?'

'The Ferry Tap.'

Alison stared at her. 'He was in the Ferry Tap on his own?'

'Yes.'

'And no one recognised him, no one realised we've been worried sick? I don't believe you.'

Ellie shrugged. 'It's true.'

'What were you doing in the Tap?'

'Drinking.'

'On your own?'

'Yes.'

'Do a lot of drinking on your own?'

Ellie looked around the room, then back at Alison. 'Do you?'

'What does that mean?'

'I can smell it on you.'

'Fuck you.'

Ellie turned and nodded at the picture of Sam in his blazer. He seemed a lot younger in the photo, an innocent wee boy waiting for the world to happen to him.

'Don't you want to know about Sam?'

Something softened in Alison's voice. 'Tell me.'

'He didn't have any money so I bought him a drink.'

'He's only seventeen.'

Ellie nodded. 'That's old enough.'

'Why won't he come home?' Alison's voice wavered, real concern, her fists clenching at her side.

'Why do you think?'

Alison rubbed at the back of her head. 'I wish I knew.'

Her breathing was shaky and her body swayed.

Ellie suddenly felt sorry for her. 'Maybe we should sit down.'

Alison nodded, moved backwards till her hand found the arm of the sofa, then lowered herself. It was the motion of a woman in trouble.

Ellie sat on the other sofa. 'Look at me, Alison.'

Alison raised her head.

Ellie spoke. 'What happened here?'

Alison's eyes flitted round the room as if she might find the answers in a dusty corner.

'You saw it on the news, you know what happened.'

'I want you to tell me.'

'What did Sam say?'

Ellie shook her head, stayed silent.

Alison took a deep breath. 'Someone came into our home, that's what happened, and they stabbed my husband and left him for dead.'

'Were there any signs of a break-in?'

Alison pressed her lips tight and frowned. 'No, but the front door was unlocked, they could have just walked in.'

'And why would a stranger do that?'

'How should I know? Jack is a police officer, maybe some maniac criminal had it in for him.'

'And what about Sam?'

'What about him?'

'Why do you think he's been missing for two days?'

Alison's head went down. 'I don't know. He's my little boy and I don't know where he is.' She was almost crying. 'Maybe he saw something and got scared. I just want him to come home. Where's he been since Monday?'

'He told me he was sleeping rough.'

'Whereabouts?'

Ellie shook her head. 'He didn't say.'

'Does he have his phone? I've tried it a hundred times. Why doesn't he answer? Why would he speak to you and not me?'

'Maybe because I'm a stranger. Maybe there's stuff at home he can't face.'

Alison wiped at her eyes. 'What do you mean?'

'How's Libby?'

Alison stared at her hands.

'I came here yesterday to see her,' Ellie said. 'Did you realise that?'

Alison pulled a hand over her face, rubbed at her skin.

'Sam asked me to check on her,' Ellie continued. 'Why would he do that?'

'Because he cares about his little sister.'

Ellie looked round the room, at the doorway. 'Maybe he thinks she's in danger here.'

Alison stood up, her hands balled tight. 'What are you getting at? Why would Libby be in danger?'

Ellie stayed in her seat. 'You tell me.'

Alison took a step forward. 'I think you'd better leave.'

'Then you're not going to hear from Sam again.'

Alison hesitated.

Ellie nodded at the sofa. 'Sit down.'

Alison obliged.

Ellie played with the wedding ring on her finger.

'Sam told me about something that happened here, in this house. Your home. Libby told me as well.'

Alison frowned. 'When did you speak to Libby?'

Ellie ignored the question. 'Do you know what I'm talking about?'

Alison shook her head.

'Try harder,' Ellie said.

'I can't,' Alison said. Her hand gripped the arm of the sofa.

Ellie sighed and looked at the family photos on the mantelpiece. 'I understand what it's like, that feeling of the kids getting away from you. Trust me, I know. One day they're toddlers following you from room to room, asking for snacks or needing their noses wiped. The next minute they're monosyllabic zombies, locked away in their rooms, faces buried in their phones. Then the next moment they're gone.'

She stopped, regained her composure.

'But how could you not know?' she said.

Alison shook her head but didn't speak.

'How could you not know?' Ellie repeated.

Alison's eyes were wet. 'Know what?' she whispered.

Ellie felt her heart in her chest, a trapped animal. 'That your husband is abusing your daughter, right here under your roof.'

Alison's eyes widened. 'No.'

Ellie nodded. 'Upstairs, in her bedroom.'

'Don't say that,' Alison said.

'He goes into her room and plays with her until he gets hard, then he makes her suck his cock.'

Alison shot out the sofa. 'How dare you . . .'

Ellie cut her off. 'He's been doing it for years. When you're out, when he's alone in the house with her. How does that make you feel?'

'Get out,' Alison shouted. 'Get out of my fucking house.'

'Are you proud of your good policeman husband now?'

'I said get out. Now.'

'Standing by your man, that's nice.'

'He would never do anything like that,' Alison said, voice shaky. 'My Jack would never harm a hair on Libby's head.'

'Ask him.'

'I don't need to ask him, I know.'

'Ask Libby,' Ellie said.

'You're sick,' Alison said. 'That's what this is. You've seen our story on the news, you've somehow found out about my kids, and you've come here and made all this up for attention.

Get the hell out of my house, I'm calling the police.'

'Just ask Libby.'

'Get out.'

Alison came towards Ellie, reached for her arm but Ellie shrugged her off. She stood looking at Alison, staring at her.

'Get out,' Alison said again.

'I'm going.' Ellie walked out the room to the front door, opened it, Alison behind her.

Ellie turned before she took a step outside.

'Open your eyes, Alison,' she said. 'Before it's too late.'

25

She ran. She had no idea where she was going, just wanted to get away, feel her feet pounding on the concrete, her body moving away from Inchcolm Terrace and Alison, from confrontation, away from Sam and Libby and the mess she was involved in.

She ran so she didn't have to think, her body took over, she had to concentrate on breathing, the molecules going in and out of her mouth, her bloodstream, her pulse pumping energy from her heart through her stomach to her legs. She ran to feel the rhythm of it, settled into the thud, thud of her heels on the ground. She was wearing the wrong shoes, casual trainers, and the wrong clothes, clinging to her as she began to work up a sweat, but she didn't care, she just kept on.

Gradually she began to be aware of where she was. She'd gone in the opposite direction from it all, up the back roads of the Ferry, east towards Dalmeny, vaguely aware of the A90 somewhere behind the trees on her right, sweeping towards Edinburgh. She turned left and found herself on a farm lane, views of Dalgety Bay across the Forth, her legs aching and her arms still thrusting away, as if she knew what she was doing, where she was going.

She turned at the end of the track, passed some cottages and realised where she was, heading back into the Ferry from the east side, close to Dalmeny railway station. Her breath was short, a wheeze in her chest. She headed towards the train station. She'd waited on that platform hundreds of times for trains into the city, always looking the other way, over the bridge. In the last six months whenever she'd stood there, she imagined jumping on to the tracks, not suicide, not that way at least. She imagined leaping on to the gravel between the rusty rails and sprinting in the direction of the bridge, it wasn't far, she could make it easily. She wondered if she could run all the way over the rail bridge before a train came and crushed her, or before railway security managed to stop her. She imagined the bridge from Iain Banks' book, an entire civilisation living inside the legs and arms of the structure. Everyone in the Ferry knew that book, Iain had lived over the water in North Queensferry, he was one of their own.

She didn't stop at the station now but pounded on, pulled towards the shoreline by the gravity of the sea, the power of the water that had taken Logan, her home calling her as she leapt down the steep stairs below the rail bridge, through the thick trees, coming out on Shore Road at the east end of the village by the legs of the rail bridge.

Without looking she ran across the road to the bridge leg, where she stopped and placed her shaking hands against the stonework. Her breath heaved and her lungs ached, her legs trembled as she used the bridge for support. Three tourists walked past, sauntering into the village, staring at her. She wasn't dressed like a jogger, so why was she out of breath? What was she running from?

As she stood there, that comforting rumble of the train overhead, click-clack of wheels on rails, the rattle of people going places a hundred feet above her head.

If she'd run on to the bridge like she imagined, the train would be bearing down on her now. She wouldn't even be halfway across. Maybe she would've just lain down and let it crush her. Maybe she would've jumped over the side, like her son. Maybe she would've stood tall, a character in a superhero movie, and the train would explode on impact. She would walk away unharmed, to save the planet from annihilation.

*

Back home and the water was calling her as she stood in the kitchen gazing out the window. She had a note from Ben in her hand, he'd gone out flyering again, somehow convinced after their boat trip yesterday that something was up with the new bridge.

She jogged upstairs, stripped and got changed into her wetsuit, stretching the material and pulling her limbs into it. There was a little more room than before from the weight she'd lost, the rubber rippling and bunching at her stomach and thighs.

She went out the back door, not bothering to lock it, pulling the cap over her head, pushing stray strands of hair under the silicon. She didn't stop to think, just dived in, the best way to acclimatise, the body used to the cold within seconds. She began stroking straight away, stroke and push, stroke and kick. She was already tired from the run but she had to feel empty, wanted to keep going until there was nothing left inside her. Swim until you can't see land.

She concentrated on her breathing again, in out, in out, angling her head to the side, then face in the water, up to the side, down, pushing the slick Forth behind her, overwhelmed by the grey swells, the waves making her adjust her stroke, constantly monitoring her body, checking her strength, her muscles talking to her.

Before she knew it she was two hundred yards out. She pictured a huge ocean liner or ferry bearing down on her, the sharp edge of the bow splurging the water aside as it thundered over her, pummelling her body, whipping in the force of the undertow, ripping her to shreds in the wake of the engines. She imagined Logan falling from the bridge directly on top of her, the two of them spiralling downwards with the force of it, held in each other's embrace, tumbling to the silt and sediment of the bottom, sucked into the mud, unable to break free, kissing each other one last time before they let the ocean into their lungs.

She stopped and treaded water, taking in her surroundings. It felt so free to be out here, unshackled from earth for a moment. But then she began to think about Sam and Libby, Ben and Logan, Jack and Alison, all of them leaking in through the cracks. She started swimming back to shore, breath shortening, limbs stretching, muscles screaming. She concentrated on staying alive and moving, always moving forward.

She was a hundred yards out from shore, arms and legs burning, a good burn. She had slowed down but that was fine, she was still going forward, pushing the past behind her, pushing the waves behind her, pushing her life behind her one stroke at a time.

She spotted Ben standing on shore, cup of coffee in one hand, towel in the other. She couldn't make out his face yet, too far away, as she pummelled through the water, the surface splash salty on her lips, the taste of it like sweat and fish and freedom.

Then she was only twenty yards out, able to put her feet down and wade the rest of the way. She stumbled on the pebbles underfoot, her legs jelly from the exertion, and wiped her eyes. She saw now that Ben was frowning. He held out the towel and stepped to the side, his head nodding back to the house, where two uniformed police officers were sitting at the kitchen table drinking tea.

26

'This is not a formal interview, Mrs Napier, we just want a little chat.'

Ellie looked around. This wasn't an interview room, didn't look anything like she'd seen on television crime dramas, they were just sitting in the corner of a regular open-plan office, computer and paperwork on the desk, spreadsheets and forms pinned to a noticeboard, a couple of framed awards mounted on the wall.

They were at the back of the police station, so the view out the window was of someone's garage and an overgrown lawn. Round the front of the station were the Forth and her house, where Ben was waiting.

She'd told him not to come. The police wanted to talk to her about her visit to the McKennas' house, and Jack's attempted murder. They seemed happy to talk at her kitchen table but she wanted them out, wanted to distance the whole thing from what was left of her family. So she told Ben not to come to the station. He'd mentioned getting a solicitor but the female officer said there was no need, it was strictly informal. And anyway, Ellie thought, they didn't have a solicitor. Who has a criminal lawyer in real life?

She'd gone upstairs, dried off, changed into her clothes and walked with them to the station. Now she was sitting in this or-dinary office, facing the two cops. She didn't recognise either of them, she'd thought she might, from Logan's suicide, or just from around town. She was surprised about that, it couldn't be much of a police force in such a small station.

The female officer was about the same age as her, maybe a little younger, auburn hair pulled into a ponytail, sleek, well conditioned. Her nails had been done recently, she took care of her appearance. Ellie saw a wedding ring and wondered if she had kids. The male officer was younger, just a kid really, mid-twenties, confident, sharp haircut, smelling of cologne, expensive, chunky watch on his wrist.

'Ellie.' It was the woman officer, a sympathetic note in her voice. Were they going to do good cop, bad cop, did police really do that?

'My name is PC Macdonald, this is PC Wood. Do you know why you're here?'

'No.'

'Alison McKenna contacted us,' Macdonald said. 'You know who I mean?'

Ellie nodded.

'She said you've been round to see her.' Macdonald had a notepad and pen at the ready. Ellie noticed she'd already written Ellie's name and the date at the top of the page and underlined it. 'Have you visited her home?'

Ellie nodded again.

'Why?'

Ellie rolled her wedding ring round her finger. She felt something like tears beginning to well up inside her, felt her stomach lurch, bile rise in her throat.

'I don't know.'

'You don't know?' This was the young guy, Wood, incredulous. He got a look from the woman. Ellie wondered about the power balance between these two. He would resent having a woman as his boss. They were the same rank but she was older, more experienced, in charge.

Ellie kept looking at her hands in her lap.

Macdonald stared at her. 'Mrs McKenna says you made accusations about her husband, Police Sergeant Jack McKenna. Is that true?'

Ellie lifted her head and looked at the certificates on the wall.

'Mrs Napier?'

Ellie shook her head, sniffed. 'No, I never said anything about her husband.'

'Do you know PS McKenna?'

'No.'

'Do you know Mrs McKenna?'

'No.'

'Then why go to her house?' Macdonald flicked a page back in her notebook. 'She says you've visited twice in the last two days, is that correct?'

'Yes,' Ellie said.

'Why?'

'I wanted to offer sympathy.'

'Sympathy?'

Ellie rubbed at her palm with her thumb. 'I know what it's like to have trouble in the family.'

Macdonald cocked her head to the side. 'Your son Logan.'

Ellie nodded.

'But this is very different,' Macdonald continued. 'This was a violent assault, attempted murder. What's it got to do with you?'

'Nothing,' Ellie said. 'I just felt . . . I get confused. I'm on medication, you see. Since Logan.'

Wood leaned forward, he'd had enough. 'Alison said you made accusations about her husband. A good cop.'

Ellie shook her head.

'She also said you'd been in touch with her son, Sam. Is that true?'

Ellie shook her head again. 'I made that up.'

'Why would you do something like that?'

Ellie felt tears well up in her eyes. 'I don't know.'

'You don't know,' Wood said. 'This is ridiculous.'

'Have you been in touch with Sam McKenna?' Macdonald said, voice softer.

'No.' Ellie sniffled as she spoke. 'I made it all up.'

'Why?'

'I saw in the news that he was missing,' Ellie said, tears down her cheeks now. 'I imagined what it must be like for him, alone out there somewhere, not wanting to go home.'

'What do you know about the attack on Jack McKenna?' Wood said.

Macdonald shot him a look.

'Nothing,' Ellie said.

'Were you anywhere near Inchcolm Terrace two days ago?'

Ellie shook her head. She wondered about CCTV, Neighbourhood Watch, if there was evidence. She had been all over that place, if they could just find out. It was only a matter of time, surely, but the fact they were asking meant they didn't have anything yet.

'Can you account for your activities that day?'

Ellie thought. Closed her eyes, opened them, stared out the window at the weeds. 'I went for a walk.'

'A walk?' Wood's voice sounded like he'd just been personally insulted.

Ellie nodded.

'Whereabouts?'

'I don't know exactly,' Ellie said.

'Do you go on walks often?'

'All the time. It's what I do now, walk for miles, go running, swimming. It's how I cope without Logan. I walk all over the Ferry, beyond as well, out to Hopetoun House or Dalmeny, even to Crammond.'

'You walk to Crammond?'

'Sometimes.'

'Did you walk to Crammond on Monday?'

'No.'

'Then where?'

'I don't remember,' Ellie said. 'I go all over the place, I can't remember specifics.'

'Did anyone see you on this mysterious walk?'

'Plenty of people,' Ellie said. 'But no one I know, I don't think.'

'Very handy.'

Macdonald butted in. 'Look, I understand you're dealing with a lot. But you can't turn up at strangers' doors, making accusations and getting them upset.'

'I didn't make any accusations.'

'Mrs McKenna insists that you did,' Wood snarled.

Ellie thought about how the police had found her. She'd given Alison a false name, but it wasn't exactly hard. She'd mentioned Logan jumping off the bridge, that was in the local paper, she would've been named in that. Easy to find the address. What must they have thought when they realised she lived fifty yards along the road from the station? Nice easy job for the officers.

'I'm sorry,' Ellie said. 'I shouldn't have gone to see her. But I was confused, that's all. I don't know why I did it.' Tears were really flowing now. Was she putting it on for them, or really crying? She wasn't sure any more. It didn't make any difference.

'It's OK,' Macdonald said.

Ellie heard Wood snort derisively. She didn't blame him. She pulled a tissue out of her pocket and dabbed at her cheeks, her nose. Sniffed loudly.

'Can I go?' she said.

Wood was shaking his head, but Macdonald had a soft look on her face.

Ellie thought about fingerprints. They were all over the house, but then she'd been there to talk to Alison, surely that was her cover. If anyone saw her the day Jack was stabbed, that was different. And if the police checked her phone records they would know about her and Sam. The phone was in her pocket now, hot against her thigh. She imagined it buzzing with a message from him.

'You can go for now,' Macdonald said. 'But we might well be back in touch, depending on our enquiries.'

Wood leaned forward, trying his best to be intimidating. 'And we'll definitely be in touch if you go near the McKennas again. Got it?'

Ellie nodded. 'I understand.'

She got up, her legs weak, and headed for the door, wondering where Sam was and when she could see him next.

27

Ellie was on Rose Lane trying to get herself together when a car pulled up ahead of her. She recognised it straight away, the silver BMW from the driveway in Inchcolm Terrace. She stared at the brake lights as the passenger-side window buzzed down, then she stepped forward and bent over to look in.

Jack McKenna.

'Can we talk?'

Ellie looked behind her. The police station was round the corner, he must've been waiting for her to come out.

'I've nothing to say to you,' she said.

'Please.'

He was leaning forward, clutching his side. She could see under his Hugo Boss T-shirt where it was thick with bandages. How was he out of hospital so soon?

Ellie felt her house key in her pocket, thought of Ben waiting at home for an explanation. She thought of Sam in the boat, Libby at school hoping beyond hope this man wouldn't get out of hospital any time soon. Yet here he was, wheezing and grimacing in pain.

Ellie shook her head. 'I don't think so.'

Jack nodded at the passenger door. 'It's for the best, for Sam and Libby. For everyone.'

His skin was pale, dark rings under his eyes. His black hair was greying at the temples like Ben's, but closer cut, neatly shaved round the back and sides. He looked smaller than when she'd seen him in hospital, smaller than when she'd found him on his kitchen floor.

In her pocket she pushed the house key between her fingers and made a fist, a makeshift knuckleduster. She pulled the door open and got in. She looked in his eyes for a moment, but couldn't see anything there. She imagined sticking the knuckleduster in his face, blood spurting out. He smelt of hospitals, antiseptic and bleach, and she could smell his sweat underneath.

She pulled the door closed and put her seatbelt on.

He put the car into gear and drove to the car park at the end of the road, did a three-point turn and headed back. He turned right at the junction and for a moment she thought he was going to take Shore Road to the marina, but instead he turned along Hopetoun Road heading out of town.

He was clearly in pain, his movements slow and tentative. She couldn't imagine him overpowering her, one quick punch to his bandaged side would double him over.

They picked up speed as they left the Ferry, the road bending towards the coast beyond the marina, flowing with the contours of the land where it met the sea.

Was that the face of a child abuser, someone who could rape his own daughter? She remembered Libby telling her what he'd done, and her fists tightened in her pockets.

They drove over a makeshift crossing, a workman in a hardhat and hi-vis jacket leaning on a STOP/GO sign. Muddy tracks to their left, the building site for the new bridge on the right. This was where the approach road was going to go, through the fields and woods, stretching out over the water.

Jack kept driving. Ellie could see Rosyth docks and the naval base across the firth. The road widened and there were thick gravel verges on either side. Jack pulled in sharply and stopped, pushed the handbrake button. Ellie tensed her muscles, ready.

Jack looked out over the water and pulled his hand down his face as if he was trying to wipe it clean. The engine was still running.

'I saw you,' Jack said. He was still looking out the window, away from her.

Ellie stared at him. 'What do you mean?'

'I saw you in my house.' He turned to her. 'In the kitchen, when I was lying there. You spoke to me, said something about Sam. Right?'

Ellie tried to remember exactly what she'd said.

'You went out the patio door.' His face was drawn, exhausted. 'When Alison came home.'

Ellie shook her head. 'I don't know what you're talking about.'

'Come on, no lies.' Jack looked beaten by the world, so tired.

Ellie didn't move or speak. Jack pushed himself up in his seat a little, gave a grunt of pain.

'I'm not supposed to speak to you,' he said. 'Macdonald and Wood are handling the case. I'm meant to be at home resting. By the time I got out of hospital, Alison had already talked to them about you. If she'd asked me, I would've told her not to.' He shook his head. 'You know, I could have forensics check those patio doors. But I don't think it's in either of our interests for that to happen, do you?'

He squinted, brushed at something on the steering wheel.

'I'm sure we both want what's best for Sam,' he said. 'And Libby.'

'Do we?'

Jack turned and frowned. 'I'm not quite sure how you're involved.'

'I'm not involved.'

'This is such a mess.' He sighed. 'Let me tell you what I think. After he stabbed me, Sam left in a panic. You found him somewhere, upset, he told you what he thought he saw and what he'd done. You came to the house to see for yourself, then you left when Alison came home. You know where he is now, and you're trying to work out what to do.' He looked her in the eye. 'Am I close?'

She said nothing.

'I'm close,' Jack said.

'You said, "what he thought he saw", about Sam.'

Jack lifted a hand, palm up. 'It was all a stupid misunderstanding.'

'Are you trying to tell me you weren't raping your daughter?'

Jack's eyes widened. 'Of course not, I love Lib.'

'What were you doing, then?'

'She was upset about something in school. I was just comforting her. I'm allowed to hug my own daughter.'

'So Sam got the wrong end of the stick and stabbed you.'

Jack sighed. 'I don't want him to get in any trouble over this.'

'It's you who's in trouble,' Ellie said. She was trying to keep her voice level.

'It escalated out of control. I don't know what he thought he saw, but it was totally innocent. Honestly.'

'He said your trousers were at your ankles.'

'He's been very difficult recently, big mood swings, struggling with mental illness.'

'Really.'

Jack shook his head. 'We've been to see a psychologist, and he's taking different medication, but he's tried to overdose twice. Talks about seeing and hearing things, hallucinations, maybe that's what happened the other day.'

Ellie remembered Sam standing on the bridge, in a trance.

'I don't believe you for a second,' she said.

Jack narrowed his eyes. 'You've been speaking to him. Has he seemed rational the whole time?'

Ellie thought about that. 'Yes.'

'I know you're covering for him and I know why. Because of Logan.'

Ellie didn't say anything.

'But Sam isn't Logan,' Jack said. 'He's my son.'

Ellie shook her head. 'You've been abusing Libby for years.'

Jack looked shocked. 'Sam made that up.'

'Libby told me, not Sam.'

Jack stared at her. 'When did you speak to Libby?'

Ellie shook her head.

'She's lying,' Jack said. 'I don't know why, but she's lying. Maybe she's covering for Sam, maybe she thinks if she says that, Sam won't get in trouble for stabbing me. Maybe she wants to hurt me and her mum. I don't know. She can be a very difficult girl.'

'I don't believe a word you say,' Ellie said.

'It's the most hurtful thing a kid can do, accuse their parent of something like this. She doesn't realise, she's only young, but it breaks my heart. You must know how it would feel. Imagine if Logan had said that about you, or Ben.'

'How do you know my husband's name?'

Jack shrugged. 'I'm a police officer.'

She pictured herself at her kitchen table, Logan coming in, sheepish look on his face, avoiding eye contact. She asks if something is wrong, he skirts around it, not wanting to tell but yes, wanting to tell, confronting something horrible, then blurting out that his dad has been doing things to him, terrible things, touching him, making him do things he didn't like. Ellie felt her stomach flip and the muscles in her shoulders tighten.

What if it was all made up? What if Sam was struggling with medication, with mental illness, what if Libby was covering for him? What if this was an innocent man sitting next to her – imagine what she or Ben would feel like if false accusations were made against them, if Logan had written something in a suicide note that said he'd killed himself because of them, because of abuse?

No, this is what abusers do, they manipulate people. It's all about power, being in control, and Jack didn't like it because for once he wasn't in control, things were spiralling away from him and he couldn't contain them any longer.

'I need to get some air,' Ellie said.

She opened the door and felt a hand on her arm. Her fingers tightened around the key in her pocket.

'Wait,' Jack said.

Ellie looked at him. He was worried. If she was honest, he didn't look dangerous, sweating from the pain, he looked nervous and downtrodden, an underdog.

'You have to believe me,' he said. 'I've never done anything to Libby. I would never harm her, I swear on my mother's grave. The same goes for Sam.'

Ellie pressed her mouth into a thin line. 'I need to go.'

'I just want my family back,' Jack said. 'Things back the way they were. You of all people must understand that.'

Ellie shook her head and looked at his hand on her sleeve. He followed her gaze then lifted his hand away, letting her go.

'Please help me get my family back,' Jack said. 'That's all I want.'

'I have to think.'

Jack nodded like a puppy. 'Of course.'

Ellie undid her seatbelt. 'I'm getting out.'

Jack frowned. 'I'll give you a lift back.'

Ellie got out the car.

'It's miles back to town,' Jack said. 'Don't be stupid.'

'I want to walk.'

She shut the door. She didn't want any more words, she needed space and time. She looked up and down the road. Several miles of nothing, scrub grass on the verge, the Forth over the other side of the road, hedges and fields behind her.

The BMW sat next to her for a long moment, the engine turning over. Then she heard revs and it swept round in a U-turn towards town. The crunch of gravel and the throb of the engine receded until there was nothing, just the gentle shush of waves lapping at the shore.

Ellie waited until the car was out of sight then began walking back to the Ferry. She pulled out her phone. It rang three times then she heard Sam's voice.

'Your dad's out of hospital,' she said.

28

Ellie strode fast, the Forth to her side as she cut along Society Road, past the old house and the handful of new-builds by the water. She wondered if more developments would spring up in the shadow of the new bridge, or if people would stay away, put off by traffic and noise.

She cut down the back way on to Shore Road and came to the marina from the west end. The disused lane was blocked to traffic, old concrete tank-defences placed across it, but still accessible on foot.

She emerged at the harbour still thinking of Jack. She put herself in his shoes, what would it be like to be accused of something like that by your own kid?

It came down to trust. Did she trust Jack? Why should she? But he hadn't seemed like a man who would do something like that, he'd seemed like one of life's losers, just like her, struggling to get by, trying to keep his family together. He was right, she could relate to that. But what about Libby and Sam, she trusted them, didn't she? Libby had been visibly upset, in tears when she spoke about her dad. And where did Alison fit into all this – did she suspect and cover up for her husband, or was she really in the dark? Maybe there was nothing to know, maybe Jack was telling the truth.

She walked past the warehouse where Sam had decamped, turned towards the pier. The wind was up, the rigging clattering away on the boats rocking in their berths. She took the stairs three at a time down to the pontoon then along to the Porpoise.

She scanned the horizon as she clambered on board, but there was no one in sight, the place shutting down for the day.

She went below deck. Sam and Libby were sitting either side of the table. Strewn across the surface were a half-finished loaf of bread, empty crisp packets and chocolate wrappers, juice bottles. Ellie realised that she yearned for Sam, her arms ached to hold him. Her heart swelled at the sight of him, still wearing Logan's clothes, flicking his hair out of his face. Libby was slouched on the opposite bench, shoving the last of a crisp sandwich into her mouth. Ellie was overwhelmed with something, the ordinariness of this, kids being kids, the three of them on a boat, snacking and chatting, normal, boring family shit. Except it wasn't her family.

Sam stood up. 'What are we going to do?'

Ellie put a hand on his forearm.

'I spoke to your dad,' she said.

She'd only given Sam the thinnest detail on the phone, just enough for him to warn Libby to get out the house.

'How is he?' Sam said.

He said it blankly, and Ellie couldn't work out what he meant, was he worried about him, or sorry he wasn't dead?

'He's in pain, but OK I think.'

'I wish you'd killed him,' Libby said.

Ellie looked at her. She was so confident about life, no concept of mortality yet.

'And what if he had?' Ellie said. 'Then your brother would be a murderer. Is that what you want?'

Libby lowered her head.

'Take it easy,' Sam said, putting a hand out. 'How did he get out of hospital so quick?'

Ellie shook her head. 'I don't know, maybe he checked himself out. He's heavily bandaged around the stomach.'

A brief look passed between her and Sam, acknowledging his role in that.

'He seemed exhausted,' Ellie said. 'I don't think he should be out of hospital.'

'How did he find you?' Libby said.

'He met me when I came out of the police station.'

Sam frowned. 'Why were you in the police station?'

'They asked me in for questioning. Just routine.'

'Routine?'

Ellie sighed. 'I went to see your mum.'

'What did you say to her?'

Ellie showed her palms. 'I wanted to speak to her about what's been going on, about Libby and your dad.'

Libby's face fell. 'Oh my God, you didn't tell her, did you?'

'I thought that's what you wanted?' Ellie said.

Libby shifted on her seat, agitated. 'Things are going to be so much worse now.'

'Why?'

'They just are,' Libby said. 'I can't go back there.'

Sam looked at her. 'You don't have to go back there, don't worry.' He turned to Ellie. 'She can stay here, right?'

Ellie rubbed at her forehead. 'For tonight. But tomorrow we have to sort this out.'

'How do you mean?' said Sam.

Ellie paused for a moment. 'Libby, you have to go to the police, tell them what your dad's been doing to you.'

'No.'

'You have to,' Ellie said. 'It's the only way this can be finished.'

'I can't.'

'Why not?'

Libby rubbed at her arm. 'I told you already. He's one of them, they won't believe me.'

'They will.'

'They won't. And then things will be a hundred times worse. They won't do anything, and I'll have to go back home and live there with him and Mum, and they'll both know I told on him.'

'My God, Libby, this isn't about telling on people,' Ellie said. 'This is child abuse and rape. Your dad is a criminal.'

'I'm not going to the police,' Libby said.

Ellie walked over and sat next to her. 'I'll come with you, I'll be there the whole time. If you don't want to continue at any point, then we don't have to. There's a nice policewoman there, I met her today, PC Macdonald, I'll insist we talk to her. It'll be fine.'

Libby shook her head.

'It makes sense, Lib,' Sam said.

'I can't do it.'

Ellie looked at her. 'You want it to stop, don't you?'

Libby stared at her. 'Of course.'

'Well?'

Libby sighed.

Ellie put her hand on the girl's. It was bony, cold, poor circulation.

'I know it's hard to talk about these things, but you have to in order to make it go away.'

Libby didn't speak.

Ellie thought about her conversation in the car with Jack. Steadied her hand.

'Are you absolutely sure about what he's been doing to you?'

Sam took a step towards them. 'What do you mean? Of course she's sure.'

Ellie looked up. 'I'm just asking because it's what the police will ask.'

Libby had her head down. Ellie felt Libby's hand move under her own.

'Libby?'

The girl began to sniff, precursor to tears. Was she turning on the waterworks, or was this for real? She nodded her head, keeping her face down.

'I'm sure.'

Sam spoke. 'What did he say when you spoke to him?'

Ellie looked up. 'He denied it completely. Said it was all a misunderstanding.'

'What a cunt,' Sam said. 'A misunderstanding? He was in her room. I know what I saw.'

Libby was crying now.

'He said he was just comforting her, giving her a hug,' Ellie said.

Sam snorted. 'A hug? With his trousers down?'

Ellie kept her gaze steady on Sam, kept rubbing Libby's hand.

'He said that you've had some problems, Sam.'

Sam looked around, fists tight. 'Fuck him.'

'Mental problems.'

Sam looked like he was going to punch a hole in the wall. 'I knew he'd use that against me.'

'He said you've been hearing voices. Hallucinating. Said you were having trouble with different pills.'

'I know what I saw,' Sam said. 'Ask Libby. This is not about hallucinations or anything like that.'

'Take it easy,' Ellie said. 'Remember where I first met you, where I found you. What you were like.'

Sam's neck muscles were straining but he reined it in, took a breath before he spoke. 'That was different, that was after. Can you blame me, after what had happened? But I know what I saw. You think I'd just go around stabbing my dad for nothing?' He looked at his sister. 'Tell her, Lib.'

Libby wiped her tears on the cuff of her cardie, the material pulled down over her hands.

'I told you already what he's been doing,' she said. 'When you walked me back to the house. I wasn't lying. I promise.'

'That's fine. I had to ask. I have to be clear, you understand?'

Libby nodded.

Ellie put a hand on her thigh. 'We have to go and report this, though, you realise that? Nothing will change unless we get the police involved. It doesn't matter that your dad's a cop. If you tell them what you told me, they'll arrest him, I promise.'

'What about Sam?' Libby said, looking up.

Ellie looked too. 'That depends.'

'On what?' Sam said.

'On what Jack tells the investigating officers.'

'You mean he hasn't told them that it was me who stabbed him?'

Ellie shook her head. 'I don't think so. He said he hadn't. And they never mentioned it when they questioned me. Obviously you being missing is suspicious, but there's no law against leaving home and not getting in touch if you're over sixteen. If Jack doesn't drop you in it you could be OK.'

'Will he drop me in it?'

Ellie thought about that. If Jack was arrested, what would he do? Fight it? Retaliate against Sam? Cut his losses and admit what he'd done? She couldn't untangle it in her mind. He said he just wanted his family back. But he'd been raping his own daughter.

'I don't honestly know,' she said. 'I hope not.'

This was the only way forward. If Libby reported Jack, he'd surely be taken into custody, then Libby and Sam could go home. Ellie tried to imagine the atmosphere in that house, between the two of them and their mum, under the cloud of Libby's accusations. It wouldn't be easy, but whatever path they took now wouldn't be easy.

Ellie put an arm around Libby, who hunched up under the touch.

'The pair of you stay here tonight,' she said. 'Then first thing tomorrow I'll come and get Libby, and we can go to the police station together. You won't have to see your dad. We'll talk to someone there and they'll deal with it. OK?'

Libby nodded. 'OK.'

Ellie stood up and walked towards the stairs. Sam walked with her.

'Just sit tight,' Ellie said, then turned to look at Libby. 'Will she be OK?'

Sam nodded. 'I'll look after her.'

'You're a good brother,' Ellie said.

She reached up and stroked his cheek, felt him flinch.

'See you tomorrow,' she said.

29

It was dark now as Ellie stood at her front door. She brushed the familiar black wood with her fingers. She'd lived here for so long she knew every knot and whorl, every grain in the surface, every loose floorboard in the hallway, every cracked tile in the bathroom. The dent in the living-room wall where the Wii remote had flown out of Logan's hand, narrowly missing Ben and the television. The stiff drawer on the wardrobe in her room where he'd stuffed a piece of Lego into the mechanism.

Her home was made up of a million reminders, its character shaped by the people who had lived in it. The house at Inchcolm Terrace must be the same. What did Sam and Libby know about that place that no one else did, what secrets did they have from the world?

She closed her eyes and imagined the front door opening, Logan bustling past with his bag and a banana in his hand, in a rush to get to school. No time to chat, hardly even looking up, that eternal teenage hurry, locked in a world of his own importance.

She opened her eyes, unlocked the door and stepped inside.

'Honey, is that you?' Ben's voice from the kitchen.

He appeared in the doorway. Dishevelled, still needing a shave and a haircut, his hoodie frayed and dirty. He was the love of her life, though, she just had to try really hard to remember how all that worked.

'God, I was worried sick.'

It was the kind of thing they used to say as a joke if one of them was late back from work. Hamming it up for Logan's benefit, an in-joke about being a real, proper couple who didn't need to have overblown displays of affection. One of them would rush to the door, overdoing it, showing off, like something from *Gone with the Wind*. But this wasn't a joke and anyway there was no one else here, no audience to appreciate it.

He came over and put his arms round her. He needed a shower, but the smell of his sweat was so comforting she was glad he hadn't washed. She felt her shoulders shrug with the beginning of a sob, tears in her eyes as she reached round his waist and linked her fingers together.

'It's OK,' he said.

But he was wrong, it wasn't OK.

'Come on through,' he said.

She didn't want to let go, but allowed herself to be led to the kitchen. The overhead light seemed too bright after the gloominess of the hallway, and she squinted.

He pulled a chair out for her then put the kettle on.

So much in their lives had happened in this kitchen. She remembered wandering around here in the night, half asleep, trying to measure baby powder into a bottle, boiling the kettle, shaking it together then cooling it down in a bowl of water. She remembered dabbing at Logan's knee with antiseptic wipes, blood dripping on the laminate, soaking through the ineffectual plaster she put on, then grabbing her keys to take him to A&E when the cut wouldn't stop bleeding.

The rush of the kettle boiling filled the room.

'They kept you for hours,' Ben said as the kettle clicked off.

173

Ellie turned to him. 'Sorry?'

'The police. It's four hours since you went to the station. They weren't interviewing you that whole time, surely?'

Ellie shook her head. 'Lots of waiting around.'

He placed a mug of green tea in front of her then pulled out the chair opposite.

'So,' he said. He had a kind but worried look on his face.

'What?'

Ben angled his head and narrowed his eyes. An expression she was so familiar with, like looking in a mirror.

'I presume you're going to tell me what that whole police thing was about, and why you didn't want me to come with you.'

Ellie picked up her tea and brought it to her lips but it was too hot to drink. She blew across the top, watching the ripples as they pushed away from her. She clutched at the warmth of the mug with both hands, her thumbs through the handle.

She took a long breath. 'It was about that police officer who was attacked.'

Ben looked confused.

'The one up at Inchcolm Terrace,' Ellie said.

Ben frowned, his mouth squint. 'Yeah, I know, it's not like we have loads of cops getting stabbed around here. But what's that got to do with you?'

Ellie wanted to be somewhere else. Tucked up in bed, or at the bottom of the ocean, maybe. But she needed to be here and she needed to tell him.

'I went to see his wife,' she said.

'Why?'

'To speak to her.'

'What about?'

'About what's been going on in her house.'

Ben shook his head, still not understanding. 'What has been going on in her house?'

'Bad things.'

'How would you know?' Ben's face was crumpled. 'You don't know them.'

Ellie shook her head. 'I didn't, before all this.'

'But you do now?' Ben said.

Ellie nodded. 'Kind of.'

She put her mug down and laid her hands in her lap. She rubbed at her thumb with her other hand. Ben reached over and placed a hand on top of hers.

'Why don't you start at the beginning?' he said.

Ellie hesitated then looked up and saw Ben's face. She swallowed.

'I met the missing boy,' she said.

'His son?'

'Sam, yes. On the road bridge, a few days ago. He was about to jump.'

Ellie felt Ben's grip on her hands tighten.

'I brought him back here. He was all over the place. He had blood on him, not his own.'

'His dad's?'

Ellie nodded.

'He stabbed him?'

Another nod.

'You should've turned him in,' Ben said.

Ellie took her hands away from his and stared at him. 'I couldn't.'

Ben held her gaze for a long time. Rubbed at the stubble on his chin.

'OK,' he said finally. 'But you should've told me.'

Ellie looked down, spoke under her breath. 'I know.'

'Why did he do it?' Ben's voice was soft, mirroring Ellie's.

'His dad has been abusing his little sister.'

'Jesus. Are you sure?'

Ellie looked up. 'Yes. I've spoken to both of them.'

'The girl too?'

Ellie nodded again. It felt like all she ever did, nod in agreement.

'They have to go to the police.'

'I know,' Ellie said. 'They will. I'm taking Libby tomorrow morning, first thing. It's just taken us a while to get to this stage.'

Ben frowned, thinking. 'What did the mum say?'

'She doesn't believe it.'

'Are you sure the kids are telling the truth?' Ben said.

'I think so.'

'You think so?'

'They are.'

'Are they back home?' Ben said.

Ellie shook her head. 'Jack is out of hospital already. I couldn't let them go back there.'

'So where are they?'

Ellie looked past Ben to the black water out the window.

'In the boat.'

'Our boat?'

'Yeah.'

'Christ, since when?'

176

No point complicating things. 'Just today.'

Ben shook his head. 'What have you got yourself messed up in, Ellie?'

She put her hands on the table. 'I know, it's ridiculous. But you understand, don't you? When I saw him on the bridge . . .'

She felt her breath getting short and the words caught in her chest.

'It's OK.' He rubbed her hands. 'You're doing the right thing. You're protecting them.'

She wiped at her eyes. 'Thank you.'

He laughed. 'Don't thank me, I haven't done anything.'

She stood up. 'Yes, you have.'

He stood up too, and she put her arms around him, kissed him, nestled into his chest.

'Do you want me to come with you tomorrow?' he said.

She didn't speak for a moment, weighing it up. 'No, I'll do it myself.'

'If that's what you want. But I'm here if you need me for anything. You know that, right?'

She looked him in the eye. 'I know.'

30

The wind was up, whipping her hair into her face so that she had to pull a strand away from the corner of her mouth. She looked down.

She'd swithered this morning. For the first time in the months since she'd been coming to the bridge, she thought about walking out on the west side, not the east. The east was Logan's side, the expansive spread of water out to the rail bridge, the North Sea and Norway beyond. But from the east side she couldn't see the marina, the Porpoise. If she'd walked out the west side she could see the boat, imagine Sam and Libby curled up asleep in the forward cabin, unaware of the stress today would surely bring. Out west it was all industrial, the new bridge, the ferry port, the naval base, the oil refinery upriver. It was a diminishing view, the Forth getting narrower, the banks edging closer, squeezing the body of water, reducing it to a trickle.

Looking this way, east, the firth got wider and wider, endless possibilities out there in open water, the chance to get lost in the enormity of it all. It was that sense of freedom that had brought her on to the east side if she was honest, not the nagging dedication to the place Logan fell from. Or maybe it was both. She couldn't let go of that moment, that instant when her life ended with his, one simple act reducing her to dust.

Up over the railing, drop on to the ledge, then step off.

That's all it took.

She got her phone out of her pocket. Couldn't resist. Flicked to Videos. There it was, the footage of Logan jumping from the spot where she was standing.

She pressed play, her stomach cramping, chest tight.

She watched the empty walkway on her phone, glanced up to check the CCTV camera was still there, watching her right now. It was. Same camera, same walkway, same bridge.

She stared at the clock running at the bottom of the screen, knew exactly when Logan appeared. Seventeen seconds. And yes, there he was, sauntering, not in a hurry, why would you be in a hurry to kill yourself, you've got the rest of your life to do it, once it's done you'll never be in a rush again.

Step, step, step, so easy, one foot in front of the other, a quick glance at the traffic out of sight from this angle, then another glance out to sea, two more steps then he slowed and turned, rested against the railing with both elbows, just another tourist or local taking in the view, feeling the size of the planet under his feet, his insignificance in the face of it all, the kind of feeling everyone gets in the presence of something big. That simple factor of scale can make a human being feel like an insect, a microbe, a virus, can make them ponder their own existence, the meaning of it all. Or maybe Logan was standing there thinking nothing at all, his mind blank like a Zen master, an empty bowl waiting to be filled with ideas. Or maybe he was tormented, a million thoughts jumbling his brain, voices telling him to jump or not jump, evil, paranoid devils, convinced that his mother and father hated him, all his school friends were laughing at him behind his back, the voices telling him he was a worthless individual who didn't deserve to live, constant mental anguish and pain and the best way to escape was to end it all, stop existing.

Logan pushed his elbows away from the railing and hoisted his feet sideways on to it. A slight hover there, his body in equilibrium, his poise, like a gymnast preparing for the dismount, then he was over on the wrong side of the railing, standing on the ledge, facing out, the toes of his shoes at the edge, almost dangling over the drop.

Ellie pressed pause. The two thick vertical lines of the pause sign flashed up in the middle of the screen, partially blocking the view of her son. Logan, at the moment of decision, the split second before it was all over, the infinitesimal increment of time before his life blinked out of existence.

Ellie took a shaky breath and looked away from the screen. Cars roared at her back, strangers she would never meet going places she would never visit. The surface of the Forth was choppy with the wind. The water was sepia today, a thin muddiness, white smudges of waves everywhere. It gave the impression of constant movement. She spotted a train heading south across the rail bridge, a small two-carriage affair, and beyond that three oil tankers were lined up at the fuelling depot. Ellie imagined pressing pause on the world, two vertical lines flashing in front of her eyes, the train freezing on the track, waves stalling, traffic behind her suddenly motionless, caught in that instant, the glorious moment before everything went to shit. She imagined the silence of it, no traffic roar, no rush of the ocean, no clack of train wheels. No thoughts in her head, none whatsoever.

She looked down at the screen.

Pressed play.

Logan stepped off the bridge and dropped out of view of the security camera.

She closed her eyes. Counted in her head.

One elephant.

Two elephants.

Three elephants.

Four elephants.

Five elephants.

Six elephants.

He had hit the water.

She went online months ago and found out how long it took. Easy enough to get an answer. Falling from a forty-five-metre bridge took approximately 5.6 seconds. Less than six elephants.

What went through his mind? Happy and serene as he plummeted through the air, or full of regret? Panic and terror, or his mind still racing with all the clutter and debris that we each carry around with us? Maybe he passed out, pissed or shat himself, screamed until his throat was torn.

She looked out over the firth and breathed. Put a hand against the railing to steady herself as a gust of wind swept up the walkway.

She looked at her phone, swiped off Videos, opened Facebook, went to his page. Two messages since last time, both girls, just kisses and hearts. Girls were better at that than boys, better at remembering, not caring about looking soft. She didn't recognise either of the girls who'd posted. That was Logan's world, not hers. They had the same world to begin with, but we all make our own worlds as we grow up, create our own universes, propagate our way through the madness alone.

She typed quickly:

Miss you more every day. Love you always.
Mum xxx

It was pathetic and insignificant and inadequate.

She stared at the words for a few seconds then typed Sam's name into the search box, clicked through. Checked his page for messages then flicked through his pictures. Zoomed in on a few. He had a cute smile, beautiful eyes that he hid behind that fringe. He would be a handsome man someday soon.

Ellie put her phone away and strode off the bridge. It was time for action.

31

The marina was quiet. After the roar of the bridge Ellie always felt an emptiness, a vacuum in her waiting to be filled. She walked past the Bosun's Locker, not open yet, then Karinka's Kitchen, no one inside. The door to the sailing clubhouse was padlocked, and the only place she spied activity was in the coastguard Portakabin where a guy was hanging up his bulky jacket, starting his shift.

She pictured Ben back in bed. She liked being up and about while he slept, enjoyed being awake before the world, something about the isolation gave her power, a subtle authority. She imagined Sam and Libby in the boat, still wrapped in bedcovers, maybe just coming round. She tried to picture Jack and Alison at Inchcolm Terrace. Had Alison believed anything Ellie told her? If so, surely she couldn't share a bed with him. Or maybe she'd ignored the accusations, put them to the back of her mind. Maybe she'd brought it up but Jack had talked her round. He was persuasive, Ellie knew that from the car yesterday, he could make you feel sorry for him, as if he was the victim. She was glad she went straight to Sam and Libby afterwards. The look on Libby's face wiped away any sympathy she might've had for Jack, any doubt she harboured about what had happened.

She was at the gate to the pier now. Keyed in her number, Logan's birthday, reminders everywhere. The door clicked open and she walked down the steps. She wasn't looking forward to today. Libby would have it tough, but Ellie would be there, support her. She wouldn't let any harm come to Libby or Sam.

She made her way along the pontoon, the ebb of the waves making it rock underfoot. The wind was stronger at sea level, a westerly straight down the Forth into her face as she walked, twenty knots maybe. Decent sailing weather, as long as it didn't get any stronger.

She got to the Porpoise. No sign of activity on deck. There was one old-timer on his dinghy further up the pontoon, someone Ellie knew to say hello to, and she nodded and raised a hand in reply to his greeting.

She pulled the painter rope attached to the bow, the boat nudged against the pontoon and she stepped on board. Over the secured rigging and round to the door of the cabin. The door was slid back, the two of them must be up and about inside.

Ellie started down the stairs.

'Morning,' she said. A flash of memory came to her, shouting into Logan's room as he lay under his covers, motionless. Time to get up for school and all that.

Ellie reached the bottom of the stairs and stopped.

Three people were staring at her.

Sam, Libby and Jack.

'Hello, Ellie,' Jack said. He had his hands out in supplication, almost pleading.

Ellie looked from him to Libby, who was cowering on the edge of the bench. Sam was standing between Jack and Libby. The four of them now in the cabin made it cramped, the air thick.

'Get out,' Ellie said.

Jack shook his head. 'I just want to talk to my kids.'

He put one hand to his stomach, pulled his face into a grimace.

'They don't want to talk to you,' Ellie said. 'Get off my boat.'

'They're my kids,' Jack said. 'Of course they want to talk to me. This is all a misunderstanding.'

Sam had his hands tense at his sides. 'You heard her, get the fuck out of here.'

Jack raised his eyebrows. 'Don't talk to me like that, please.' His voice was level, quiet.

'I can't believe you're here,' Sam said. 'I can't believe you have the nerve to look either of us in the eye after what you did.'

'I haven't done anything,' Jack said. 'Ask Libby.'

He turned to her. She was like a turtle trying to duck inside its shell, her legs pulled up tight, shoulders hunched, head turned to the side.

'She's scared to death of you,' Sam said. 'Leave us alone.'

'I can't do that,' Jack said. 'You're my kids.'

'We don't want anything to do with you,' Sam said.

Jack turned to Ellie, pleading. 'Can't you speak to them?'

Ellie took a step forward. 'Why should I?'

'This is all a mistake.' Jack's voice wavered now, breaking up. It looked like he might start crying. He took a step towards Libby. 'Lib, come home with your dad, please. It'll all be fine, I promise.'

Sam moved closer to Jack. 'Get the hell out of here.'

'How did you find us?' Libby said.

The sound of her voice made everyone pause.

Jack looked round the cabin, like a quiz show contestant searching for the right answer.

'I'm a police officer, honey,' he said. 'It's my job to find out things. I discovered Ellie had a boat. As soon as it was light I came down, on the off chance. I got lucky.'

'Unlucky for us,' Sam said.

Jack reached out to him but Sam batted the hand away. 'Sam, I know you've had problems.'

Sam shook his head. 'Don't turn this round, this isn't about me.'

Jack was still talking. 'I know you've heard voices, been depressed, tried to kill yourself.'

Libby sat forward. 'What?'

'Three times, Lib, that we know of.'

'You mean apart from the bridge?' Libby said.

Jack looked puzzled. 'What happened on the bridge?' He turned to Ellie, a look coming across his face. 'That's where you met him. He was going to jump. I bet it was the morning he stabbed me.'

'I can't believe I didn't finish the job,' Sam said through his teeth.

Jack was still staring at Ellie. 'You see how unstable he is? How he talks?' He turned to Sam. 'Son, it's OK, we can get you help. I haven't told the police about the stabbing, I said I couldn't remember.'

Sam shook his head. 'That's only so they don't find out why I did it.'

'That's not true, nothing happened.' Jack looked at his daughter. 'Tell them, Lib.'

She didn't speak. She cowered back, trying to squeeze her body into the crevice at the side of the cabin.

Jack took a step forward. He could almost reach out and

touch her. Sam intervened, put a hand on his dad's chest. Jack looked at the hand, then at Sam's face.

'Don't,' he said.

'Or what?'

Jack's eyes were welling up. 'I just want my family back.' A crack in his voice.

'It's too late for that,' Sam said. 'We're going to the police, right now. That's why Ellie's here, she's taking Libby to tell them everything you've done to her.'

Jack reached out to the girl. 'Libby, honey, don't do that. Don't lie to them.'

Sam pushed Jack in the chest and he rocked back on his heels. 'Fuck off.'

Jack still had his eyes on his daughter, crouched in the corner.

'If you tell them those lies, I'll have to tell them about your brother trying to kill me,' Jack said. 'It'll all come out.'

'Shut up,' Libby said, shaking.

'He'll probably go to prison,' Jack said. 'Is that what you want?'

'That's enough,' Ellie said.

Sam looked at his sister. 'Don't listen to him, Lib. He's just trying to save his own skin.'

'I'm not, honey, honestly,' Jack said. 'Come home and we can put all this behind us.'

He inched closer to Libby. Sam pushed at him but Jack didn't budge. Ellie stepped closer, took hold of Jack's arm but he didn't respond, didn't even seem to notice.

'Your brother won't survive in prison,' Jack said.

'Shut the fuck up,' Sam said.

'He's already tried to kill himself all those times,' Jack said. 'He won't get the right treatment in prison, the right medication. He'll either kill himself or someone else will do it.'

Libby's face was scrunched up, tears on her cheeks.

'I don't believe you,' she said. 'I don't believe you.'

'You heard her,' Ellie said. 'Leave. Now.'

Jack turned. He looked for all the world as if he was sorry, a lost little boy looking for his parents.

'I can't leave without Libby,' he said.

'You'll have to,' Sam said, his hand still on Jack's chest.

Jack reached past Sam and grabbed Libby's wrist. She tried to wriggle free but he held on easily. Sam pushed at his arm as Ellie had her hands on his shoulders trying to pull him away.

'Get your hands off me,' Libby shouted, the sound echoing round the cabin.

'Come on.' Jack yanked at her arm and Libby was lifted off her backside, sliding on to the floor then staggering to her feet. Ellie thought she saw something glint on the bench behind her. Libby was feeling at her back, fingers grasping air then scrabbling across the top of the bench.

Jack gave her wrist a heave and Libby lurched forward. Sam pushed Jack who stumbled but then righted himself, Ellie still tugging at his back, trying to pull him away. Libby took a step back, picked up the scissors she'd been searching for on the bench, and gripped them tight in her fist. She lifted them above her shoulder and plunged them down into Jack's stomach just below his ribcage.

'No,' Ellie shouted, reaching for the scissors.

'Get off,' Libby screamed, pulling the scissors out then thrusting them back in again. She repeated the movement, in and out, in and out. Ellie grabbed for the scissors and felt a slice of pain up the palm of her hand. Jack fell backwards making Ellie lose her balance. She pushed a hand out to catch herself from falling. Jack went forward again, but he fell right into Libby's fist gripping the scissors.

'Keep your hands to yourself,' Libby said, pushing the scissors into Jack's stomach one more time.

Sam hauled her back. 'No, Lib.'

The scissors clattered to the floor. Jack roared and threw Ellie off his back, launching himself at Libby. His hands went round her throat and he squeezed, Libby's neck straining as she tried to take in air. Sam pushed at his dad's face and neck, trying to prise him off, then shoved at his arms, but he couldn't release Jack's grip. He reached to the floor and picked up the scissors then plunged them into the flesh of Jack's neck just above his collarbone. Jack staggered backwards, grasping at the handle of the scissors, blood spraying between his fingers. He couldn't get a purchase on them, kept fumbling at it, his throat gurgling, eyes wild, snot dripping from his nose. He stumbled to the doorway of the cabin, his palms slapping on the banisters, then began hauling himself up the stairs, moaning and grunting.

Ellie looked around. Libby and Sam were on the bench, wide eyed. She darted forward, grabbed a cable from the equipment box then lunged at Jack halfway up the stairs, wrapping the cord around his neck, criss-crossing it over and heaving herself backwards, pushing against the wall with her feet until Jack's grip on the banister came loose and he fell on top of her. The boat rocked with the force of their landing, Jack's hands reaching behind his head, scratching at Ellie's face as she pulled the cable tighter. She held on as his breath shortened, his legs thrashing at the bottom of the stairs, trying to get purchase on anything. He pushed himself into Ellie, sending them both shunting along the floor until Ellie's head bumped the leg of the table, but she held on, struggling for breath under his weight. Jack's hands reached for the cord around his neck, pushing his fingers against it, trying to pull it away from the skin, blood pulsing out the wounds in his stomach and neck. But he couldn't get any relief. Ellie pulled tight, the muscles in her arms burning, her neck taut, every sinew stretched as far as it would go, every ounce of strength in her body used.

Jack stopped struggling and slumped, his head falling back and smacking Ellie in the mouth. She moved her head sideways, spitting his hair from her teeth, gasping, her chest struggling to rise and fall under his weight. She kept tight hold of the ends of the cord, waiting, listening, expecting something, but nothing happened.

She let go of the cable. Heaved air into her lungs. Shoved at Jack's body, rolled it to the side and began shuffling out from underneath, sliding away from him.

She was covered in blood. She panted, gulping in air, her legs shaking, her body trembling from shock and adrenalin. She looked at the bench. Sam had his arms round Libby, her face buried in his chest. She was sobbing, hands pressed into her lap. Sam was staring at Jack. He turned to Ellie with a look.

Ellie held her hands out in front of her and stared at them. The skin was raw and moist where she'd gripped the cable. Jack's blood was smeared in the creases and folds of her skin. One palm was sliced by the scissors.

She crawled on her hands and knees over to Jack's body. Blood was oozing from his collarbone, pooling under his back, his clothes wet from the wounds to his stomach and chest.

Ellie put two fingers to his neck, felt for a pulse. Then she took his wrist, did the same. Waited, trying to regulate her own heart rate. Finally she knelt by his face and put a hand over his mouth and nose, feeling for breath.

She slumped down on her haunches and looked at Sam. Shook her head.

Libby lifted her face out of her brother's chest and saw Ellie. Ellie looked at the scissors sticking out of Jack's neck, the cord still digging into the skin around his throat. She put one hand against his shoulder and pulled the scissors out, dropping them on the floor. Blood came bubbling out the wound and down his back. Then Ellie lifted the back of Jack's head and unwrapped the cable. It was only with the cable in her hand that she realised what it was. The kill cord, for cutting the power to the engine if you fell overboard, so you didn't get chopped up by the propellers.

Libby was crying, shaking, trying to squirm into Sam's body. Sam had a glassy look on his face, staring at his dad's corpse in the middle of the cabin.

'What do we do now?' he said.

Ellie wiped her hands on the thighs of her jeans, felt the pain on her palms as she did so. She looked round the cabin, shook her head then pulled her phone out.

32

They waited on deck. It was risky out here, the kids could get recognised, but none of them could stay another moment below with Jack. Libby had been freaking out, hysterical, Sam just staring, so Ellie had shoved caps on their heads and pushed them upstairs and out the cabin. Now the pair of them were hunched in the stern, Ellie pacing up and down the starboard side, pretending to check the rigging, trying to stop her hands shaking as she looked out for him.

And there he was. Ben.

She watched him approach the boat and tried to freeze-frame the moment, imprint it on her memory, the instant before she dragged the man she loved into this shitstorm. Maybe she should still protect him, turn him away, stop him coming on board. She hadn't told him anything on the phone, just that she needed him straight away. She could force him to turn round right now but the truth was she needed him, she couldn't do this alone.

She didn't stop him climbing on board.

He frowned when he saw her face. 'What's up?'

She felt herself close to tears.

He looked at Sam and Libby. 'That's them?'

Ellie nodded.

He turned to them. 'Hi.'

They didn't reply, just nodded. Libby had a wild look on

her face. She turned her gaze from Ben to the hatch of the cabin.

Ben spoke to Ellie. 'I thought you were taking her to the police.'

Ellie shook her head. 'Something happened.'

She walked towards the hatch.

'Come on,' she said, then turned to Sam and Libby. 'Wait there.'

She took careful steps down the ladder, heard Ben's footfall behind her. She got to the bottom and moved aside so he could take it in.

Jack was where she'd left him, blood blossomed round his body, draining through the floorboards and gathering in the hull below. His eyes were open, his lips already a little discoloured, skin greying. The blood flowing from the wounds in his neck and stomach had slowed.

'Holy shit,' Ben said.

Ellie didn't look at him, kept her eyes on the corpse.

Ben turned to her. 'Holy fucking shit, Ellie.'

The boat rocked in the water making them both spread their feet and shift their weight.

Ben rubbed at his head and stared at the body, eyes wide.

'It was self-defence,' Ellie said.

'Is he dead?'

Ellie nodded.

Ben shook his head. 'Oh shit. Fucking hell, Ellie.'

Ben pulled a hand down his face, scrunched his eyes then opened them. He peered at the wounds on Jack's body. Part of the stomach a shredded mess, the gaping hole in the neck, livid strangulation marks on the throat.

Ben looked at Ellie. 'Self-defence? Really?'

Ellie avoided catching his eye. 'He tried to take Libby away. He was violent.'

'Who did this?'

Ellie thought. Libby first in the stomach, then Sam in the neck, then her stopping him from leaving.

'We all did.'

'Tell me the truth,' Ben said. 'It's me, Ellie.'

'He attacked Libby. She panicked. She stabbed him in the stomach with scissors. He kept at her. Sam stabbed him in the neck. Then I did the throat.'

Ben shook his head and took a step back from the corpse. 'This is so fucked up.'

Ellie put a hand out and touched the table in the middle of the room to steady herself. 'What do we do?'

Ben looked at her, then at Jack, and shook his head. He walked round the body as if it might seem less dead from the other side.

'Was it really self-defence?'

'Yes.'

'Then we go to the police. Tell them everything.'

'They won't believe us.'

'Yes, they will, they'll have to.'

Ellie nodded at Jack's body. 'This doesn't look like self-defence.'

Ben shook his head. 'But it was. I believe you.'

Ellie looked at him. 'The police won't. A jury won't.'

Ben shrugged. 'We have to take that chance.'

'We can't do that to Libby and Sam,' Ellie said. 'We just can't. We have to protect them.'

Ben looked out the cabin hatch. 'What the hell are you say-ing? Are you suggesting we cover this up?'

He stepped back from Jack's body and stumbled over the scissors on the floor, recoiled from them. 'Jesus Christ.'

Ellie looked at her husband.

'We can do it,' she said.

Ben stared at her. 'Have you lost your mind? Think about what you're saying for a minute.'

The only noise was the clank of the rigging against the mast, a coded signal beamed into the atmosphere, a proclamation of guilt to the world, like the conspiracy of Ben's mobile-phone signals, poisoning the minds of locals.

'I don't think he would've told anyone he was coming here,' Ellie said. 'He didn't want the police involved, for obvious reas-ons.'

'So what?'

'So if no one knows he was here, there's nothing linking us to him.'

Ben snorted in disbelief. 'Except the fact he's lying dead in a pool of his own fucking blood in our boat.'

'We can clear this up,' Ellie said. 'Make it go away.'

'No chance,' Ben said. 'It's insane.'

'What's the alternative?' Ellie held a hand out to him. 'We all get done for murder. Libby and Sam would be guilty of killing their own father. God knows what would happen to them. They've already suffered enough, I'm not putting them through that.'

Ben nodded towards the cabin door. 'What about those two?'

Ellie followed his look. 'What about them?'

'If we try to cover this up, they would have to go along with it.'

Ellie shook her head. 'I know.'

Ben stared at the corpse. 'Self-defence or not, they've contributed to the death of their own dad. That's a lot to handle. Didn't you find Sam on the bridge?' He waved his hand around the room. 'How will he cope with this? And the girl is just a kid.'

'Maybe we should ask them,' Ellie said.

A long silence.

'OK,' Ben said.

He stepped carefully around the body and up the stairs, Ellie behind him.

Sam and Libby were sitting at the stern, arms around each other, looking out to sea. Gulls dive-bombed the breakwater, splashing at the surface with their beaks.

Ben stood over them as Ellie crouched down to eye level.

'This is Ben, my husband. We have a decision to make.'

Her voice was level. Ben had always been the calm one with Logan. Ellie used to fly off the handle, shouting upstairs to the boy, but she never heard Ben's voice raised in anger. Now it was her turn to be calm.

'What decision?' Sam said.

'We need to work out what to do,' Ellie said.

Libby's eyes were wide with panic, her breathing erratic. 'What do you mean?'

'We have two choices. Either we go to the police and tell them everything, or Ben and I make this go away, but you two would have to play along. This never happened, you were never here, you haven't seen your dad since the morning he was stabbed at your home.'

Libby scratched at the back of her hand, shot scared glances at her brother. 'We can't go to the police,' she said. 'We just can't.'

Ellie put a hand on top of hers. 'It wouldn't be easy, but if we told them the truth, all of it, it might be OK.'

Sam shook his head. 'You don't believe that.'

Ben looked at Sam. 'There's a lot of uncertainty here. It would be rough, and we'd all get in trouble, but at least we'd be telling the truth.'

Their four faces were close now, huddling like conspiring witches.

Libby shook her head, swallowed. 'No way.'

'What's the alternative?' Sam said.

Ellie looked at him. 'Ben and I can get rid of the body.'

'How?'

'We just will,' Ellie said, her voice flat. 'But that's not the hard bit. The hard bit will be staying quiet about it. Forever. You can never tell anyone what happened here. Especially your mum. We'd need to come up with a story and you'd need to stick to it. That won't be easy.'

Sam looked at his sister. 'Lib?'

Libby stared at the cabin hatch. She looked like a fox caught in a snare, ready to gnaw her own leg off. She glanced at her brother, then out to sea. She chewed on her lip and rubbed at her wrist.

'I can't go to the police,' she said.

Sam touched her shoulder and nodded at Ellie.

Ellie stood up. 'OK.'

Ben took her shoulder and led her away. 'So that's it? We're just going to do this fucked-up thing on the say-so of a frightened girl?'

Ellie stopped and put a hand on his arm. 'We don't have any choice. I said I would protect them and I meant it. I will not put them through anything more. This is my second chance and I'm taking it. And I need you, Ben, I can't do this alone.'

Ben stared at her for a long time, then finally sighed. He got his car key out of his pocket and handed it to her. 'It's parked round the back of the boat sheds. Take them to our place, get them settled, then come back.' He turned to Sam and Libby, who were getting up. 'Stay at our house until we come and get you.'

'What are you going to do?' Sam said.

Ben looked around the boat for an answer.

'I'm going to work out what to do next,' he said.

33

Having teenagers in the back of the car, her hands on the steering wheel, made Ellie remember times with Logan, giving him lifts to McDonald's to meet his mates, to school on rainy days, home from football, the car filling up with the earthy stink of mud and grass.

Ellie's fingers trembled on the gearstick as she shifted up, leaving the marina and turning left. Under the bridge once more, always back and forth under the damn bridge. She remembered when Logan was little, she and Ben read *The Three Billy Goats Gruff* to him at bedtime and it became a favourite. Later they got a CD with the story on it. The troll lived under the bridge, trolls always lived under bridges in fairy tales, and that became a running joke. One time with Logan still in a car seat, not yet promoted to a booster, so he must've been five or so, they drove under the bridge to the marina to go and meet Daddy from work, and Logan wondered aloud about trolls living under the Forth Road Bridge. Ellie laughed and played along, the in-joke between them escalating every time they passed the same spot. They set up 'trollwatch', keeping eyes peeled, Logan in the back making the shape of binoculars round his eyes, peering at the fenced-off area around the bridge legs, the tangle of wire, the slabs of concrete, the diggers and other works vehicles that were always parked there doing nothing. Maybe it was a troll den, a lair where a bunch of hairy,

199

warty creatures slept and ate and farted and picked their ugly noses, feasting on goats and little children.

Ellie thought about Sam and Libby. Did they have in-jokes like that in their family? A million secrets, meaningless stuff, between Libby and Sam, Alison and Jack. Were they a happy family, despite it all, despite what Jack had done? What Ellie, Sam and Libby had done today had destroyed that family forever, no chance of redemption, cursed now, a lie that the kids would have to tell their mum forever. Ellie wondered how they'd cope.

They were already home. She pulled into the drive, felt the gravel crunch under the wheels, then stopped and switched the engine off. She ushered Sam and Libby out the car, opened the front door and pushed them inside.

Libby pulled her cap off and flapped at her mussed-up hair. Sam removed his cap too, ran a hand through his hair and looked around. Ellie wondered how much he remembered from his first visit here, that morning. She remembered him half-naked in Logan's room and felt ashamed. She'd led them to this, hadn't protected them like she promised that first day.

'I'll put the kettle on,' she said, heading for the kitchen. She nodded at the living room. 'Make yourselves at home.'

This was ridiculous, no amount of hot tea could make things normal.

Ellie placed her forehead against a kitchen cupboard, one hand on the kettle. She weighed it in her hands, it was half full already, so she switched it on. She placed both hands on the metal surface of the kettle, felt the heat rise quickly, kept her hands there until she couldn't stand the pain any more.

She looked at her hands. Dried blood caked in the lines on her palm, the joints of her fingers. Burn marks beneath her thumbs from the kill cord, the cut from the scissors across the flesh. She went to the sink and squirted washing-up liquid, rubbed hard, rinsed them off, repeated until they were clean, revelling in the stinging, throbbing pain.

She got the first-aid kit out a cupboard and opened it. Rubbed at her hand with an antiseptic wipe. The cut wasn't deep, a plaster would do, no need for a bandage. She raked in the box and pulled out the biggest one she could find, about half the size of her palm. She peeled the adhesive off the back and pushed the edges down on her skin, flexed her fist a couple of times to work the stiffness out.

She made mugs of tea, took them through to the kids in the living room like a normal day, two young visitors in need of sustenance. She put the mugs down on the coffee table. Sam stood at the back window, looking at the sea carved out between the bridges. He turned to stare at the road bridge.

Libby was looking at Logan's most recent school photo on the mantelpiece.

'Are you two OK?' Ellie said.

They both turned and nodded but neither spoke.

'I mean physically,' Ellie said, squeezing her hand tight. 'Are either of you hurt?'

Sam rolled and cricked his neck. 'We're fine.'

'What about . . .' Ellie didn't know what to say. 'You know, back there.'

Libby shook her head and looked down. Ellie put an arm round her. Libby flinched and shirked it off, and Ellie was left with her arm hanging in midair.

Libby touched the picture of Logan, lifted it from the mantel-piece.

'Is this your son?'

'Yes,' Ellie said.

Sam spoke. 'Libby.'

'It's OK,' Ellie said.

'The one who killed himself?' Libby said.

Ellie nodded. 'Jumped off the bridge.'

'When was that?'

'Six months ago,' Ellie said.

'What's his name?'

'Logan.'

'He's cute.'

'Yeah, he is.' Ellie was aware of the present tense.

'You must miss him,' Libby said, putting the photograph down.

'All the time,' Ellie said.

Libby looked at Sam, then past him out the window.

'I won't miss Dad,' she said. 'He was evil.'

Ellie wondered if it was as simple as that. Just decide someone is evil, then you never had to care. But Jack must've been nice to his daughter sometimes. Did the bad behaviour annihilate the good, wipe it away so all that was left was a monster?

Ellie thought about the fight on the boat. Jack had been aggressive, trying to reclaim his daughter, his family. Libby made accusations about him, he was stressed. Did that mitigate his aggression? Or theirs? They killed a man, and Ellie wasn't entirely sure why. She knew what Sam said he saw, but what if Jack was right, what if Sam was unstable, imagining things? What if Libby was lying?

It didn't matter now, it was done, they just had to deal with it the best they could.

'I better go,' Ellie said. 'Stay in the house until Ben and I come back. Don't answer the door to anyone. Understand?'

Libby stared at her for a moment.

'We understand,' she said.

34

Ellie took a lungful of air as she stood at the berth. This felt like it might be the last time she'd see the marina, her small world, before the weight would be too heavy on her shoulders, the pressure on her chest too much to breathe.

She was standing next to the Porpoise. She ran her hand against the name, painted in blue on the bow. It was faded and chips of paint fell away as she swept her hand along it, catching on her fingers. She turned to the sea and took in the size of it, the span of the bridges, the workmen on the new foundations in the distance.

She went on board and down into the cabin.

Ben was sitting at the table, head in hands. He turned when he heard her footsteps. He looked flushed, blood just under the skin, a sheen of sweat on his forehead. He wiped at it with his sleeve.

On the floor next to Jack's body were a kit bag and two rucksacks.

Ellie nodded at them. 'What's going on?'

Ben got up.

'Ballast.'

Ellie shook her head. 'We use water ballast, I don't get it.'

'Not for the boat,' Ben said. 'For him.'

Ellie looked at the bags, then at Jack, then at Ben. She knelt down and opened one of the rucksacks. It was full of rocks and broken bricks. She opened the other two bags and they were the same.

'Where did you get this?'

Ben lifted his head. 'From the old warehouse over there. Took three trips.'

Ellie zipped the bags and stood up. 'We're going to dump his body in the firth?'

Ben nodded. 'It's the only way.'

'We'll have to make sure the weights stay attached,' Ellie said. 'If they come loose he could wash up anywhere along the coast.'

'Let's just make sure we attach them properly,' Ben said. 'We can tie knots, can't we?'

Ellie laughed despite herself. She raised a hand to her face and covered her mouth, ashamed, then felt tears come.

'This is fucking awful,' she said.

'I know.'

They sat like that for a few seconds in silence.

'We'll have to scuttle the boat,' Ben said.

Ellie looked round the cabin and sighed. There was blood all over the floor, soaked into the boards, seeped into the hull. Forensic trail everywhere, there was no way it could be cleaned without leaving evidence.

'I know.' She looked at Jack. 'But we do the body separately?'

Ben nodded. 'If we leave the body in the boat and scuttle her, it's too big a target to find. It can be spotted on sonar, or by diving teams. If we do the body first, make sure it's weighed down, we can dump Jack further out in the middle of the firth, away from prying eyes, then bring the boat in closer to shore, so that we have a chance of getting back to land.'

'But we'll have the life raft,' Ellie said.

Ben shook his head.

'Draws too much attention,' he said. 'The coastguard would be called out. Then we'd have to explain what happened with the boat.'

Ellie stared at him. 'You're saying we swim to shore?'

Ben nodded. 'Will you manage?'

Ellie was the better swimmer. 'Will you?'

'I'll be fine,' Ben said.

'OK.'

They were both silent, thinking. Ellie looked at Jack's body. Images flashed into her brain, the smell of his sweat as she tightened the kill cord round his neck. The sound of his breath catching in his throat. The red swill of blood around them. The scratch and scrape of his feet against the wall as his legs thrashed about.

She turned away. 'We have to get this right.'

'I know.'

They had to think it through. This was a logistical problem to be solved, nothing more, they couldn't let it be anything else.

'Do we wait until dark?' Ellie said.

Ben frowned. 'Too suspicious, who goes out on the Forth at night? It'll draw attention.'

'But it's more risky in daylight.'

Ben went over to a drawer and pulled out the OS map of the firth. It was folded over at the area around the marina, the creases worn and weathered. He flattened it out on the table and they both studied it.

'We have to get away from the bridges,' Ellie said. 'Upstream.'

Ben nodded. 'Less traffic on the water.'

They were talking it through so they did it right. It was how they always planned sailing trips, back when they used to take trips together. The planning was the most important part, that way if anything unexpected happened, they were ready. It felt good to be doing this, like a proper couple again. Ellie touched Ben's arm.

'And we'll need to go past the new bridgeworks, quite a bit past.'

'But not too far, because we'll have to walk home once we get ashore.'

Ellie nodded. 'So not on the north shore either, obviously.'

She traced her finger along the south shore of the Forth.

'But the coast road runs up here for miles,' she said. 'Anyone driving along it could spot us.'

Ben put his finger down on a little blue symbol.

'Not here,' he said. 'The road goes inland round Hopetoun House. They've got all those grounds around the castle. We could come ashore at Bog Wood or North Deer Park.'

Ellie nodded. It made sense. There were woodland walks in the grounds of the big house, but none of them went down to the shore, leaving space for the deer to roam.

'OK.' She looked at Ben, held his gaze. 'Are we really going to do this?'

'We have to.'

Ellie nodded.

35

The wind was freshening as they made their way past the breakwater into the firth. They'd run the engine out this far but now Ellie cut the power as Ben untied the main boom and hoisted the sail. It had to look like a normal sailing trip if anyone on shore or the bridge saw them. It made sense to do everything as if they didn't have a dead body down below, that way no one would remember them, just another couple out on the waves, enjoying the freedom.

They tacked west, Ellie at the tiller, Ben scurrying up to the foredeck to fiddle with ropes and the smaller sails. The breeze had them scudding across the surface of the water in good time. There was no great swell in the waves, so the hull eased through the water with little resistance.

They headed into the middle of the firth, giving the new bridgeworks a wide berth. It was more risky sailing out here in the middle of the Forth, the main shipping channel up and down the river, but there were no large ships in sight.

As they got further out Ellie looked back the way they'd come. She lifted the binoculars from the seat and examined the coast. All the problems of everyday life back there, all the worries and stresses of the world left ashore, as they headed into open water. Who was she kidding? As if they were free of anything out here. You carry that baggage with you wherever you go and no amount of fresh air and sea spray changes that.

She swept the binoculars past the new bridge foundations. They were busy pouring concrete into the cofferdam. She'd read somewhere that the process took days, millions of tons of the stuff poured continuously. She imagined heaving Jack's body into that, destroying the evidence forever, making him a permanent part of the new bridge. But it was a stupid idea, how could they get the body up the side of the cofferdam? There were security guards patrolling it and workmen on top, everyone paying close attention, obeying health and safety. No, what she and Ben were doing was the only way.

She dropped the binoculars and turned to him. He didn't have his lifejacket on, and she realised that she didn't either. She imagined the boom arm swinging round and catching him on the head, knocking him overboard. She locked the tiller, darted into the cabin and grabbed two lifejackets, turning away from Jack's body on the floor. She ran back up and shouted to Ben, threw a lifejacket his way.

They made good time heading west. They stayed nearer to the south than the north bank, no point getting too close to the Rosyth naval base, they had tight security there.

There were hardly any other boats on the firth, and the ones that were out were a good distance away. People tended to sail under the bridges, sticking close to the icons, while the Porpoise was heading the other way, upstream towards solitude.

Ellie watched Ben work the sails and smiled. For a moment this felt like the old days. They were a man and a woman in love, working together towards a goal, getting on with their lives. Ben looked up, saw her face, smiled back.

After twenty minutes more sailing they were on their own. Ellie couldn't see another craft anywhere. They were a long way past the workmen on the bridge, an equally long way from Rosyth on the opposite coast. The bridges looked like models from this distance. Ellie imagined Sam and Libby sitting in her living room right now, looking out the window. She had a flash of Logan jumping, the footage of him stepping into nothingness, 5.6 seconds of gravity.

Ben took in the main sail and tied the boom as Ellie locked the tiller. She scanned the horizon with the binoculars. A couple of sailing boats miles away, over near North Queensferry, but nothing else.

She felt a hand on her shoulder.

'Let's do it,' Ben said.

They went into the cabin and stood over Jack's body.

Ellie picked up his hands, held them tight, as Ben lifted the legs and tucked the feet under his armpits.

'After three,' Ellie said. 'One, two, three.'

He was heavier than she expected. Not a big man, but solid enough. Their first heave barely lifted him off the ground. Ellie staggered backwards towards the steps, Ben shuffling after her, the body sagging between them. Ellie felt her palms sweat, the pain in her hand where she'd been cut, the rope burns. She bumped into the first step then lowered her backside on to a higher one and slid herself up, gripping tight. Ben stepped closer into Jack, getting a better grip on his thighs as Ellie bumped herself up the stairs one at a time. As she went up, Jack's head reached the bottom step, so that Ellie had to heave his weight up and over, his skull bumping on the steps with a solid clunk.

Seven heaves and she was at the top of the steps, sitting on deck, pulling at Jack's arms. Ben had changed his grip and was pushing at Jack's arse, lifting it over the top step. Ellie imagined the corpse farting in Ben's face. Didn't bodies piss and shit themselves when they died? She was sure she'd read that somewhere.

Jack was on deck. Ellie and Ben slumped at either end getting their breath back. Ellie stood up and did a three-sixty. No sign of any boats. She grabbed the binoculars and scanned again. She wondered about people on shore, if anyone was paying them any notice, just a normal sailing boat on the firth. A high-powered telescope or binoculars would be able to identify them, but no one could see Jack's body from anywhere except up close, as he was nestled in the footwell of the deck.

She looked at him. His hair was dark and slick, the water around him pink with blood. The wound in his neck was raw and open, a ragged mess of skin and flesh.

She heard a sound. Something alien, electronic. It was so out of place it took her a moment to realise it was a ringtone, a descending scale of notes, coming from Jack's body. She exchanged a glance with Ben, then crouched down, tilted her head. She went into his trouser pocket and pulled out a mobile. 'Alison' flashing on the screen. Calling to find her husband. Ellie thought about GPS, could it be tracked? She switched the phone off and slipped it into her pocket.

Ben headed back into the cabin and she followed. He took one handle of the kit bag and looked at her. She lifted the other handle and took the strain. The two of them waddled with the weight between them to the step, then Ben went up backwards, pulling as hard as he could, Ellie placing her hands under the back end of the bag, pushing as it slid up the steps in short yanks and spurts until it landed on deck with a thunk.

Then she and Ben lifted a rucksack each. Hers was too heavy to get on her back so she heaved it up and cradled it in her arms, using her elbows on the stairs to lever herself on to the deck. She dropped the rucksack with a clack of bricks from inside.

Ben went into one of the small lockers on the side of the deck and pulled out spare ropes and ties. He looked up, checking the water around them, then down at the body.

'We need to get him on the side here, before we tie the weights on.'

He nudged past the body to Jack's legs as Ellie took the hands again. The skin of Jack's hands felt rubbery. They hauled him out of the footwell and up to the port side of the deck. The effort of it made the boat rock, and Ellie and Ben fell on to their knees next to the body, sliding close to the edge.

Jack was in view now if anyone came by. From here, they could just give him a little push and he'd be in the water.

Ellie was down at the kit bag, waiting. Ben took the other handle and they heaved it up and on to Jack's body. Ellie winced as the weight squashed Jack's chest and stomach. She picked up a rope and tied the handle of the kit bag to Jack's arm, then forced the rope beneath him, slid it under his neck and round the other side, connecting with his right arm then the other handle of the bag.

Ben had the rucksacks up and was tying them to Jack's thighs and torso.

She tested her handiwork, pulled on the rope and it seemed secure. She looked around. A small dinghy was heading down the firth, but way over on the north side, too far away to be any bother. Ben saw it too and shook his head. He yanked on the ropes tied around Jack's corpse, checking them, and everything held well.

He ran his hands through his hair and stood up. Ellie looked at her hands. She had pulled on the ropes so tight she'd given herself more burns. All these little reminders.

'Let's do it,' she said.

Ben nodded.

The two of them pushed at Jack's body with the bags on it. For a moment nothing happened, the mass of it creating inertia, but slowly he began to inch towards the edge of the deck, and as they shoved harder he gained momentum against the slippery surface, then slid over the edge legs first, hitting the water with a thick splash and disappearing straight down.

Ellie stared at the waves where he'd gone in. No sign of anything untoward amongst the brown chop and swell of it. She imagined Jack sinking to the bottom and wondered how long it would take. More than 5.6 seconds anyway. She turned. Ben was rubbing at his stubble. A thin trail of pink water led from the edge of the deck into the footwell, then along to the cabin door.

Evidence everywhere.

36

They ran the engine for ten minutes, puttering closer to the coast, heading further west until Ellie couldn't see the road on the shore through the binoculars. She took Jack's phone out of her pocket, slid the back off and removed the battery and sim card. Snapped the sim in half, weighed all the pieces in her hand then hurled them as far as she could into the water. She scanned further west, past the small copse of oaks and beech that made up Bog Wood, then the open shoreline of North Deer Park. Sure enough, she spotted half a dozen deer, male and female, grazing on a patch of grassland by the beach, stopping to chew and look around.

The Porpoise was about half a mile from land when she cut the engine. The boat bobbed and swayed. She thought about that phrase 'sea legs'. It was a real thing, some people naturally more able to cope with the constant shifting of weight, the continual balancing act. And it worked the other way round, after a long day's sailing the first quarter of an hour on dry land was disorientating, the flatness of the world under your feet, the banality of a solid planet. Her body missed the shifting of the sea when she was away from it.

Ben went into the cabin and came back out with wetsuits. He threw one to her. She took her lifejacket off and stripped, pulling the rubber against the skin of her legs, feeling the tension of it.

She watched Ben do the same, admiring his body. He'd thickened over the years but not unpleasantly. There was no potbelly or love handles, just a stocky torso, a welcome solidity. She pictured Sam semi-naked in Logan's room, so lithe and skinny. Entirely different creatures.

She looked down at her own body. Gazed at the tattoos covering the real her. She scratched at the new one of the bridge on her arm, it was starting to heal. She looked at Logan's name and dates of birth and death on her left wrist, touched the ink under the surface. Not that she needed a permanent reminder, of course, the tattoos were more than that, a penance.

Ellie pulled her arms into the suit, stretching the fabric till her hands were free. She zipped up, feeling the looseness at her hips. She went over to Ben who was frowning, looking past her at the shore. She kissed him firmly on the mouth and stroked his arm.

'We'll make it,' she said.

She stepped over the discarded lifejackets. They would be no use to them in the water – they were for floating, not swimming. They kept you alive if help was coming, but if you wanted to save yourself, the only way was with your arms and legs, willpower and stamina.

Ellie and Ben went into the cabin. She pulled up the hatch in the floor, and Ben lifted another hidden hatch at the bow. Ellie reached in and took the wrench from a hook and began opening the through-hulls, small valves built into the bottom of the boat. They were used to expel excess water or sometimes to let water in to cool the engine, but if they were left fully open the hull would fill with water. She undid one, seawater rushing in over her hand, pouring into the hull. She quickly did three more, the water up to her ankles already. She looked up and saw Ben doing the same at his end.

'I'll cut the sink drain,' Ellie said. 'You do the hoses at the front.'

She had to shout over the water rushing in, up to her shins already, a sudden sense of urgency in the cabin. They'd started this thing, it had to be done quickly.

She reached over to the emergency pack behind her and opened it. Lifted a small axe and a serrated knife. Scuffed the knife along the cabin floor to Ben who grabbed it with a splash. She shifted her weight and picked up the axe, swung it down at the sink drain. Cutting it meant nothing would prevent the cabin from filling up. Two quick hacks and it was severed. She shunted herself out the cubbyhole in the cabin floor and reached for the bilge pump. She turned it off then went back to the trap door. She took a couple of quick practice swings, then brought the axe down on the bottom of the boat, next to the through-hulls she'd opened. Everything they'd done so far was fine, but the boat might not fill quick enough, better to make sure.

She hacked at the hull, water splashing in her face. She felt the wood splinter and crack so she swung again and again, heaving her arms, putting her weight behind it, feeling the planks of wood break open, one giving way under her foot and making her slump forward. She dropped the axe, throwing her hands out to regain balance, pulling her foot out of the hole.

She looked up and Ben was standing above her holding out his hand. She took it, stood up. The water was already halfway up the legs of the table in the middle of the cabin. The boat lurched to the port side. With the water rushing in, the balance was shifting and erratic.

They went upstairs.

Ellie looked around, then up. 'We should drop the mast. It might show at low tide.'

She went over and disconnected the forestay, then pulled the mast pin out and dropped it. Ben joined her and together they pushed at the mast, watched as it toppled, bounced and clattered off the deck.

They stepped over it as they went back to the stern, Ellie looking out, making sure no one was around to offer them help. If they got assistance, the boat might be salvaged. They would have to explain everything to the coastguard, the police. She looked at the shore. Small brown dots of deer munching on grass were the only movement.

Ben was at her side, resignation on his face.

'The end of the Porpoise,' he said.

Water was already at the top of the cabin, a slurp of it washed around their feet on deck. The boat sat low in the water, it had filled much quicker than Ellie imagined, she thought they'd have to wait a while. It was as if the boat wanted to sink to the bottom, give up battling against the waves every day, struggling to tame the wind whipping down the Forth. Their boat wanted to be at peace at the bottom of the sea.

'Yeah,' she said. 'Our little purpose.'

Ellie knew it was stupid to fill an object with memories, to connect it to other things in your mind, but she remembered the first time they'd taken Logan out on the boat when he was five. A dead calm day, a short potter round the bay with the motor running, Ellie panicking every time he got up or bumped on to his bottom, every time he ventured near the side of the boat. She followed him like a shadow that day, hands outstretched, prepared to catch him if he fell, ready to jump in after him if he went in the water. He had a mini life-jacket on but all the protection in the world wasn't enough for a mother looking after her son, making sure he came to no harm.

The water had filled the footwell of the deck and was creeping up the sides. About three quarters of the boat was underwater, the whole thing swaying with the roll of each wave.

'She's going down fast,' Ellie said. She hugged Ben and turned to shore. 'Ready?'

Ben took a breath. 'As I'll ever be.'

Ellie looked at him. 'Stay together in the water. Look out for each other. No matter what.'

Ben nodded. 'Of course.'

They climbed on to the stern, only a few inches clear of water now, looked at each other one last time, and dived in.

The shock of that first cold stab to her heart when she went in the water never reduced. The breath hammered out Ellie's lungs as she stroked, feeling the chill in her bones. She kicked to the surface. Ben was just ahead, turning back to check on her. She waved briefly, pointed to shore, then began swimming, even strokes in the water, pushing the body of it behind her with every touch, every kick of her feet, every swish of her rubber-clad legs. Already she was warming up with the effort, her breath short but regular, heart thudding, the pulse in her ears mingling with the slosh of the water, the splash of waves, the wind whistling overhead. She was in Ben's wake now, feeling the ripples from his body, the slipstream connecting the two of them like an invisible thread.

She heard a noise and turned back. The Porpoise had slumped on its side, taking on more water with a thwack and slurp, the port side of the hull exposed, but only a little, most of it already underwater. This could work, she thought.

She pushed towards land, imagining herself a porpoise gliding through the water as if it wasn't there, at one with the sea. The water was her plaything, hers to manipulate. Her arms and legs were aching, but it was a good ache, it felt righteous and worthwhile.

Up ahead Ben was splashing through the waves. As the shore got nearer she could make out individual deer, their heads turned away, not worrying about anything approaching from the water.

She closed her eyes and breathed, head in, head out, breathe, just keep going. She pictured Jack sinking to the bottom of the Forth, weighed down by rocks. She pictured Logan falling through the air, less than six elephants to destruction. She imagined Sam doing the same, meeting up with his father and Logan at the bottom of the ocean, a crowded bustle of all the people who ever died in the Firth of Forth, all suddenly alive and sharing their stories, the terrible, ordinary lives that had led to their deaths, a thousand people jumping off the bridge since it was built, more than the congregation of a church, or the entire roll of a school, all waiting on the seabed for others to join them, for Ben and Ellie to join that blissful release.

Ben was slowing down ahead of her and she caught him up. They were still a hundred yards from shore. He said something to her but she couldn't make it out, then his head went under. She stopped, treaded water. His head and one arm came back above the surface, his other hand reaching down to his lower leg, grabbing at his calf muscle.

Cramp.

His head went under again.

She waited a few seconds.

This time he didn't come back up.

She dived under, trying to see through the murk, the saline stinging her eyes. She powered over to where he had disappeared, grasping at the water, pushing downwards, turning and stretching her hands out. She saw movement out the corner of her eye and spun round again, kicked and stroked towards the swirl in the gloom. She spread her arms and made wide sweeping movements from left to right. Eventually she felt the material of his suit brush against the back of her outstretched hand and grabbed at his body. She got a hand under his armpit and hauled him upwards, kicking furiously to get back to the surface. She could feel his heartbeat through the wetsuit.

They broke the surface, Ellie gasping, Ben coughing and choking.

'I've got you,' she said.

She leaned back and pulled him with her arm around his chest, her other arm making deep strokes in the water, her legs kicking hard under his body. Ben was limp in her embrace to begin with, then slowly began to stroke with his right arm, the one he had free of her body. Between them they started to get some momentum, small surges through the wash, every stroke taking them a few inches closer to land.

'Sorry,' Ben spluttered through the water.

Ellie shook her head and whispered in his ear. 'Don't speak.'

She shot a glance behind her. The shore was seventy yards away. She felt the muscles in her thighs and calves begin to cramp up, burning spasms. She rested a moment then kicked again, the pain returning stronger, her arms thrashing in the water, the waves bobbing over their mouths as they slipped under then came back up for breath, salt on her lips. More strokes, more kicks, the last of her energy draining, Ben's too, she could feel it, just keep going, keep stroking and kicking and breathing. Stroke, stroke, stroke. Gasp for air. Her lungs heaving, legs on fire, arms like jelly, Ben's back on her chest, the two of them a single entity fighting to stay alive.

She snuck a glance behind. Forty yards. They were moving excruciatingly slowly now, hardly making headway, their heads dropping below the surface, then back up, necks strained to gulp in air. All Ellie could hear was her heartbeat in her ears, roaring. She kicked and kicked but her muscles refused to respond, constant cramp and spasm, no energy left. They ducked under the water again and Ellie thrashed her arm and legs, trying to get back to the surface. Ben was a dead weight on top of her now, pushing down on her chest. Her lungs ached and she longed to breathe, the urge to open her mouth almost overpowering. She kicked through the pain, through the cramp, sweeping her hand out, moving upwards inch by inch, so close to the surface she could almost smell the salty air, her muscles seizing up all along her legs from her groin to her toes.

She broke the surface, heaved in air, thrashed her limbs, panic filling her mind, kicking and pushing through pain like she'd never experienced before, Ben still in her grasp, his head lolling backwards.

They went under again, Ellie gulping in a mix of air and water as they sank. Her body was empty, utterly drained, as she stroked weakly and tried to muster her legs to move.

She kicked out for what felt like the last time she could manage, and felt pebbles scrabble and tumble under her toes.

She threw her leg out again, scuffed her heel against the bottom, tried to get purchase, kicking towards shore, kicking to get her footing. She lost balance and sank down again, Ben's body pressing on her, then she began to get a solid footing on the stones, eventually managing to dig her heels in until she was suddenly standing, her feet on the ground, her body connected with the solid earth, as she hauled Ben with her.

'Ben,' she said. 'We've done it.'

He didn't speak, didn't open his eyes.

She felt ground under her feet as she walked backwards. The cramp surged through her calves and thighs. She grabbed Ben by the scruff of his wetsuit and dragged him towards the beach, staggering and stumbling as her legs gave way, her arms numb.

She got him to the edge of the beach and collapsed next to him.

'Ben.'

Nothing.

She rolled him on to his side, hit his back hard.

Nothing.

'Fuck's sake.'

She put him on his back, pinched his nose, tilted his head and placed her mouth on his. She'd seen in an advert somewhere that you didn't do that any more, but fuck it, that's the way she'd been taught.

Stopped and pushed on his chest six times. Six elephants.

Went back to his mouth, did the same again.

Then the chest.

Nothing.

She slapped his face hard. 'Come on, Ben.'

She pinched his nose again, breathed into his mouth, taking large gulps of air in between and blowing till her cheeks burned.

She hammered his chest, six thrusts, this time pushing with all her might, imagining his chest cavity collapsing under the force, her hands grasping through the ribs, her fingers wrapping tight around his heart, squeezing it back to life.

Still nothing. She punched his chest.

'Don't leave me, you fucker,' she shouted.

She gave him mouth to mouth once more. Pictured her breath streaming into his lungs, dissipating into his bloodstream.

She pushed on his chest, throwing all her weight behind it.

One. 'Come on.'

Two. 'Live.'

Three. 'Fucking live.'

Four. 'I need you to live.'

He coughed and gasped, seawater spouting out his mouth as his chest began to rise and fall. He wheezed air into his lungs then turned his head to the side and puked into the pebbles, gulping in air and groaning.

Ellie slumped over his body, spent.

'Jesus,' he gasped.

'Thank God,' Ellie said, her body shaking.

Ben lay there for a long time with his eyes closed, drawing breath like it was the sweetest taste on earth.

Eventually he opened his eyes and turned his head.

'You saved me,' he said, his voice just a whisper.

37

She didn't know how long they lay there getting their breath back, trying to stop their arms and legs from shaking. The relief was overwhelming and Ellie found herself laughing as she stared at thick white clouds flitting across the sky.

'What are you laughing at?' Ben said.

She turned to him as if they were lying in bed together, a couple making small talk. 'I don't know.'

The sound of her laugh scared the deer. There was a shuffle of hooves, legs swishing through grass and the herd scattered into the woods.

Ellie stood up, her footing uncertain on the pebbles, and looked out to sea.

She couldn't see the Porpoise.

'We did it.'

Ben pushed on to his elbows then sat up, holding his hand out for help.

'Here,' Ellie said, pulling him up.

He got his balance and followed her gaze. Just the grey-brown motion of the water, the never-ending undulations of it, the shifting patterns of waves, forever restless.

But no boat. No hull sticking out, no rigging slapping the waves, nothing.

'It sank,' Ben said.

'It did.'

Ellie scanned the grounds behind them. No one about. A small beach, a grassy field next to it, then some thin forest along the coast heading east.

'We need to get back,' she said. 'Are you OK to walk?'

Ben nodded.

They picked their way off the beach and into the field. It was a couple of miles straight back to Port Edgar, but they'd have to take a detour once they left the grounds of Hopetoun House, avoid the coast road by heading up through higher fields and woods. The stately home hosted expensive weddings and business meetings, and Ellie smiled as she imagined a wedding party coming across two strangers in wetsuits and bare feet staggering into shot for their photographs outside the big mansion.

They walked to the end of Bog Wood then left the grounds of the house, sticking to the coast. After a while they cut round the back of Society Point, the same houses Ellie had walked past when Jack dropped her off out this way. She thought of Jack lying at the bottom of the Forth, weighed down, fish nosing at him.

They cut across the road and into a field, picking their way between cowpats. Only a thin row of trees gave them cover from a factory and office to their right. To the left was East Shore Wood, but they couldn't risk going further in, Ellie knew from jogging that dog walkers used it. They cut across Linn Mill and through more fields. Under tree cover they scurried across Society Road and walked down until they met Shore Road, the back way into Port Edgar.

Ellie had left the car parked at the other end of the marina, so they had to take the high road round the busy centre, avoiding the clubhouse and coastguard. The car was sitting in an isolated corner of the overflow car park, in the shadow of the bridge. The noise from there now was morphine to Ellie's mind, calming her, making her feel at peace, like she belonged. She realised right then that she would always feel at home here.

The car park was uneven gravel and it hurt her feet as she picked her way across. No one else was around. Just her, Ben and the bridge. She looked at the enormous legs supporting the structure and imagined trolls heaving round from the other side, smelling their blood and coming to gobble them up.

She reached the car and pulled the door open. She'd left it unlocked, the key in the glove compartment. She opened it and took the key out. Ben opened the passenger door and got in. The wet arses of their suits made damp patches on the seats as they sat down. She pulled her door closed and put the key in, turned the ignition and felt the engine bump into life, vibrations through her body.

She laid her head back against the headrest and turned to Ben. He looked so tired. She couldn't imagine what she must look like to him. She wiped gravel off the soles of her feet then revved the engine and put it into gear.

38

Ellie stood at the front door and wavered. Despite what they'd done, it felt good being out on the water, just her and Ben, like old times. As soon as she opened this door the real world would come pouring back in.

Ben put a hand on her back. 'Come on, we're almost done.'

She turned to him. 'You think?'

He shrugged. She loved that he didn't even try to bullshit her, another reason they were meant for each other. She opened the door and they went in. Sam met them in the hall, looking at their wetsuits and dirty feet.

'Are you OK?' he said.

Ellie touched his shoulder and ushered him into the living room. Libby was sitting on the sofa watching a cartoon. She turned and frowned.

'We need to talk,' Ellie said. 'But Ben and I have to get changed first. Wait here.'

They went upstairs and stripped out the suits, dumping them in the bath. They towelled themselves off then threw on joggers and T-shirts. The stink of brine was all over them. Ellie rinsed her feet with the showerhead, then Ben did the same.

They went downstairs and Ellie headed into the kitchen and filled the kettle, a reflex action. As it began hissing, she walked through to the living room.

Not my family, she reminded herself. This is not my family.

The end credits were rolling as Libby switched the television off.

'Sit down,' Ellie said to Sam.

Sam felt for the arm of the sofa and lowered himself.

'We got rid of the problem,' Ellie said.

'You dumped his body?' Libby said.

Ellie nodded.

'Out at sea,' Ben said.

'Won't he just float back to shore?' Sam said.

Ellie rubbed her cheek, felt the burns on her hand. 'We weighed him down.'

'What with?' Libby said.

Ellie frowned as Ben spoke. 'Don't worry, he won't be found.'

Sam stared at Ellie then Ben. 'Why were you in wetsuits?'

'We had to ditch the boat,' Ellie said. 'Too much evidence.'

'You sank your boat?' Libby said.

'Yes,' Ben said.

'And swam to shore?'

Ben nodded.

Libby pointed out the back window. 'Just out there?'

Ellie shook her head. 'Further along the coast, away from prying eyes. I'm pretty sure no one saw us.'

Silence for a long moment.

'Thank you,' Sam said.

Libby looked awkward. 'Yeah, thanks.'

Sam stood up. 'So what now?'

Ellie glanced at Ben. 'You two go home,' she said.

Libby shook her head. 'I want to stay here.'

'That's impossible,' Ben said.

228

'Why?'

She was really just a kid, didn't get the way things worked.

Ellie sat next to her on the sofa. 'Alison is your mum, your legal guardian, you have to go back.'

'I don't want to,' Libby said. 'She knew what Dad was doing.'

Ellie shook her head. 'You don't know that.'

'Trust me, she knew.'

'It's not that simple,' Ellie said. She didn't want to defend Alison, but found herself in that position all the same. 'Maybe on some level she suspected, but you can't say she knew. She's your mum, Libby, think about that.'

'And he was my dad,' Libby said, hands in her lap. 'Think about that.'

Ellie placed a hand on hers. 'Look, you have to go back. It's the only way. At the moment, no one even knows your dad's missing. And there's no law against going missing, not for grown-ups. If he chose to wander off and start a new life, that's that. That's what we play up to.'

Sam frowned. 'I don't know how this is going to work.'

Ben looked at Ellie.

'You and Libby go home,' Ellie said. 'Sam, you say you've been sleeping rough since the day Jack was stabbed. You could say you were in that old warehouse, that way it's more like the truth. Say you panicked in the morning when you came downstairs and saw your dad had been stabbed by an intruder, and you ran away. Say you've been confused and worried this whole time.'

Ellie turned to Libby. 'You say you got in touch with him, then went to make sure he was OK. You stayed last night at the warehouse with him. Now you've both decided to come home.'

'It won't work,' Sam said.

Ellie stood up. 'It will as long as they don't suspect you. At the moment, why should they? Your dad didn't tell them anything. You ran, but you were scared. That's a reasonable reaction for a teenager. Especially one with your issues.'

'I don't know.'

Ben turned to Sam. 'What's the alternative?'

'How do you mean?'

'If you don't go home, what are you going to do? You can't stay here. You'll have to keep running forever. Start a new life somewhere people don't know you. Never see your sister again.'

'I could go with him,' Libby said.

'Then you'd really be in trouble,' Ben said. 'That would be abducting a minor, you'd definitely have the police after you.'

'It's the only way,' Ellie said. 'It won't be easy, but you can ride it out. Just don't say anything, keep the information to a minimum. Don't tell them about the abuse, don't tell them about the stabbing, don't tell them about me or Ben. Just don't say anything you don't have to.'

'And what about Mum?' Sam said.

Ellie held out her hands. 'What about her?'

'What do we tell her?'

'Nothing.'

'Really?'

Libby spoke up. 'Are we supposed to keep up the lie forever?'

Ellie walked to the mantelpiece and looked at the picture of Logan, ran a finger along it and shrugged. 'The alternative is to go to the police station and tell them the truth.'

'Then what would happen?' Sam said.

'God knows,' Ben said. 'But we'd all be in a lot more trouble.'

'I'd happily go to jail for you both,' Ellie said. 'For all of you. I couldn't give a shit. But you have to decide, Sam, you and Libby. You have to make a decision and stick to it.'

Sam shook his head and looked at his sister. 'What do you think, Lib?'

Libby stood up.

'I'm not going to the cops,' she said.

39

Ellie stood at the door to Logan's room, her finger tugging on the skelf of loose wood on his name sign. When he was alive she used to go in his room every day to tidy up, a ritual of motherhood. She barely had the time, holding down a job, all the other stuff that went with being a parent, but she would sneak in when Logan was out or even just downstairs and pick dirty clothes off the floor for the wash, scoop stuff off his desk into the top drawer, empty out the bin full of crisp packets, crumpled up pieces of paper and Irn Bru cans.

Then one day there was nothing left to tidy. Two weeks after it happened, all his clothes were put away in the drawers, the bin emptied, the desktop clean, the room caught in a moment of time forever, preserved for the future.

She went in now and closed a drawer. Earlier, she'd given Sam a new set of Logan's clothes. A quick inspection of the stuff he had on, the clothes he'd borrowed three days before, and she spotted dark stains on the trousers, the top as well. Could be blood, could be something else, either way best to get rid of them, give him a new outfit. She chose the most innocuous stuff she could find, blacks and greys, and if Alison spotted they weren't his clothes, he was to say he stole them off a washing line when his own clothes got too dirty. It wasn't ideal, but then none of this was ideal.

She'd given Libby some of her own clothes – a loose sweat-shirt and plain jeans. They were about the same size, which had given Ellie a wry smile. Libby made a face at the clothes, but she took them and handed over her own when she realised her father's DNA was all over her T-shirt and trousers.

How would Ellie feel if her two missing kids turned up on the doorstep just like that? If they were wearing strange clothes, had been hiding out for days, and didn't know anything about their missing dad. She'd just be glad to have them back. She imagined her doorbell ringing, Logan standing there dripping wet after swimming to shore. She'd pictured it countless times. But maybe Alison wasn't like her, being a mother didn't guarantee anything.

Ellie and Ben had ushered Libby and Sam out the door a few hours ago, sending them up the road to their house. There were no hugs on the doorstep, both kids too awkward for that, everyone still in shock.

When the door was closed Ellie stood with her back to it and burst out crying, tears quick to her eyes, her shoulders heaving. Ben hugged her until she had it under control, then she went and gathered all the clothes Libby and Sam had been wearing and stuffed them into a bin bag. She walked out to the Binks, stopping to pick up half a dozen heavy stones from the beach on the way and adding them to the bag. She tied the knot at the top of the bag tight, checked no one was around, then hurled the bag into the water with as much strength as she could muster. The black plastic ballooned as the bag floated for a few moments, then as the water seeped inside and the rocks made gravity do its work, the bag sank like a deflated ball. It wasn't exactly lost forever, it could be found if anyone was looking, but then that was true of everything they'd done, everything they'd tried to cover up. If someone was really look-ing, they'd find out. The trick was to not give anyone a reason to look.

When she got back to the house Ben was in the bathroom soaking and rinsing the wetsuits. He put them on a radiator af-terwards, not ideal for the neoprene but it was best to get them dried quickly.

Ellie checked her phone. She deleted all the call notifica-tions to and from Sam's mobile. Wouldn't make a blind bit of difference if they checked the records, but it was all she could do for now. Before she deleted his number from her contacts she scribbled it down on a piece of paper and hid it under an ice tray in the freezer. She'd thought about throwing the phone away, joining all the other evidence at the bottom of the Forth, but then she pictured the CCTV footage, Logan stepping off the bridge. She couldn't do it, not yet.

Ellie looked round Logan's room again. Same posters, same games consoles, same bedsheets. There was a small dent in the pillow where Sam had put his head down to sleep that first day. She sat on the bed and smoothed it with her hand. Lifted the pillow to her nose and breathed in.

She remembered a night, maybe a year before the jump. It was summer and Logan had been hanging out with his mates along the prom on their bikes. They must've persuaded someone to go into the offy and get them a carry out, cider by the reek of it. She'd done the same when she was a kid, small-town teenage drinking hadn't changed over the years. He stumbled in the door half-cut, not hammered, he was too sens-ible for that, too in control. Even his suicide smacked of con-trol, when she thought about it. The ending of his life looked like a clear and conscious decision, rational thought. She didn't know if that made it better or worse.

That night with the drink in him he'd popped his head round the door, mumbling about going straight to bed. It was so obvious, it was hard for Ellie and Ben not to laugh. They listened smiling as he clumped around upstairs, a wall shuddering as he bumped off it. Then after a few minutes of silence, Ellie crept upstairs to find him curled on the floor next to his desk, snoring away. She got Ben to help get him undressed and into bed. Then once he was stripped and under the covers she stayed sitting on the bed, right where she was sitting now, for a long time, stroking his head and whispering that she loved him. It'd been so long since he needed her, since he had to be put to bed, since he allowed himself to be touched like that. It felt like coming home, being allowed to touch his face, stroke his hair without complaint.

Ellie stood up and went to the window. The bridge still there, the Firth of Forth still there, the whole of the Ferry still out there, twinkling in the twilight, going about its business, carrying on.

The doorbell went.

Ellie looked at the clock on Logan's bedside table. Half past seven. It was four hours since she pushed Libby and Sam out the door.

She was surprised it had taken this long for the police to come round.

40

'Hello, Mrs Napier, we'd like to speak to you for a moment. Can we come in?'

PCs Macdonald and Wood. She wasn't going over to the station, then, not yet anyway.

'Of course,' Ellie said, widening the door and pointing them through to the kitchen. 'I'll put the kettle on.'

She busied herself filling the kettle, switching it on, throwing teabags into mugs, getting milk out the fridge. She tried to focus on her hands, keeping them steady.

'Has something happened with the McKennas?' she said, turning to face them.

'That's what we're here to talk about,' Macdonald said.

She gave Ellie a soft, sympathetic look. Behind her, Wood was mooching around, looking at the shelves of cookbooks, fiddling with the bowl of car keys and other rubbish in the middle of the kitchen table. He looked like he thought he was in a television crime drama, waiting for his *Columbo* moment.

The kettle clicked off and Ellie poured the tea. Squeezed the bags, fished them out and added milk. She realised then that she hadn't even asked how they liked it.

'I hope you take milk,' she said, turning with two mugs in her hands.

Macdonald and Wood took them.

'Sit down,' Ellie said.

Ben appeared in the doorway. 'Everything OK, love?'

Ellie nodded. 'It's about the McKennas.'

'Ah.'

Ellie faced Macdonald. 'I told him about our last conversation. He didn't know I'd been to see Mrs McKenna, but I explained about it. He understands. He knows what I'm like at the moment, we don't have any secrets from each other.'

'Mrs Napier . . .'

'Please, call me Ellie.'

Macdonald gave a deferential nod of her head. She had the same notepad in front of her, the one she'd had at the station. Ellie wondered what she'd written in it since then. A list of suspects, maybe, with Ellie's name at the top.

'When we spoke before, it was because you'd been to see Mrs McKenna.'

Ellie nodded.

'You said you'd been in touch with her son.'

'Yes, but that wasn't true, I told you about that.'

'Quite. And is that still the case, that you've never been in touch with Samuel McKenna?'

Samuel, his Sunday name, so quaint. It felt like something out of the Old Testament. She couldn't imagine the gangly teenager crying on the bridge as Samuel.

'That's correct,' Ellie said.

Macdonald shot a glance to Wood. 'The boy is back home,' she said.

Ellie smiled. 'That's good news. I was worried about him, as I explained when we spoke before. It must've been scary, being out there on his own.'

'Don't you want to know what he said?' Wood said. 'Where he's been? Why he ran away?'

Ellie shrugged. 'I'm sure he had good reason. As long as he's back home and safe, what does it matter?'

Ben stepped further into the room. 'But he does back up my wife's statement, yes? That she's never met him.'

Wood raised his eyebrows at the interruption. Scanned Ben up and down. He was just a kid who thought he had more authority than he really possessed. When your teenage son has committed suicide, when you've killed a man and dumped his body in the sea, that gives you a certain authority. That gives you the power to truly not give a fuck, to not be intimidated by jumped up little pricks.

'He's not been all that communicative,' Macdonald said. 'Although he did say that he'd never heard of your wife, yes.'

Ellie looked at her hands. 'So where was he all this time?'

Macdonald and Wood both eyed her closely. She was risking it, but she didn't care. Macdonald referred to her notes, but it was just for show, she knew the details already.

'In a lock-up garage beneath the rail bridge,' she said. 'I believe it belongs to the family of a friend of his sister.'

That was good, a piece of misdirection away from the marina, keep them from looking there. Ellie should've thought of that.

Wood spoke. 'The sister came back too, they were together.'

Ellie looked surprised. Wood was trying to catch her out.

'His sister was missing?' she said, voice natural. 'That wasn't in the news.'

Macdonald looked at her colleague. 'Not for long. She didn't come home last night. Said she spent it with her brother in the garage, then persuaded him to come home today.'

'I'm so glad,' Ellie said. 'The family's all back together.'

Wood snorted. 'Not exactly.'

Ben came over and put a hand on Ellie's shoulder. 'What do you mean?'

'Jack McKenna might be missing,' Macdonald said.

Ellie looked surprised. 'Isn't he in hospital?'

Wood shook his head. 'He checked himself out, against the advice of doctors.'

'What do you mean, "might be missing"?' Ben said.

'It's unclear at this stage,' Macdonald said. 'He left home on foot very early this morning, told his wife he was going to look for Samuel and Libby. She hasn't heard from him since.'

'And the children didn't see him?' Ellie said.

'They say they haven't,' Macdonald said.

Wood narrowed his eyes. 'Have you seen him?'

Ellie shook her head. 'No.'

'Have you ever seen him?' Macdonald said. 'Before today, I mean.'

'Never, only a picture on the news.'

Wood sat back in his seat, pleased with himself. 'That's interesting, Mrs Napier. Because we have a description of someone who sounds very much like you visiting Jack McKenna in hospital the day after he was stabbed.'

Macdonald looked at her notebook. 'Several nurses in his ward described a woman claiming to be his sister who spent several minutes alone with him.' She looked up. 'Jack doesn't have a sister, Ellie.'

Ellie felt Ben's grip on her shoulder tighten. She concentrated on her breathing, looked down at her hands and back up.

'OK,' she said finally. 'I did go and see him in hospital.'

Wood smiled. 'Why?'

'I can't explain it,' Ellie said, her voice shaky. 'It's part of the same thing, the reason I went to see the mother and lied about her son. I felt involved somehow. It made me think of everything that happened with Logan. I felt sorry for the police officer, worried about him. I didn't want those children to lose a father, I didn't want Mrs McKenna to lose her husband.'

Macdonald frowned. 'But he was a complete stranger to you, correct?'

Ellie nodded, felt Ben rubbing her arm. 'I just . . . I haven't been sleeping. The pills I was taking weren't working. After Logan jumped, I haven't been able to cope. When I saw the story on the news, I felt like it was my family. You wouldn't understand. I don't understand myself, really. I felt like if I could just make the McKennas' lives OK, just get them all back together, then that was a second chance for me. Does that make sense?'

Wood sucked his teeth. 'Not really.'

Macdonald stared at him.

Wood ignored it. 'So how does this family love tally with the accusations you made about PS McKenna to his wife?'

'I never made any accusations.'

'You never said he was abusing his daughter?'

'I told you last time, I never made any accusations.'

'Why would Mrs McKenna make something like that up?'

'You'd have to ask her,' Ellie said. 'She's under a lot of stress. Maybe it was just a case of crossed wires.'

Wood snorted. 'Really?'

'Her son was missing,' Ellie said. 'Her husband in hospital.

Unless you have a family, you can't understand the strain of that.'

'Oh, come on,' Wood said.

Ellie looked at the wedding ring on Macdonald's finger. If she had kids maybe she could understand the loss, the need to be useful, involved in the lives of others. That's what Ellie was banking on.

'Can you tell us what you've been up to since we spoke to you yesterday?' Wood said.

Ellie thought for a moment. She wiped at her eyes and nose, buying time. Felt Ben's hand still on her shoulder.

'I think my wife has told you everything you need to know,' he said.

'No, she hasn't,' Wood said.

Ellie looked up, put a hand on Ben's. 'It's OK. I'm fine.'

'Since the interview yesterday,' Wood said.

Ellie remembered getting in the car with Jack, walking back to the marina, coming home. Then all of today, back and forth in the car, out on the water. Everything.

'I've just been at home mostly,' she said.

'I can vouch for that,' Ben said.

'Mostly?' Macdonald said. She was still trying to be kind, trying to give Ellie options.

'Maybe I went for a walk today,' Ellie said.

'Maybe?' Wood said.

Ellie nodded. 'I did. This morning.' She remembered telling the cops the same thing in the station. Try to be consistent.

'Another of your famous big walks,' Wood said. 'Can you re-member this time where you went rambling to?'

She couldn't say Port Edgar, didn't want them even thinking

of that place, going there and asking around. But she couldn't say the other direction, along the High Street and the prom, because that led to the lock-up where Sam said he stayed.

'The bridge.'

'The road bridge?' Macdonald said.

'Yes.'

'Why?' Wood said.

'I go up there every day.'

This was good, this was true. She was up there yesterday, first thing, she could use the truth to make a lie. She gave Macdonald a look, mothers together.

'I go up there every day,' she said. 'Ever since Logan jumped.'

Wood shifted in his seat. 'That's a bit sick, isn't it?'

Macdonald turned to him. 'That's enough, Jay.'

Her voice was sharp, and Wood slumped in his seat.

'It's something else I can't explain,' Ellie said. 'I just have to go up there. It's a compulsion. It's the only connection I have with Logan now, that's how it feels. My God, I sound crazy.'

Macdonald reached out and touched Ellie's hand. 'You don't sound crazy, Ellie.'

Wood made a noise in his throat suggesting that's exactly what Ellie was, but he didn't say anything.

'I need to get help,' Ellie said.

Macdonald took her hand away, looked at her notebook.

'You think?' Wood said.

Macdonald glared at him.

'It might be a good idea,' Macdonald said. 'Didn't anyone offer you counselling after your son's death?'

Ellie nodded. 'I went for a while. Didn't help. Nothing helps. Except walking and running and swimming.'

Ellie could feel the muscles in her arms and legs ache from the swim earlier. She was suddenly aware of the acid building up in them, and she longed to soak in a hot bath for hours.

'That clearly hasn't worked either,' Wood said.

'Jay, I told you already,' Macdonald said.

Wood turned to her. 'What? We get these crazies all the time, people hanging around victims or criminals, deluded folk who see stuff on telly and think it's real, it's part of their lives. She's been hassling this family since it started. It's a waste of police time.'

Macdonald had a look on her face that said Wood was going to get a solid bollocking as soon as he was out the door.

Ellie pressed her lips together in a sign of meekness. If she was just another crazy person wasting police time then that was fine.

Macdonald smiled at her. 'I think we're done here.'

'But we might be back in touch,' Wood said.

'If there are any developments,' Macdonald added.

They all stood up.

Ellie put an arm out, showing them towards the kitchen door.

'I hope Mr McKenna shows up soon,' she said. 'I hate to think of that family without him.'

'We have other lines of enquiry,' Macdonald said in the hallway.

Ben spoke. 'Like what?'

Wood made a noise, bringing yet another look from Macdonald.

'It seems there might be some irregularities with PS McKenna's police work,' she said. 'Internal Affairs are investigating. That's all I can say.'

'I'm sure he'll show up soon,' Ellie said, opening the door.

They were outside when Macdonald turned. Ellie thought of Wood and his *Columbo* moment, but he didn't speak.

'Thanks for your time, Ellie,' Macdonald said.

'Not at all,' Ellie said, her hand on the doorframe. 'Thank you for being so understanding. I'm sorry for any trouble I've caused.'

She closed the door with a trembling hand then kept it there for a long time, feeling the grain of the wood under her fingers.

41

She couldn't sleep. Too much going through her mind, so much so she found herself grabbing at the bed sheets beneath her, her fingers like witches' claws. She thought about Sam and Libby in their house, in their beds. Were they able to sleep? What about Alison, standing at the kitchen window with a glass of red wondering where her husband was? Ellie thought about the trail they'd left getting rid of Jack, but she honestly didn't care, she would take whatever came her way.

She got out of bed and padded downstairs. Put the kettle on and made green tea. Seemed like half her life was spent tied to the kettle, the kitchen, cooking and cleaning up. It was her space in the house, a room her two men only entered to open the fridge or a cupboard and stuff their faces. And while she always used to moan about that, the stereotypical domestication of a woman in the home, she loved the headspace, the corner of isolation it provided. She longed to see Logan loping in, flinging the fridge door open too hard and shoving slice after slice of ham into his mouth.

She stared out the window and thought of him. In hindsight she began to think there had been signs, just maybe towards the end. Nothing specific and nothing like you hear about in other cases. No cries for help, no near misses, but there had been a closing down, perhaps, a withdrawal from his family and, it turned out, his friends too. Nothing drastic, no fights, no throwing himself on his bed in tears or rage, or smashing his room up. Just a gradual build up of resistance to life, like he was becoming petrified, slowly transforming from flesh to stone. She tried to talk to him but could never get him to open up. She should've tried harder, but how could she have known? She thought it was that worst of clichés, 'just a phase', and he'd come through it like 99 per cent of teenagers did.

But he was the one per cent. She tried to see what marked him out as different, as special, but there was nothing. That was the worst thing, what happened could've happened to any child, any teenager, any person on earth. It just happened to be him. Whether he was in his right mind or not didn't matter. That didn't even mean anything, 'right mind'. In the end words completely failed to explain any of this experience, any of her son's emotions or actions, any of Ellie's reactions or distress, anything at all.

Words were useless, utterly useless.

You just had to try to keep living. Continue being in the world, keep on acting as if it meant something, there was a reason, behave like your actions were meaningful. It was much harder than it sounded.

Ellie finished her tea, slipped upstairs and got dressed. She patted the keys in her pocket, put her jacket on and left the house, pulling the front door behind her.

She started walking. Not aimlessly, this wasn't just a way of freeing her mind. No, this time she had a purpose, she was compelled, there was somewhere she needed to go.

She checked her watch. 2.35 a.m. She walked past the police station to the end of Hopetoun Road then hooked right, following the road up the hill. Her stride had vigour as she passed the two churches and the turn off for Station Road, then the primary school and the park. What did it mean to know a place so well? To know every bench in every park, every bin and post-box on every corner. Did it amount to anything?

She turned off Kirkliston Road at Viewforth and headed into the warren of residential streets. A left then a right and she was on Inchcolm Terrace. She hadn't walked past a single soul since she left her house down by the water. Not even a car or a taxi had swished past in the streetlights. The town was hibernating.

She got to number 23 and stopped. Glanced up and down the street then looked at the house. The lights were off. She opened the gate and walked up the path. When she got to the front door she stopped. Looked at the glass and wood of the door, the doorbell, the handle she touched that first time.

She got the keys out of her pocket, Jack's keys, slid the Yale into the lock and turned. The door clicked open and she stepped into the McKennas' home.

42

She stood with the door closed at her back and listened. Just her own breath in her throat, a pulse in her ears. She took a step forward and heard her ankle click. Just a joint thing, it happened occasionally after she'd been swimming, but the sound of it was outrageous in the dark.

She angled her head to listen upstairs. Nothing. She crept towards the kitchen and stopped in the doorway. She looked at the floor to the left, where Jack had been lying that first day. She walked over to the spot and knelt down. Rubbed at the laminate flooring. No sign of blood. She brought her fingers to her nose and smelled. Particles of dust and grit between her fingers, nothing more. She stood up and looked along the work surfaces. A knife block with one knife missing. Presumably still at the police station as evidence. She wondered what they'd been able to make of that.

She went to the patio door at the back of the kitchen. Looked at the handle, the one she touched. People must've come and gone out this door since then. She wondered how many remnants of fingerprints had been left over the years. If the house was fifty years old, say, think of the hundreds of people passing through, new owners, friends, family, parties, a slice of mundane humanity in this insignificant corner of the world.

She went into the living room and did a circuit. Looked at

the family portraits on the wall, the school photos of Sam and Libby, the holiday snaps, a picture of Alison holding a baby. Ellie couldn't tell which child it was, and it seemed unfair that there was only one baby picture on the wall.

She went to the bottom of the stairs and began walking up. She'd read somewhere as a kid that the way to sneak upstairs was to place your feet at the sides of the steps, as the centres were more inclined to creak under your weight. She had no idea if that was true but she did it all the same, spreading her weight and placing her feet carefully on the edges of each stair as she went up.

She stood at the top, her hand on the banister, and cocked her head again. She could hear breathing from one of the bedrooms, the one to her right. It sounded male, though she wasn't sure. Not quite snoring but close, a peaceful, rhythmic sound.

She went in the other direction to the bedroom nearest the bathroom. Stood looking at the door for a while, then pushed it open and stepped inside.

Libby's room. It was a midden, as Ellie's mum would've said. There were clothes scattered all over the floor, magazines and books in three tumbling piles next to the bed. Make-up, cheap bracelets and necklaces were piled on top of a chest of drawers, along with hair straighteners, and half a dozen bottles of grooming products. The desk was strewn with empty Coke cans, biscuit wrappers and crisp packets, schoolbooks buried underneath.

Libby was lying on top of her covers in a short T-shirt and skimpy pants, only her legs under the duvet. She was on her back with her arms behind her head, like a soldier surrendering.

Ellie walked over. Her breathing was deep but gentle, her

face peaceful, her skin so fresh and smooth that Ellie wanted to pinch it. She stood watching the girl for a few moments, then rubbed at her own eyes and left the room. She headed for the snoring next, waiting for a moment at the door before going inside.

Sam. The smell of him straight away, not the deodorant but really him, earthy and animalistic, like a fox. She breathed it in. His room was more organised than Libby's, but not much. Clothes on the floor, football stuff in one corner, an Xbox and television in the other.

Ellie stood over him. He was half-out from under the covers, and she could see he was only wearing pants, the pair of Logan's that Ellie had given him. She gazed at his bare torso, wiry and hard, ribs ridged up his sides, his elbows and wrists thin and delicate, like they would break easily. He shuffled in his sleep, shifting his weight, turning his face away from her. Ellie's body tensed. Sam's back was to her now, a bony spine, the shoulder blades like nascent wings. She wanted to touch them, see them flutter free. She watched his shoulders rise and fall with his breathing then turned and walked out the room.

That left Alison.

Ellie stood at the door and listened. All she could hear was Sam's breathing from the other direction. She swallowed and pushed open the door.

Alison had her duvet pulled up to her chin. Asleep on her back, a hand hanging over the side. She was tucked into one half of the double bed, hadn't spread out. Maybe over time she would get used to the extra space and claim it. Ellie imagined having a double bed to herself – freeing or lonely?

An empty bottle of white wine and a glass were on the floor

next to the bed. A lamp, clock and a packet of painkillers for the morning. Her clothes discarded on a chair in the corner of the room. A large mirrored wardrobe along one wall, a print of stones on a beach from IKEA on the wall above the bed. Nothing out of the ordinary, just a normal married couple's bedroom.

Ellie stood over Alison, watched her. Imagined picking up Jack's pillow and placing it over Alison's face. She sat on the edge of the bed and put her hand over Alison's mouth.

'Wake up,' she said.

She gave Alison's rump a shake through the covers and Alison's eyes pinged open. She grunted and squirmed but Ellie pressed down on her mouth, felt the hard enamel of her teeth and the skin of her lips.

'Shhh,' she said. 'I'm not here to harm you, I just want to talk.'

Alison's eyes were wide. She shoved Ellie's hand away from her mouth.

'What the fuck are you doing in my house?' she hissed. 'I'm calling the police.'

Ellie shook her head. 'No.'

'Fuck you.'

'I know about your family.' Ellie looked behind her at the bedroom door. 'I want to talk to you, but I think it's best if we don't wake Sam and Libby, don't you?'

Alison stared as Ellie got up. She could see that Alison was wearing silky underwear, burgundy with lace trim.

'Put something on and meet me downstairs,' Ellie said, walking out the room.

43

She sat at the kitchen table in the dark.

Alison came in, tying a dressing gown around her waist. She put a light on, a recessed spotlight near the fridge, went to a cupboard and took out two wine glasses then lifted a bottle of Rioja from the worktop. She poured, slid one across to Ellie, then glugged at her own, half of it gone already. She topped it up.

'Well?'

Ellie examined her. Her skin was crumpled from sleep, but there was more to it than that. The drink was beginning to show on her face, thin red lines under the surface on her cheeks and nose. Her eyelids were puffed and heavy, hanging over her eyes as if trying to keep a secret. Thick lines across her forehead and bags under her eyes from worry and stress. Ellie could see her body relax as the wine began to work, her shoulders slumping, her breathing regular, but she still had her guard up, still ready for combat. This crazy woman had broken into her house in the middle of the night, after all.

'I want to speak to you,' Ellie said. 'One mum to another.'

'We're nothing alike,' Alison said.

'You think?'

A gulp of wine and a shake of the head. 'No.'

Ellie took a sip. Just a sip, she wanted to stay in control.

'You love your kids,' she said.

'Of course.'

'I loved my Logan.'

Alison took another drink.

Ellie stared at her. 'I know what you're thinking.'

'What?'

'How could I love my son the way you love your kids, if I let him kill himself?'

Alison's head went down for a moment. 'I wasn't thinking that.'

'I don't blame you,' Ellie said. 'Everyone thinks that. I see it in their faces when I walk down the street. Oh sure, there's pity and sympathy, but underneath is the animal in us, the bad side of humanity. It's my fault, I did something wrong, that's why my boy did it.'

Alison took a drink, but a sip this time. 'I promise, that's not what I was thinking.'

Ellie sipped too. 'You're the exception then.'

Alison lifted the Rioja and filled both glasses. A little splashed out the top of Ellie's, a dribble down the side of the glass. She thought of Jack lying in the corner of the kitchen, his stomach oozing. She pictured him lying on the ocean floor, blood droplets infinitely diluted by the billions of gallons of water on the planet until there was nothing left of his essence. She thought about Logan's ashes, dissolved and now part of the sea.

Alison took another big gulp from her glass.

'Aren't you going to tell me I'm drinking too much?' she said.

'I'm not in a position to have a go at anyone about their coping mechanism.'

'Who says it's a coping mechanism?'

'Isn't it?'

'And what do I have to cope with?'

'The collapse of your family,' Ellie said.

Alison stared at her across the table. 'You don't know anything about my family.'

'I know that Libby and Sam are back home. And Jack's gone.'

'How?'

'The police came to see me. They said Sam had confirmed I was never in touch with him.'

'He's lying.'

Ellie looked Alison in the eye. 'Of course he is. And of course you can tell. No one knows a boy like his mum.'

'I should tell the police.'

'If you send the police to me again, I'll deny I was here,' Ellie said. 'And I'll come back for you. I have keys.'

'How do you have keys?'

Ellie waved a hand, as if that was of no importance.

'I'll change the locks,' Alison said.

'It won't matter.' Ellie took a sip of wine. 'You really shouldn't get the police involved.'

'Why not? They need to find my husband.'

Ellie shook her head. 'No, they don't. Jack isn't coming back.'

'How do you know?'

'He told me.'

'When did you see him?'

'He picked me up after my first police interview. Told me he was leaving.'

'Why would he do that?'

'You know why.'

Alison drained her wine. She poured the last of the bottle into her glass, her hand trembling.

'Not this again,' she said. 'Jack never did anything to Libby.'

Ellie grabbed Alison's hand and pulled it towards her. Alison jumped at the sudden movement, her chair scuffing the floor.

'You knew what he was doing,' Ellie said.

'I didn't.'

Ellie leaned across the table and touched Alison's temple. 'Maybe not up here.' She moved her finger to the woman's chest. 'But you knew it in here.'

Alison shook her head as tears came to her eyes. She lowered her face and her shoulders shook. Ellie was still gripping her hand in her fingers, like a buzzard with its prey.

'Why do you think Sam stabbed him?' Ellie said.

Alison was snivelling now, trying to pull her hand away.

'My boy would never do that,' she said.

'Look at me.' Ellie yanked Alison's arm. Alison's head came up.

'Sam was trying to protect his sister. Your daughter. Do you understand? He's a good boy, the son you've raised. He was protecting his family from harm.'

Alison's tears landed on the table. 'No, someone broke in.'

Ellie dropped Alison's hand then slammed her fist down.

'No one broke in, you know that. It was Sam. Because of what Jack was doing to Libby.'

Alison covered her face with her hands as she sobbed, elbows skidding on the table, her body shaking.

'I swear I didn't know . . . I couldn't . . . how could he . . . ?'

Ellie watched her. She tried to put herself in Alison's position. It was something the counsellor had said about empathy, trying to imagine what life was like for someone else. But that was useless in Ellie's case, how could you possibly put yourself inside the head of someone suicidal? How could you empathise with that? And yet she did. Ironically, the very thing Logan had done put her in the same mindset. She wanted to die, she had wanted to die every day since he killed himself. She had all the empathy in the world. If she'd had any kind of religious belief she would've done it by now. If she had even the slightest feeling in her heart that she would see him again in some kind of afterlife, she would run over and grab a knife from the worktop right now and plunge it into her belly as deep as she could, right up to the handle, and she would feel good about it. But the truth was, she knew she would never see him again. She knew he wasn't waiting for her with the angels, in a better place, all the clichés that get trotted out when someone young dies. They just die, end of story. They just create an unimaginably huge hole in the lives of everyone they left behind. That was the reality, and it was only once you embraced that and owned it that you had any chance of carrying on.

Alison was still crying, her sobs racking her body. She knew about what her husband had done, had admitted it to herself for the first time. What must that be like? A betrayal, of course, and massive guilt. Ellie understood both those things so well.

She couldn't help herself from speaking. 'How could you not do anything?'

Alison looked up, her face a crumpled mess. 'I didn't know.'

'You did know, and you did nothing.'

Alison shook her head.

'Libby tried to tell you,' Ellie said. 'She told me. She said you kept avoiding it.'

'I don't know about that. No . . .'

Ellie felt her anger rise. 'Yes.'

She landed a fist on the table that made Alison jump. She looked scared. She should. Ellie thought about those knives in the block, a few feet away. She breathed, tried to control her body. Her fist ached.

'I did something about it,' Ellie said.

Alison narrowed her eyes. 'What did you do?'

'I made Jack go away.'

'What do you mean?'

'Just that. I made your husband go away.'

'How?'

Ellie laid her hands in front of her, held Alison's gaze. 'I persuaded him. I can be very persuasive when I need to be. I told him I would take Libby to the police. I said I had evidence. He understood it was over.'

She pictured him pleading with her in his car, saying it was all a mistake, that he hadn't been doing anything. She saw Libby sticking the scissors into her dad's stomach, then Sam planting them in his neck. Then herself strangling him as he tried to escape.

'He said he was sorry,' Ellie said.

Alison was crying again. 'How could he?'

'He won't come back. Ever.'

'Where did he go?'

Ellie shook her head.

'He must've said something.'

257

'Forget about Jack,' Ellie said.

Alison stared at her. 'After what you've just told me?' Something hardened in her face. 'Why should I trust you, who the fuck are you anyway? Why are you even in our lives?'

Ellie sighed and ran her fingers down her neck. She leaned in towards the middle of the table and lowered her voice, like a conspiracy.

'I found your son on the bridge.'

'What do you mean?'

'Sam. I met him the morning he stabbed Jack. He was on the Forth Road Bridge. He was going to jump.'

'No.'

Ellie nodded. 'He was over the railing, looking down. He was about to step off when I stopped him. I spoke to him. If I hadn't been there, your son would be dead. Just like mine.'

Alison lifted her wine glass and finished the dregs in the bottom. Both her hands shook on the glass. She looked like a drowning woman clutching at a piece of driftwood.

Ellie pushed her chair back and stood up.

'You're lucky,' she said.

Alison shook her head. 'I don't feel lucky.'

'You've got a second chance. Both your children are tucked up in bed and you've got a chance to live a new life with them. You've got a chance to make their lives better, make it up to them. To talk to them, and listen to them when they want to talk. Don't you know how precious that is? I would give anything to have that. Anything.'

Alison stared at Ellie, her head nodding as she tried to get her crying under control.

'Don't waste it,' Ellie said.

44

Ellie stood at her kitchen window watching the sunrise. From here you could see the light bleeding over the water before you saw the sun, hidden by the rocky outcrop to the east. The rays splayed up the Forth, diffracted through the criss-cross grid of the rail bridge, reaching across the amber surface of the firth to the road bridge. Cars and vans glinted as they caught the light, bouncing the energy outwards, dispersing the power of the sun to everyone.

There was a knock at the door.

She sighed. Alison had called the police after all. It was a risk, Ellie knew. She'd hoped Alison would take this opportunity to start again, but no, they were going to get dragged through the squalor of what they'd done. She would protect the children, though, would never involve them, even if it meant going to prison for the rest of her life. She didn't care about that. She thought of Ben upstairs in bed. She would protect him too if she could. If anyone took the blame for all this, please let it be her alone.

She went to the door and opened it.

Sam stood there with a Tesco carrier bag under his arm.

'I brought Logan's clothes back,' he said.

Ellie looked down the street and ushered him inside.

'You shouldn't have come.'

His face fell and she touched his arm.

'But I'm glad you did,' she said. 'Come through.'

Sam stood in the middle of the kitchen just like that first time, the start of this. The boy she saved from the bridge.

'Sit down,' she said.

He handed her the bag.

'You didn't have to return these,' she said.

He pulled out a chair and sat down. 'I wanted to. They're too small for me anyway.'

She made tea and placed a mug in front of him. He was sitting with his back to the window, looking away from her, eyes flitting round the room. He wasn't distressed, like that first time, more in control. But he was still shy, still felt awkward around a middle-aged woman who wasn't his mother.

'You really shouldn't be here,' she said. 'If the police find out.'

Sam smiled. 'The police don't give a shit.'

'We can't be complacent. What if they followed you, or were watching the house?'

Sam shook his head. 'They don't want to find him. He was up to all sorts of shit, apparently. Taking protection money, misplacing evidence, selling drugs. The young cop told me on the sly. He enjoyed it, thought he was shocking me, telling me bad things about my dad, like I gave a shit. He even suggested Dad had been sexually assaulting women in custody.'

'I'm sorry,' Ellie said.

'Don't be.'

Ellie examined his face. 'He's still your dad.'

Sam gave her a look. 'He was, you mean.'

Ellie shook her head. 'Don't ever feel proud about what we did. Don't turn into that person.'

'But he was evil.'

Ellie thought about that. 'I'm not sure evil exists, not like you mean.'

'Of course it does.'

'He did bad things,' Ellie said. 'Very bad things. But we all make mistakes.'

Sam frowned. 'Don't make excuses for him.'

'I'm not,' Ellie said.

She blew on her tea. Maybe it was easier if they thought of Jack as evil, it justified what they did. But she couldn't swallow that, she couldn't believe it was right to take someone's life. She couldn't accept it was impossible for him to change. Given the right circumstances, Jack might've turned his life around. But Sam didn't need to hear that. He was seventeen and he'd helped to kill his own dad, the last thing he needed was Ellie throwing moral ambiguity around. It was easier to think they killed an evil man, then maybe at least some of them could get to sleep at night without pills.

Sam gulped at his tea like he had a thirst.

'How's Libby?' Ellie said.

He lowered his mug. 'OK, I think.'

'She's been through the most,' Ellie said. 'Don't forget that. She'll need her big brother more than ever.'

'We had a chat a few hours ago,' Sam said, nodding. 'I think she's going to be OK.'

'You were chatting in the middle of the night?'

Sam nodded. 'It was weird, Mum woke us both up. Said she wanted to let us know she loved us very much, that she was going to take care of us, all that guff. Kept hugging. Especially Libby.'

'How did Libby take that?'

'Not great.' Sam rolled some stiffness out his neck. 'Mum seems different somehow.'

'How do you mean?'

'Like she knows Dad isn't coming back. She kept talking about a new life, the three of us, a fresh start, all that rubbish.'

Ellie smiled. 'They're clichés because they're true.'

'I suppose.' Sam took a final gulp of tea and stood up. 'I better go.'

It was too soon. Ellie didn't want him to leave, she was getting used to having him around.

He shuffled on the spot, looked out the window, at the cooker, down at the table.

'Thank you,' he said, raising his face. 'For saving my life.'

'There's no need.'

'But I want to say it.'

Ellie looked at him, this beautiful boy who belonged to someone else. She got up and put her arms round him, felt his long, thin arms go around her waist. She rubbed at his back and placed her cheek against his chest so she could hear his heart. Just a human heartbeat, there were billions of them on the planet, but this one meant everything to her.

After a few moments she felt him squirming free. She released him and placed a hand on his face. She went on tiptoes and kissed him on the lips. She registered the look of surprise on his face but didn't care, then stepped back, raising a hand as if to say he was free to go, to get on with his life.

'Take care, Sam,' she said.

He nodded and smiled, taking a step towards the door.

'I will.'

She saw him to the door and watched him walk down the path, on to the street, his loping gait, rolling shoulders, typical teenage boy. He didn't look back.

She closed the door and turned.

Ben was at the top of the stairs in his pyjamas, face bleary and hair ruffled.

'Was that Sam?' he said.

'Yeah.'

'What did he want?'

'Just returning Logan's clothes.'

Ben rubbed at his scalp. 'Everything OK up the road?'

'I think so,' Ellie said. 'Put some clothes on, I want us to go for a walk together.'

45

That first step on the bridge, the thrum of the traffic shuddering through her feet, like a homecoming. She kept walking, Ben at her side. It was rush hour, cars and vans, trucks and buses filling all four lanes, thudding past in a blur, a mass of metal and plastic, humanity on the move. Ellie slid her hand along the railing, the vibrations of the bridge running up her arm. A couple of cyclists overtook them heading to Fife, as Ellie felt Ben's hand slip into hers. She turned and saw him smile. They walked on without speaking, the roar all around them, a gust of wind trying to throw them off balance. It was squally out on the firth, if it settled a little it could be a decent day for sailing.

Ellie's pace slowed as she approached the middle of the bridge. She felt Ben's hand tighten in her own. He hadn't been up here since Logan jumped, didn't see the point. They had their own ways of dealing but maybe that was changing, maybe there was a way forward together.

She stopped when she reached the spot, hesitated, then turned.

'Is this it?' Ben said, raising his voice over the noise.

He'd seen the footage, but only once. Said he never wanted to see it again, then weeks later confessed that he regretted ever watching it, couldn't get it out of his mind.

Ellie nodded. 'This is it.'

Ben watched the cars storming past. 'It's so exposed.'

They both looked out to sea. The sun was up, no clouds. The colours of everything seemed ultra-sharp, like the world had finally been pulled into focus. Ellie felt as if she could almost see the rusty paint flaking off the rail bridge from here.

Ben turned and looked back at the Ferry. He was squinting, searching for their house. His face relaxed when he spotted it. He looked straight down at the drop.

'Jesus,' he said, lifting his head back up. He turned to Ellie. 'I still can't believe he did it, you know. I expect him to walk through the front door every day. I wake up in the morning and think he's going to need shaking out of his bed again.'

'I know,' Ellie said.

They both had their hands flat on the railing. She moved hers until it was touching his.

'Nothing helps, does it?' Ben said.

Ellie shook her head. 'No.'

'Why do we try?'

'What else can we do?'

Ben looked down. 'Jump?' He turned to her. He wasn't serious, but a tiny part of him meant it, she understood that.

'We aren't brave enough,' she said. 'We couldn't go through with it.'

Ben stared at her for a long moment, their eyes locked.

'He was a brave boy,' he said. 'Our boy.'

Tears filled his eyes. Ellie felt the same coming to her.

'We have to keep living, don't we?' she said.

Ben wiped at the wetness on his cheeks. 'Yes.'

They were both silent for a while, hands touching on the railing. Ellie wondered if there were any of Logan's atoms here, on the railing, perhaps a single molecule of him rubbed off on the bridge before he went over. Or not even a part of his body, a fleck of rubber from the sole of his trainer, a thread from his hoodie.

She'd come here every day looking for a second chance. Finding Sam wasn't what she had in mind, but it was something. She'd tried to help. She felt needed for the first time since Logan died, and it felt good. She was in charge of her life again, responsible for others. She had no idea how to recapture that control.

She turned to Ben.

'I'll stop coming up here if you stop with the conspiracy theories,' she said.

Ben didn't speak, kept looking at the water.

Ellie followed his gaze and spotted something. She imagined for a moment it was a porpoise, a sign from the universe, but she couldn't make it out.

'I'll try,' Ben said. 'I'll try.'

46

Swim until you can't see land.

The song ran through her mind again as she pushed her arms through the soupy water, kicking her legs, feeling the burn from yesterday in her thighs and arms, the tension in every muscle. Her breathing settled as she got used to the rhythm of the strokes, and she began to feel at home in the water.

She wasn't aiming for anywhere, just heading into the Forth, powering through the choppy waves, feeling the ebb and flow, the tug of the tide underneath. The beat of her heart was a drum in her ears, the gulp of her breathing, in out, in out. As her head lifted to the side she could see the road bridge towering over her, legs in the water, its span defying gravity, the grey towers reaching to heaven.

She dived under and pushed downwards. She imagined seeing the wreck of the Porpoise drifting slowly back up, its mast magically upright again, breaking the surface and reaching skywards, signalling its existence to the world. She imagined Jack coming back to life, wriggling free of his bonds, slipping the knots used to weigh him down, laughing as he propelled himself towards land to tell his story.

She stroked and kicked, ever downwards.

She imagined a splash above her, the thunk of a body hitting the water and plummeting past her. Logan, her little baby, come to join her on the ocean floor. She pictured him reaching the bottom of his dive then opening his eyes, his body still intact, smiling at her then swimming over, embracing her, pulling her with him to the surface.

She couldn't see anything around her any more, she was deep enough that the sunlight didn't penetrate.

She stopped swimming for a long moment.

Then she pushed upwards, shoving herself towards the surface, flexing her feet like a propeller, making her body as sleek and streamlined as possible. Her lungs ached and she longed to breathe, but she held her mouth clamped shut as she came closer to the surface. She could see it now, the light glimmering up there, the sun beaming down on the planet, and she craved to be part of that world, to stand on the shore and soak up the energy like a lizard on a rock. She stroked and kicked, stroked and kicked, the shimmer of the surface closer and closer, her lungs burning, the oxygen in her blood thinning and dispersing, her muscles screaming.

She broke the surface and gasped in air, felt the molecules enter her lungs. As long as she kept breathing she was a part of the universe. She took a deliberate mouthful of water, swallowed it, imagining atoms from Logan's ashes slipping down her throat, being absorbed into her blood, her heart, her bones.

She looked at the shore. She was a long way out, but she could make it back. On the beach in front of their house she could see Ben holding a towel. He had a hand shading his eyes, searching for her.

She threw an arm into the air.

Waving not drowning.

Then she began swimming back to shore.

Also by Doug Johnstone

ff

The Dead Beat

If you're so special, why aren't you dead?

The first day of your new job – what could possibly go wrong?

Meet Martha.

It's her first day as an intern at Edinburgh's *The Standard*.

Put straight onto the obituary page, she takes a call from a former employee who seems to commit suicide while on the phone, something which echoes events from her own troubled past.

Setting in motion a frantic race around modern-day Edinburgh, *The Dead Beat* traces Martha's desperate search for answers to the dark mystery of her parents' past. Doug Johnstone's latest page-turner is a wild ride of a thriller.

'Riveting. Fearless. Twisted. If Tartan Noir was a family with an irreverent rebel child, his name would be Doug Johnstone.' *Daily Record*

'There's a tangible sense of expectation and excitement to this rollercoaster tale of dark secrets.' *Lancashire Evening Post*

'A twist-laden tale of family secrets.' **Howard Calvert**, *Mr Hyde*

ff

Gone Again

A missing wife –
A father and son left behind

As we learn some of the painful secrets of Mark and Lauren's
past – not least that this isn't the first time Lauren has
disappeared – we see a father trying to care for his son,
as he struggles with the mystery of what happened
to his wife . . .

'A major discovery.' *Spinetingler*

'Excellent . . . sharp and moving.' *The Times*

'Calling to mind the best of Harlan Coben, Johnstone shows us how quickly
an ordinary life can take one dark turn and nothing is ever the same again.'
Megan Abbott, author of *Dare Me* and *The End of Everything*

'Deeply poignant and compelling . . . it's hard to take your eyes off the page.'
Daily Mail

'Riveting from start to finish.' *The Skinny*

ff

Hit & Run

The worst night of your life just got worse . . .

High above Edinburgh, on the way home from a party with his girlfriend and his brother, Billy Blackmore accidentally hits a stranger.

In a panic, they drive off.

The next day Billy, a journalist, finds he has been assigned to cover the story for the local paper.

'A great slice of noir.' **Ian Rankin**

'This noirish crime novel builds into something more substantial: an existential thriller where a man crumbles as he tries to scream the truth in a house of liars. Thus *Hit & Run* becomes a grisly parable for our times.' **Irvine Welsh**

'With this book, Doug Johnstone hits YOU and then HE runs, and you never catch him until the last word of the last sentence on the last page. Cracking stuff.' **Alan Glynn**, author of *Graveland*

'Fantastic: sparse and fast-paced but believable and emotionally satisfying. You feel you could be Billy – and you thank God you're not. His best yet.' **Helen FitzGerald**, author of *The Cry*

ff

Smokeheads

Four friends. One weekend. Gallons of whisky. What could go wrong?

Four friends, spurred on by whisky-nut Adam, head for a weekend to a remote Scottish island, world famous for its single malts. They have a wallet full of cash, a stash of coke, and a serious thirst. Determined to have a good time and to relive their university years, they start making friends: young divorcee Molly, whom Adam has a soft spot for, her little sister Ash, who has all sorts of problems, and Molly's ex-husband Joe, a control freak who also happens to be the local police.

But events start to spiral out of control and soon they are thrown into a nightmare that gets worse at every turn . . .

'It lulls the reader with the warm glow of a good dram on a winter's night, then ambushes him with all the bitter nastiness of a brutal whisky hangover.'
Christopher Brookmyre

'A hugely atmospheric thriller soaked in the spirit of life . . . sip and savour.'
The Times

'It is so well written . . . there is plenty of flesh and blood here, much of it splashing across the page.' *Scotsman*